In A Glance

A Medieval Romance

The Sword of Glastonbury Series

Book 9

Lisa Shea

First Printing: November 2013

- 9 -

Print version ISBN-13 978-0-9855564-4-0
Kindle ASIN B00GCE9W0W

Sometimes we must release old goals
In order to achieve our greatest dreams

In A Glance

Contents

Preface

Welcome to my Sword of Glastonbury series. I'm thrilled you've joined me in this adventure! These full-length novels share my adoration for all things medieval. I've belonged to the Society for Creative Anachronisms for many years and delved fully into my medieval personae. I've researched the language, clothing, education, and outlook of medieval women. I've practiced swordfighting for years, too. I'm joyful to be able to share the fruits of this research with you!

Each of the novels in this series is fully standalone. While there is a sword passed from heroine to heroine to flow the stories together, each book can be read on its own and involves its own set of characters.

If you've read the series in order you've probably read this preface before :). If you're just joining us, then hello!

Did you know that many words like "wow" that we think of as modern are actually quite old? And that words like "hug" that we consider timeless are actually fairly recent? You can learn more about medieval language, clothing, and other related topics in my appendices in the back. Medieval people loved slang words, traded in goods from the far reaches of the Earth, and had some fairly "modern" views about what women could or could not do.

Especially during these Crusades years, when countless men were off at war, large numbers of public offices were held by women. Many keeps were ruled by women. Women fought with blades to defend their homes and keeps; some even went on the road to fight in the Crusades. Queen Eleanor of Aquitaine was a powerhouse of strength and a model for all women of these years. During this time it was wholly expected that women should be respected in positions of power and were quite capable of actively defending their lands.

It's only later, when peace moved in, the Church solidified power, and courtly love traditions developed, that women were demoted to restrictively passive roles.

It's good to shake off some of the misconceptions created by everyone from Errol Flynn to Game of Thrones and examine what our real-life history has to offer.

You might think oranges and citrus were solely in Asia – but did you know there were orange orchards in Italy in the 900s? People in medieval times had access to immense trade and a variety of products. While they used different names than 'tangerine' for their varieties, names now lost to time, they enjoyed them all the same.

In A Glance is a clean romance. The few scenes of intimacy are fade to black. The few swears are period-appropriate such as "God's Teeth" or "God's Blood." There is sword-fighting but no explicit violence. As such, it is suitable for teens and up.

If you ever have any questions or comments for me, I would love to chat! You can find me on Facebook, Twitter, Instagram, Google+, Pinterest, Wattpad, and most other social networks. Just check the 'about the Author' section or do a search for Lisa Shea in your system of choice.

So sit back, relax, and enjoy a virtual vacation in the entrancing world of medieval England!

All proceeds from this series benefit battered women's shelters. Be the change you wish to see in the world.

Chapter 1

England, 1200

"If it is not right do not do it;
If it is not true do not say it."
-- Marcus Aurelius

Joan smiled in contentment as she crossed the village green in the easing crimsons of late afternoon, walking across a carpet of ethereal white primrose flowers. May had brought a gentle warmth with it, finally chasing away the chill of the long, rough winter. She ran a hand through her chestnut brown hair, brushing it back in the breeze, then turned to the blonde at her side.

"Muriel, while the flowers you have here may be different from the ones I grew up with near Jerusalem, they are just as beautiful in their own way."

Muriel smiled in appreciation. "Someday I would like to be able to see the Holy Land," she mused, pulling her cloak closer against the soft chill. "But to have lived the life of a military child must have been rough on you."

Joan shrugged, a twinkle coming to her eye. "My father gave me free rein, and the entire camp was my playground. I would say my childhood was fairly idyllic."

Muriel raised an eyebrow. "And yet, when you turned twenty-three last year, you decided to return to a 'homeland' where you'd never set foot before."

"Lucky for you I did," pointed out Joan. "Who would you have turned to with this current problem?"

Muriel's gaze became serious. "I am grateful you are willing to lend a hand with this," she admitted. "I have heard good things about Hugh and his band, but I would still feel uncomfortable going in there alone."

Joan ran her eyes over the rough-hewn walls of the tavern before them. It was far from the finest she had seen in her years of travel. One of the shutters hung askew and the oak door was nearly split down its center. "Your elder sister is on a dangerous quest," she gently reminded the woman. "These men will ensure she gets safely to the other side."

"You are sure of that?" Muriel's voice was hesitant. "Maybe we should go to the sheriff."

Joan sharply shook her head. "It's true I have only been on English soil for a year. Still, that's been long enough to know to avoid the sheriff at all costs," she ground out. "No, Hugh's men are our best bet. They hold court in a private room at the back of this … choice establishment."

She stared at the door for a long moment, then glanced at the sky.

"It is not quite time yet," she informed her friend. "Let us go around to the side window and listen for a few minutes. The more information we can gain before we engage them, the better."

Muriel nodded. In a moment the two women had slipped through the weeds at the side of the aging structure. Joan picked up a stick and used it to detach a large, intricate spider web from the shutter. She then carefully eased the sagging wood open just an inch. Slowly, cautiously, she drew close to the opening.

Four people were seated around a large, circular oak table, with room for at least two more. Mugs of ale sat before each person. As Joan watched, a buxom waitress with stunning honey-blonde hair came pushing her way through the door, a large ceramic pitcher cradled in one beefy arm. She gave a warm smile to the group as she moved from mug to mug, filling each to the brim.

She stopped solicitously by a raven-haired woman. "Sybil, my duck, would you like that stew now, or later?"

"Later," snapped Sybil, not looking up. "You know I would not interrupt business with pleasure."

The waitress looked over at the person next to her, a middle-aged, greying man whose thick biceps reflected an active life. "You hungry for some stew, Norman?"

"Certainly," he agreed, glancing up and nodding. "With some steamed turnips on the side."

A thin, wiry man at his side eagerly leant forward, his gaze sweeping down the waitress's form. "You know what I would like," he called out in a suggestive tone, his eyes twinkling.

The waitress's mouth quirked up in a grin. "Stew is all you shall be getting," she advised him.

She turned to the fourth man, shook her head, and then headed back toward the main room. She closed the door behind her with a gentle thump.

Joan took in a long, deep breath, and then turned her gaze toward the last man at the table. It had been five long years since she had seen him. She could vividly remember that summer's day on the coast near Jaffa, with the fragrant smell of olives wafting from the kitchens of the seaside restaurant.

She had watched him for an hour, drinking him in as a dying woman submerges wholly, gratefully, in a desert oasis. And then she had turned her back and left. It had been the first time she had seen him in person – and she swore it would be the last. Her heart yearned for him too strongly. She was not free to follow the passions swirling within her.

And yet, with the twists and turns of life, the forks in paths and the cul-de-sacs, somehow she was here. She was watching him again, how he ignored the ale before him and stared steadfastly at the door, as if his focus could cause it to open before the scheduled time.

He had become sturdier in the past five years. His short-cropped hair was still light brown, but somehow it seemed darker in the depths of the gloomy inn, rather than out beneath the glowing sun of an azure Mediterranean sky. His dark eyes seemed shadowed, and she wondered if her own held that same burden. His arms and shoulders still held the muscled, toned readiness that she remembered, and she had read enough reports of his prowess in battle over the years to know he was an expert with the sword at his side.

God's teeth, she still craved him with all her being.

He suddenly looked straight at the window.

Her years of training served her well – she stayed stock still, only flicking her eyelids shut to hide the gleam. He would have noticed any sudden movement; instead all he could see would be a muddle of shadows, nothing to bring concern. After several long moments she risked opening one eye a fraction. He had returned to his perusal of the door. His fingers began a slow, rhythmic drum against the table.

The reedy man at his side gave him a nudge, following his gaze. "Hoping for Ada to come back and spend more time on you?" He shook his head vigorously. "I saw her first," he insisted. "I get first rights."

Hugh's fingers stilled for a moment, a ripple of tension moved through his shoulders, and then the coiled muscles forcibly released. The fingers went back to their even thrumming. "You can have her, Ymbert," he stated without interest.

Ymbert's smile grew wide. "She is surely the most beautiful woman I have ever seen," he extolled. "Such curves, such hair! How she ended up in a slime-pit like this is beyond me."

Sybil's laugh was harsh. "Better get her quick, then," she advised the thin man. "Before she comes to her senses."

Ymbert's face shadowed with worry for a moment, then he shrugged it off. "Another will come along, even more beautiful," he promised. He turned to Hugh. "You were off in the crusades; you have seen the world," he prodded the man. "Who was the most beautiful woman you have seen?"

"Not now," retorted Hugh, his gaze steady on the door.

"Please?" wheedled Ymbert. "I have never been more than thirty miles beyond this tavern. What are the women of the south like?"

"We have a client – "

"We have at least fifteen minutes before our client arrives," prodded Ymbert eagerly. "The church bell has not even rung yet. Tell me, are the women of the Holy Land tall and slender like angels? Are they round and soft like pillows? Are they …"

Sybil rolled her eyes. "God's teeth, Hugh, just tell him something. Anything. If he whines any more I swear I will run him through myself."

Hugh looked down at his ale for a long minute, then brought the mug up, taking a long draw. "Fine," he said, bringing his eyes back to the group. "I will tell you about the most stunning woman I have ever encountered."

His gaze drifted for a moment and he looked off into the distance. "She was wearing a flowing silk dress of tangerine and gold that rippled in the late afternoon sun. I remember she was barefoot, dancing along the waist-high stone wall which separated the cobblestone courtyard from the sea below. Seagulls, glossy white against the blue, were hovering at her side. Every once in a while she would turn and throw a bit of crust to one, laughing in delight when they picked the food out of the sky by maneuvering with just a subtle twist of the wing-tip."

Ymbert leant forward, his eyes wide. "What was her beauty? What did she look like?"

Hugh gave his head a soft shake. "Michael and I were sitting at the far side of the plaza, at one of the small tables near the restaurant. She was across the cobblestones. I could barely see her face in the summer glare. She had long, dark hair which fell in waves past her waist. She was young – perhaps eighteen – and slim. But it was not artfully made up eyes which caught me, or abundant curves, or pouting lips." He drew his gaze down to his ale again. "It was her lightness of being, the dance in her step, the sheer pleasure she took in the natural beauty of the day. And then she looked at me …"

Ymbert was practically lying on the table now. "And? And?"

Hugh took another draw on his ale. "And nothing," he cut out shortly. "And I turned to Michael, and by the time I looked back, she was walking away. She was gone."

Ymbert shook his head in bewilderment. "Why did you not go after her?"

Hugh's eyes moved back to look at the door. His voice was curt. "I was on business, as we are now."

The somber bells of the church across the green began tolling; Muriel gave a nervous tug to Joan's sleeve. "It is time," she murmured.

Joan nodded, drawing in a deep breath. She forced herself to come back from the window, to gently ease it shut again. She had not realized that the one glance had meant as much to Hugh as it did to her – but thank all that was Holy he never got a good look at her. She needed the next few days to unfurl as carefully as a field mouse peeling a nut near a sleeping cat. There was enormous potential for disaster. One misstep could plunge her hopes into an icy river, to be swept downstream, her chances lost forever.

She had to lay each stepping stone with perfect precision.

She pulled her cloak closer, drawing the hood over her head. Her years of training taught her to reveal nothing, to give away not the slightest hint beyond what was necessary.

The two women moved to the main door and Joan shouldered it open with a shove. The room within was fairly dim, with perhaps six oak tables scattered, populated with a collection of rough-looking men in leather and sword. Ada, the buxom beauty, wove easily between them, carrying a platter with several mugs balanced on it.

"Sit anywhere," she called out as she turned to wait on the table before her.

Muriel pressed closely against Joan's side with a nervous shiver. Joan patted her reassuringly on the arm before moving toward the door in the back. She could feel the attention of Hugh's gaze on it, could feel the focus of his stare before her, and she laid her hand against the oak for a long moment.

It had begun.

She lifted the latch and eased the door open, drawing Muriel along with her into the room, then turned to slide the door shut.

She deliberately slouched her shoulders, blending into the background, allowing Muriel to take all their focus.

Norman stood, smiling at his guest. "My dear Muriel, welcome. Please, have a seat. My companions here are Sybil, Ymbert, and Hugh. I am Norman."

Muriel settled nervously into the chair while Joan leant back against the wall by the door. She took a pose of quiet obedience, her eyes lowered, a non-threat. The others barely glanced at her.

Norman steepled his fingers, his weathered face gentling. "We hear you have a problem we can help with. Please tell us about it."

Muriel cleared her throat. "Well, it is my older sister, Linota. She is twenty now – two years older than I. She was always a take-charge person, even as a child. Had to be, I suppose. The fever took our parents and our two brothers when she was barely thirteen. She kept the farm going, took care of me, and somehow we hung on."

Norman nodded encouragingly. "Do go on."

Muriel looked around the table. "She married about a year ago, and I thought that fate had finally eased for us. Robin was a good man. Gentle, kind, all one could have hoped for. He and his sister, Beatrice, came to live with us." Her eyes misted. "It was just about perfect." She shook her head. "And then, a few weeks ago, Linota wanted some mushrooms."

Ymbert's thin face wrinkled in confusion. "Mushrooms?"

Muriel nodded. "Beatrice went down to the stone bridge by Kirklington to pick them. She never came back."

Hugh looked up, taking interest for the first time. "The tinker's bridge. Robin went to look for her? And was found drowned?"

Muriel instantly shook her head. "He did *not* drown," she insisted. "Robin could swim like a fish. There was a lump on the back of his head, but the sheriff dismissed our concerns. He said Robin must have fallen in somehow. Linota was furious, and said she would take matters into her own hand."

Hugh held her gaze. "What did she do?"

Muriel twined her fingers together, the knuckles turning white. "She made me promise not to send anyone in after her until Wednesday – so five days from now. She figured whoever took Beatrice would take her as well, and that way Linota could help her and any other captives escape."

Sybil's thin lips turned down. "Elias," she murmured.

Muriel's eyes grew wide. "Sheriff Elias?" she asked hoarsely.

Hugh shot a warning glance at Sybil, then turned back to Muriel. "Do not worry; we will be the assistance Linota needs. We will get Linota, Beatrice, and any other innocents out of their bondage."

Muriel brought a worn leather pouch up onto the table. Pulling open the mouth, she counted out twenty silver pennies.

Hugh's brow creased in confusion. "The cost for our help is only ten pennies," he gently corrected her.

From her position on the wall, Joan held her breath, fighting the urge to look up. Her heart caught in her throat. This was the first hurdle. True, it was minor in comparison with what was to come. Still, a challenge here could derail the entire plan. She prayed with all her heart that Muriel could see it through.

Muriel's voice was resolute. She looked up at Hugh. "I want my friend here to go with you to rescue my sister and sister-in-law."

Four pairs of eyes instantly swiveled to look at Joan, assessing her form with sharp attention. Joan did not move a muscle. She kept her gaze lowered, her cloak hanging loosely around her, shielding herself from their view.

Hugh's voice was a low rumble. "Our group works alone," he informed Muriel.

Muriel's voice was reasonable but firm. "Linota and Beatrice are all the family I have left. While you were warmly recommended, I neither know nor have a history with any of you." She glanced for a moment at Joan, then back at the group before her. "My friend does not need to have a voice in the planning or a role of any importance. But I insist she be there when you find my two relatives."

Muriel looked down, pressing the coins into the center of the table. "I am willing to pay extra for this accommodation."

Ymbert's thin fingers twitched with nervous anticipation, but Hugh gave another long look at the figure standing quietly by the door. "You there, what is your name?"

Joan pitched her voice low. She had worked hard to perfect her English accent since arriving; she now could pass in most situations. But Hugh was focused on her, attentive. Nothing could interfere with this first part of the plan.

"Joan," she murmured.

He frowned, looking down her length. "And you will stay out of the way?"

She nodded mutely.

Hugh looked back to the rest of the group. "We have several days to equip ourselves for the task, and for Ymbert to research the situation, before we set into motion on Wednesday. We can see then how we want to involve Joan in our plans, if at all."

He glanced toward the shuttered window where the light was now easing through in crimson streams. "But I am late as it is; I promised to be at Lord Weston's before sunset."

The door was pushed open and Ada bustled in, a large, wooden platter cradled in her arms. "Oh, I meant to tell you, Hugh," she apologized, laying a bowl of stew down in front of Norman. "My stableboy says your saddle is not back from the leatherworker's. It will be another day at least."

Hugh rounded on her in surprise. "What? Nobody should have touched my saddle!"

She shrugged, placing a bowl in front of Ymbert, giving the thin man a wink. "I only know what I have been told," she offered sweetly.

"God's teeth," swore Hugh, running a hand through his short hair.

Joan's heart pounded in her chest. And here came the second obstacle, so crucial.

Would Hugh follow along the path she created for him?

Muriel's voice held just the right balance of reluctance and resignation, and Joan could have kissed her for it. "I was planning on staying with Father Picot to help with his patients through Tuesday afternoon," she offered. "Joan is going near to Lord Weston's keep. It was one of Joan's horses I rode here on. If she is willing, you can have the use of that steed to get to your appointment."

Hugh's eyes turned back to Joan's and she warmed in the subtle shift in dynamics. Now she was the one who had something he wanted. She could feel it in his gaze, in the subtle dropping of his shoulders.

His voice was tight when he spoke. "I would be grateful if you would lend me the use of your steed."

She nodded in agreement.

Hugh sighed, easing back into his chair for a moment, then scanned the rest of his group. "We regroup at the bridge on Wednesday at noon," he informed them. "Ymbert, you do your usual magic to gather the background we need."

Ymbert was busy shoveling stew into his mouth; he nodded. "Of course," he mumbled between bites.

Hugh stood. "Then we are settled." He glanced at Joan. "Give me five minutes to collect my things from the stables, then we can leave." He was out the door at a steady stride.

Muriel stood, nodding to the group. "Thank you," she offered them. She turned to Joan, her eyes warm. "And thank you," she whispered.

Joan smiled back, tenderly clasping her friend's arm. "We will get both women back safely," she promised in a low voice.

Muriel nodded, then she headed out into the main room of the inn, Ada right on her heels.

The door settled closed again and Joan looked at the three remaining people at the table. They were ignoring her now, a fixed dismissiveness which drew a smile to her lips. The coins on the table were gone, undoubtedly swept up by Ymbert the moment Muriel's back had turned.

Her eyes went to the wiry man. "You seem the betting type," she murmured.

His eyes flashed with interest and he put down his spoon. "I admit I like a good wager," he agreed. "What are we betting on?"

The corners of Joan's mouth turned up. "I bet you do not want me to come along with you on your adventure."

He chuckled at that, his eyes gaining a sparkle. "You hardly need a bag of bones to divine that one."

She took a step toward the table. "Well then," she smiled, "here is my bet. I bet you, if you leave me completely alone with Hugh for the weekend, that by Wednesday he will insist you take me along with you."

Sybil burst out laughing. "Hugh? Want *you* as part of our crew?" She shook her head. "That man is not interested in women. If he had his way, I would not be here – but he needs my particular abilities to open certain doors." She scoffed, looking down the folds of Joan's cloak. "He will never want you."

Joan spread her arms wide. "So you accept my bet?"

Sybil leant forward with sharp interest. "What are your terms?"

Joan looked across the three. "If I win, and Hugh wants me with you, then you accept me without argument. I will not interfere, but I will be there when you seek out the two women."

Norman's brow wrinkled in thought. "And if you lose?"

She shrugged. "If Hugh does not want me, then I will not go with you. You can travel unimpeded."

Ymbert glanced down at the pouch at his side. "And the money?"

"I will tell Muriel that my role is separate from yours. Her terms will be satisfied and you can keep your extra money."

Ymbert's eyes lit up. "Done!" He held a hand out to Joan.

Joan ran her eyes across all three. "But you cannot say a word to Hugh, nor bother us in any way. Otherwise all bets are off."

Sybil grinned widely. "Oh, absolutely," she agreed. "We would not dream of doing anything but watching your hopeless plan unravel into frail little threads."

Joan nodded. In a moment she had clasped three hands.

Joan's eyes sparkled. "In fact," she advised the group, "I will even give you a head start and annoy him a bit before we leave."

Sybil laughed out loud. "You are already playing a weak hand and you want to make it worse? By all means, this I want to see."

The door was pushed open and Hugh strode in, a pack over his shoulder. "I am ready. We should head out – I will miss half of the ceremony as it is."

Joan slouched her shoulders, bringing a regretful droop to her eyes. "I am sorry, but I am afraid I need to use the privy before we leave. Could you please let me know where it is?"

The string of curses which followed her path out back were all she could have hoped to achieve.

Chapter 2

Joan waited a full five minutes before coming out of the small outhouse and strolling toward the front of the inn. Hugh was pacing in frustration before the structure, glancing at the waves of sunset radiating from the west. She drew in a moment, letting herself take him in.

He wore a dark brown leather tunic, stitched at the shoulder, over a midnight blue shirt. His leather leggings and boots matched the brown top, and he wore a long sword at his hip. His stride was steady, well balanced, and she knew well just how agile he was with that sword in hand. She had been the one to write out the orders for Hugh and Michael, to receive back the summaries of their actions. They were a legend in the field, with Michael's planning and Hugh's execution. They had been -

She pushed the thoughts out of mind with harsh effort. That had been five long years ago. She needed to focus on the here and now in order to see this through. But it had to be done carefully, slowly. The unfurling of a fern in the gentle spring's warmth.

She ambled at a relaxed pace around the corner of the building, and Hugh whirled at once. "There you are," he ground out. "Ready now?"

"Yes, thank you," she offered in a low voice. She meandered across the green, smiling at the field of primrose. It really was quite a sight, with the delicate white petals over the sea of darker green.

Hugh's voice was tight. "It is a full five miles to Lord Weston's keep and the ceremony was set to start immediately at sunset," he muttered.

"Not to worry," offered Joan sweetly. "I am sure everything will work out."

Hugh looked up as they approached the blacksmith shop and his shoulders slouched in despair. "Are these your horses?" he growled.

Joan followed his eyes with a bright smile. She had seen the decrepit steeds when she and Muriel had ridden in; she had wondered to her friend just what kept the two poor nags upright. They were skin and bones, with gaunt cheeks and rail-thin ribs.

She dug into the pouch at her hip, withdrawing the two apples she had bought from Ada on the way out of the back room. She tenderly offered one to each horse. "You poor things," she murmured. "Life can be rough sometimes."

Hugh's gaze narrowed. "You do not care well for your steeds," he snapped.

She innocently glanced up at him. "I suppose we all have our own standards," she countered. "In any case, these neglected creatures do not belong to me. Mine are around the corner."

Relief eased across his face and he followed her around the edge of the building. His feet drew to a halt as he stared between the two stallions.

Joan stepped past him, her heart warming with pride as she looked on the joys of her life. She was frugal in many aspects of life. She wore no jewelry and her home had neither pewter bowls nor glassed-in windows. But she believed with all her heart in the value of a strong and worthy horse. Her most important role in Jerusalem had been that of a courier, and more times than she could count it had been a sure-footed steed which saved her life. There had been instances that her messages, delivered in the nick of time, had saved Michael's life, and Hugh's as well.

She smiled, stepping forward to the horse on the left to run a hand down his mane, looking up into his large, brown eyes. "This one is Aquila," she informed Hugh, "while yours is Accipiter."

"Eagle and Hawk," mused Hugh, running his eyes over the two steeds. "They are magnificent creatures."

She turned her eyes to him in quiet regard. "So you approve of my horses, then?"

He smiled at that, nodding. "Absolutely," he agreed, stepping forward to offer a strong pat to his steed's neck. In a moment he had fastened his bags onto the back of the saddle and vaulted onto the steed.

Joan was up on her own, then swung her horse to face north.

Hugh's brows creased. "The main road to Lord Weston's is to the west," he pointed out.

Joan's brows rose in curiosity. "I thought you wanted to be there by sundown?"

He glanced at the road again. "You have a quicker way?"

The corners of Joan's mouth tweaked into a smile. "If you think you can keep up with me," she teased sweetly.

Hugh's eyes sparked with interest. "Lead on!"

Joan did not need a second prodding. She nudged Aquila, leant over his mane, and in a second he was in flight.

Aquila adored running. Joan's soul soared as they flew, skimming over mossy streams, blasting, almost airborne, through the narrow twists of the woods. A dim thought flickered in the back of her mind - she needed to take the unveiling slowly. She needed to dole out her revelations in small, gentle portions. But she could not draw in the reins. The thrill of the ride blew all thoughts of caution out of the hidden corners of her being. She threw her hood back, letting her long, chestnut-brown hair stream unfettered, laughing with the sheer joy of breathing in the world's delights.

She turned her head to the right and Hugh was immediately beside her, matching her pace. Accipiter's hooves fell nearly in perfect rhythm with Aquila's. And well they should; the horses were brothers, raised by one of the finest stable masters in Jerusalem. They had been hand-picked by her when they were wobbling colts on stick-thin legs. She knew their sires, knew their lineage, and time had borne out her faith.

Hugh smiled at her, and then they were twisting, streaming, flowing like quicksilver beneath the shimmering sunset. It seemed all too soon that the ride was behind them, that they were coming out into the open clearing around Lord Weston's keep.

Torches lit the walls at regular intervals and a row of metal lamps lit their way to the main gate in the curtain wall. A crowd of horses gathered in a stamping mob, waiting as the guards talked with the owners, checking over their identities before passing them through.

Hugh pulled up alongside her, his eyes shadowing as he looked over the blockade. "This will take a while," he sighed.

"Follow me," she instructed him, then gave her reins a gentle tug. She headed around the edge of the wall toward the right, moving easily through the growing dusk. She guided Aquila around a fallen log, then pressed forward toward a small, dark area of the wall.

A bored voice called down from the walkway. "All visitors proceed through the main gates for the security check," he intoned as if by rote. "No exceptions."

Her eyes twinkled as she looked up into the growing darkness. "And here I thought you wanted another ride on Accipiter," she mused. "Ah well. I guess I will just – "

The voice became warm and urgent. "Joan? Is that you? Wait!" There was a scurrying noise and a sharp scraping. In a moment the door was being pulled open. Joan and Hugh dismounted, then led the horses in through the opening.

The guard laid a hand reverently against Accipiter's neck, gazing up at the steed. "I will get them stabled for you," he promised. "The best grain, just the way you like it. I will take care of everything."

She smiled. "I know you will, and thank you."

In a moment he was leading the two horses away and she hitched her head toward the keep. "Shall we?"

Hugh's eyebrow went up in appreciation. "After you," he offered with a wave.

She turned right, heading away from the main keep entrance. It seemed he was learning to trust her. He did not voice an objection, simply followed along at her side, his gaze sweeping over the open courtyard. The stables were behind them, currently mobbed by arriving guests, and a collection of out-buildings filled the other sides of the open area. She led Hugh alongside the kitchen's stone walls.

A maid moved past them carrying a tray of rosy apples. Joan reached forward, plucking one off the tray. The maid glanced back, then smiled warmly.

"Just as long as you eat that yourself and do not feed it to those steeds of yours," she chuckled. "I swear they eat better than us humans sometimes."

"And well they deserve it," agreed Joan. "For they have defended me far more ably than a bodyguard many times in the past."

She followed behind the maid as she went into a side door of the keep, and Hugh was close behind her. There was the narrow spiral staircase up to the main floor where it sounded like dinner was going strong. She crossed the landing and started up the second flight. Hugh paused for a moment, his eyes going to the throng of people and the wealth of food, before following along after her.

She moved down the long, stone hall, slowing as she approached the guard stationed by the door at the end.

The guard nodded his head in welcome. "You are running late," he teased, glancing over her shoulder at Hugh.

"Business comes before pleasure," she returned, giving him a wink. Then he was pulling open the door, ushering them into the room.

The study was regally appointed in elm and oak, with glass windows along the far wall and an inlaid desk sitting to the right. Shelves of codices and scrolls filled the left wall. An elegant tapestry depicted a field of battle. The room sparkled with the light of the many beeswax candles that glittered from just about every flat surface.

A middle-aged man turned from the windows, his curly hair almost black, his sturdy muscles not yet easing to fat.

"Joan, there you are! I was beginning to think you turned me down in order to go off on another midnight race."

She smiled, moving forward into his arms. "My dear Lord Weston, I seem to recall you bet against me in that," she joked, relaxing in his embrace for a moment before stepping back.

He laughed. "I did not know better at the time," he agreed. "I have certainly made that money back several times over."

His eyes moved to Hugh, who had come up behind them. "Hugh! I did not realize you knew Joan."

Hugh put out his hand and the men clasped arms. "I only met her tonight, but she was kind enough to offer me a ride," he stated.

Lord Weston laughed out loud. "Oh, you are granted a ride on Accipiter and you reluctantly accepted?" He grinned. "Many men here would give a month's salary for that treat."

He turned back to Joan. "Here, let me take your cloak," he offered. She turned dutifully, undoing the clasp at her neck. He eased the thick fabric from her shoulders and hung it on a hook.

Hugh's eyes were on her, and she warmed with the glow in them. She had worn her marigold-colored dress for tonight, its body a rich orange, the embroidery along the seams a burnt yellow color. It fit her perfectly, and she knew her chestnut-brown hair gleamed in the candlelight.

Lord Weston turned back to them and chuckled at the look on Hugh's face. "She is indeed a beauty," he stated, "but it is her traits within that make her a rare catch."

Joan's mouth tweaked into a grin. "For example, my appreciation for your fine cider?"

Lord Weston's laughter echoed through the room. He moved to the side table, pouring out three glasses. He handed one to each of them before taking his own.

"A toast, to fine horses," he offered.

"Fine horses," agreed Joan, and they all clinked their glasses before taking a sip.

Joan sighed with pleasure. She had no idea how Lord Weston's brewery managed it, but the cider was by far the best she had ever tasted. "I think I will just stay here for the week."

Lord Weston smiled broadly. "You will certainly get no argument from me," he offered. "It would be worth the riot in the stables, with all the boys fighting over who gets to care for your steeds."

He looked over at Hugh. "And you, Hugh, I have not seen you in, what, a year? Not since you first returned from the Mediterranean, when your father passed away."

Hugh nodded, taking another sip of the cider. "Yes, and I apologize for not visiting sooner. I know you and my father were good friends. Life has kept me quite busy."

Lord Weston looked him over. "Still, it must be quite different from your times in the Holy Land. Your father said you were involved in some sort of reconnaissance work for the Pope."

Hugh's face eased into stillness. "I am afraid I cannot speak about that."

Lord Weston gave him a warm pat on the arm. "Of course not," he agreed. "I am just glad you made it back safely. That line of work claims many fine men."

Hugh nodded somberly. "It took the life of my best friend."

Hugh took up the pitcher of cider and refilled their glasses. "To departed heroes," he offered. This time the glasses were held high for a long moment before the cider was downed.

Lord Weston looked over to Hugh. "So, did you ever meet Master Martin, tonight's guest of honor, during your years in the Holy Land? His sword school was located in Jerusalem, although the weapons collection he is showcasing this weekend comes from all over."

Hugh shook his head, coming back from distant musings. "No, I never had that honor," he returned. "It is part of why I was so eager to come tonight, to hear him speak. His reputation is stunning; I only wish I had been able to train with him while I was there."

"Well, on Sunday he moves on to London to stay with the King for a while. If you are able to get free, and wish to go with him, I would be willing to put in a word for you."

Hugh's eyes brightened, but then he glanced at Joan and shook his head. "I have business to attend to," he demurred. "Perhaps after that I might seek him out."

There was a gentle rap at the door; all three turned at the sound. The door pressed open. Joan's heart thundered in her chest as a wizened, elderly man, an inch or two shorter than her, moved quietly into the room. His eyes swung to hers, and in a heartbeat she was kneeling before him, taking his wrinkled hands in her own, and moving her lips down to kiss them.

"Master Martin," she sighed in heartfelt relief. It had been over a year since she had seen him. Tears came to her eyes with gratitude that she had been blessed with more time in his presence.

"My child," he greeted her, drawing her up, holding out his arms. She moved into them with warmth, holding his body against hers. He was thin, but she knew within the frail looking exterior was one of the most skilled warriors she had ever met. She had certainly never even come close to beating him in the long years she had worked for him.

He stepped back at last, running his eyes down her body with a practiced gaze. "You have gotten thin," he gently chastised her.

"Not enough figs in my diet," she teased him with a twinkle in her eye.

Hugh looked between them with growing awareness. "Joan, you served with him in the Holy Land?"

Master Martin nodded. "She was one of my finest assistants."

"I am a student who still has much to learn," countered Joan with a fond smile. She turned to Hugh. "Master Martin, I would like you to meet Hugh Castillon."

Hugh stepped forward to drop to one knee before the elderly man. "It is an honor and a privilege to meet you."

Master Martin glanced at Joan for a moment, then nodded, touching Hugh on the head. "I am pleased to meet you as well."

He looked over at Lord Weston. "The crowds are getting restless below," he advised the man. "I think it may be time we move downstairs and begin our celebration."

He held out his left arm to Joan, and she folded her hand into it with a tender smile, moving alongside her aging master as she had done for so many years. And then they were in motion, walking down the long hall, heading toward the main stairs into the lively throng.

* * *

Joan leant back in her chair, stuffed beyond belief with the delicious turnips, goose, roast boar, and apple tart which had come and gone along with myriad other courses. She looked fondly at Master Martin who sat to her left. He was deep in conversation with Lord Weston. It pleased her to no end that her master had made it safely back to England, could live out his retirement amongst familiar surroundings, as he had always dreamed.

She gave a quiet laugh. *Familiar surroundings.* To her, the keep was an odd mix of strange and normal. She had grown up thousands of miles away, but her homes had always been military bases and forts, keeps and castles. She was clambering over trebuchets and catapults before she could ride. And once she had gotten on horseback, the men could barely keep her off them. If she had been a boy, she could have joined the cavalry, lived on her steed, and life would have been all she had dreamed of.

Hugh leaned over. "And just what are you thinking about, that has you aglow?" he asked with a wry smile.

She blushed, looking down. "Wishing I were male," she admitted.

He ran his gaze down her face and body, shaking his head. "Most women would wish they were you," he gently countered.

"Most women did not grow up dreaming of joining the cavalry," she pointed out. "The cavalrymen were all around me; the tales they told sang of glory and freedom."

He nodded, understanding drawing onto his face. "I thought I heard a trace of an accent in your voice. You were the child of a crusader?"

"Yes. My mother insisted on going with him; she was a skilled herbalist and knew her talents would come in handy. I was born in Jerusalem and grew up in various camps and posts."

He smiled in appreciation. "That must have been quite the life."

"It was amazing," she returned with enthusiasm. "The brilliantly colored sights, the cacophony of sounds, the constant throb of energy. It was like living in a whirlwind."

"You did not want to be an herbalist like your mother?"

Joan shook her head. "My dear mother passed away from disease before I was seven, and even by then it was the stables which called to me. I would spend every moment I could on horseback. I thought, somehow, if only I became expert enough … "

Master Martin turned and chuckled dryly. "Ah, my dear, would you so quickly give up your time with me?"

She fondly shook her head, leaning against him for a moment. "Not at all," she vowed. "Sometimes one has to be disappointed in a lesser dream in order to open up the space in their life for what they were meant to be."

Master Martin raised his glass to hers. "Never forget that," he stated quietly. "Your work saved countless lives."

Hugh's voice came from her other side. "Undoubtedly that is true," he added. "The sword students who went through your school often became Knights Templar or joined other protective orders. Those men became a foundation for safety throughout the realm."

Joan nodded, drinking. Surely her official work at the sword school had done its share of good. But it was the covert work she did for the Master, the delivery of messages and coordination of information, which was far more instrumental in keeping their people alive.

Her stomach gave a rumble and she put a hand down to steady it. "I think I need to leave for a moment, if you would excuse me?"

Hugh and Master Martin rose to their feet. She made her way carefully along the back of the head table, pausing as maids and servants moved past with mugs and platters. She pushed through the throngs to the back hallway. Undoubtedly the garderobes in the main halls were quite busy, but she knew where there was a private one by the sewing room.

The hallway here brought a welcome stillness and she turned the corner to find only flickering candles and silence. She breathed deeply. As much as she loved Master Martin, she preferred quiet to the cacophony of the crowd. Too much of her training over the years had focused on the dangers of the masses, the threat hidden inside a mob.

The garderobe was empty; in a few minutes she was standing outside it again, her shoulders finally easing. Perhaps she would take the walk back to the main hall at a slow pace. She was sure the raucous attendees would barely notice her absence.

There was a movement up ahead. A large, tow-headed man stumbled drunkenly toward her, his rough clothing disheveled. She shook her head. Another reason she disliked these types of gatherings. She eased to her left to let him by.

His eyes brightened as he took her in and his legs tilted toward her. His breath was so strong that she wondered if she could set it on fire and turn him into one of those performers she'd seen at the street carnivals.

"What a pretty lass," he chortled, his eyes glowing, sweeping down her form. "Gimme a kiss, won't ya?"

She looked up at him evenly, her hand settling down on the knife at her hip. "You really do not want to press me," she advised him in a low voice.

"Ah, but I do," he countered with growing enthusiasm. "It is just you and me here. Just one little kiss."

"Be on your way," she advised him. "There are plenty of other women who would be open to your offer."

"Ah, but you are not like other women," he insisted, his eyes drawing down her form again. "I think I will just have a taste." He reached out an arm toward her.

There was a movement behind him. His arm was grabbed, twisted, and wrenched high up behind his back. Hugh's voice came smoothly from behind the drunk.

"You will head back to the main room immediately. If you come near this lady again, I shall see you thrown into the mud pit before the gates," he stated with calm intention.

The drunken man opened his mouth to protest. Hugh twisted the arm up higher, causing the drunk's words to mangle into a cry of pain. With a push the man was weaving uncertainly back in the direction of the main room.

Hugh looked after him for a moment, then stepped before Joan.

"You are all right?"

Joan nodded, releasing the hilt of her dagger. "I am fine."

Hugh's eyes flickered to the dagger, and then back at Joan, his smile widening. "I forget that you trained with Master Martin. Perhaps you were not in need of rescuing?"

"I am always grateful for a friend," she returned, "no matter what the circumstance. You never know what twists lie ahead. Even the simplest fight can hold untold dangers."

He nodded, then offered his arm. "Shall we return to the fray?"

She smiled. "Lead on."

* * *

The room was finally settling down into quiet. Half of the men had curled up to sleep near where they ate. Servants moved quietly around them, gathering up empty tankards, crusts of bread, and well-gnawed bones.

Hugh looked at the mass of snoring, belching drunks and then back to Joan, his eyes shaded with worry. "I hope you are not sleeping down here for the night?"

She smiled at that, patting his arm. "Master Martin has a room upstairs and I will sleep there as well. For a night, at least, it will be like old times."

Master Martin looked over with a twinkle in his eye. "Let me guess – you had Lord Weston set up a thick fur rug in front of the fire."

She blushed, and he laughed out loud. "Ah, my child, will we never break you of that habit? Beds exist for a reason."

"I am fine with beds," she retorted with a grin. "But there is something to be said for the heat of a blazing fire on you after a long night of riding."

"I would agree," added Hugh. "The cold can seep into your very bones on a brisk night's ride. A good fire is just what is needed to ease it out again."

"See," called out Joan with triumph, "here is a man who understands me."

Master Martin rose to his feet, putting out his arm to her. "Well then, my dear, let us get you to your fire."

She turned her eyes to Hugh, and for a long moment she was drawn in to them, to their strength, their courage.

"Good night," she offered, her voice going hoarse.

"Sleep well," he returned, and it was only Master Martin's arm at her side which had her turning and walking away from him.

Chapter 3

Joan leant forward, her eyes glowing with excitement, soaking in the warm morning sunshine and the brisk breezes dancing across the jousting list. The squires were leading the horses around the ring to warm them up, carefully staying clear of the inner two tracks which were meticulously raked and ready. Joan ran her eye over each steed as it passed, assessing its form with focused attention.

There was a movement to her right, and Hugh came up the steps to the covered viewing box, smiling and nodding to himself. "I should have known I would find you here," he mused. "The joust does not start for an hour yet." He looked around at the empty stands, then back to her. "You get a private viewing, apparently."

She grinned. "Just the way I like it!"

He came over and took the seat next to her. "Did you sleep well?"

"The best I have in ages," she enthused with a smile. "Master Martin brought his cook back with him. The man made us fresh hummus as a bedtime snack."

Hugh's eyes brightened with appreciation. "As much as I love English food, I do sometimes crave those flavors of the Mediterranean."

"It was comforting having Master nearby as well," she added. "For so many years that was the way we slept – him on his bed, me curled up in the thick fur rug by the fire. It soothed my soul to do it again, if only for one night."

The corner of his mouth quirked up in a smile. "Surely there was room for a bedroom for you at the sword school?"

She shrugged, looking back out at the horses being drawn past, at the collection of dark brown, glossy black, and grey-white. "I was only eleven when I first visited. Often I would stay so late that I would fall asleep in a corner, watching the men spar. The Master would tuck me into his room for safe keeping." A sturdy grey caught her eye and she followed him for a long moment, noting his gait.

"Eleven is rather young for a girl to become a fixture at a sword school," Hugh commented evenly.

Joan looked closer at the grey's stride, then stood, stepping forward to lean against the rail of the platform. "You there, squire on the grey!"

The lad looked up in curiosity.

"Check his right front hoof; I think he has a stone in it."

He dutifully moved to the side of his horse and gave a gentle heft to the lower leg, bending the horse's hoof back to take a look. In a moment he was nodding, pulling the dagger from his hip and working the stone out. Then he was patting the horse's shoulder, taking up the reins again, and starting forward.

Joan settled herself back in her seat, her eyes attentive on the grey. "I am sorry, you were saying?"

He smiled. "That eleven was quite young."

"Well, Michael was sixteen," she answered distractedly, "and I went to watch him spar."

His eyes were steady on her. "And who was Michael?"

Hearing Michael's name on Hugh's lips shook her back to awareness. She closed her eyes for a minute, holding in the wave of emotion which swept over her. She had not meant for it to begin like this, so casually, not about the man who had been such an important part of her life. But it was done, and she would find a way through.

She blinked her eyes open. His gaze was sharp on her, and she remembered suddenly that this was no civilian she was attempting to hide her feelings from. He was trained, just as she had been, in reading people, in drawing out their innermost secrets.

His voice was a low murmur. "I apologize; he died far too young. I am sorry for your loss."

God's teeth, the man was good.

She nodded, looking away for a moment.

His voice was somber. "The holy lands were not an easy place to survive," he commented. "I know many good men who never returned from there."

Long moments passed. The only sound was the gentle fall of hoof in dirt, the soft *whoof* as the steeds let out a breath, the steady parade of squires making their circuits in the warm spring sunshine.

Finally Joan ran a hand through her hair, easing her shoulders. "We grew up together," she explained. "His father served with my father. It seemed we were always running along the wall of a keep, climbing up the chains of the portcullis, or racing our horses along the nearest patch of clear ground. He was like a brother to me; I followed him everywhere." She looked down at her hands. "When he started attending Master Martin's sword school, it never occurred to me to stay away. I simply went."

His mouth quirked up. "And stayed, apparently."

She smiled at that. "You have met Master Martin; there had always been something soothing and wise about him. I felt contented in his presence. He was the best of teachers – patient, skilled, and attentive. Being in his school was like being in another world."

Her throat tightened. "When I was sixteen, my father was killed in battle at Acre."

Hugh's eyes shadowed. "Your childhood was not an easy one."

She gave a wry smile. "You know as well as I do that life was not gentle in the Holy Land. With me now an orphan, Master Martin took me in for good."

"It sounds like he valued your assistance," mused Hugh.

"I considered every day at that school to be an honor; I poured my heart and soul into being worthy of his tutelage." Joan felt an ache of homesickness as she thought of the polished wood floor of the school's main room. "Anything he needed done, I would do it. Any skill I could learn along the way, I studied, to be the best trainer and assistant that I could be."

Hugh's voice was low. "And Michael?"

She looked down. "He was gone, much of the time, on assignment. We could only see each other once a month or so. And then ..."

She remembered vividly the day the messenger had burst into the sword school's main room, sweat from the hard ride streaming down his face. She had been sparring with Master Martin and turned at the sound. She had taken one look at the sorrow in his eyes and known instantly. The pain had speared into the centermost of her being ...

Hugh's voice was a low murmur at her side. "Again, I am sorry for your loss."

She nodded, running a hand through her hair, turning her gaze out to the steadily moving horses. "Life goes on."

* * *

Evening was streaking the sky with violet and magenta; the last jousters of the day came forward to take their bows and receive their accolades. Many in the stands were already heading indoors to the lush feast which undoubtedly awaited them.

Joan turned to look at Hugh, smiling in appreciation at the man's patience. Clearly he had been interested in going in to the keep while the weapons exhibit was open for viewing. He knew that those doors would close at sunset. And yet he had remained steadily by her side, refilling her mug of mead, talking with her about the jousters and horses, never once trying to draw her away from her passion.

His eyes warmed as he looked at her, and he nodded. "A good day, then? Was the joust all you had hoped for?"

She sighed with pleasure. "I enjoyed it immensely." She looked to her other side, where Lord Weston sat. "And your food is delicious," she praised. "No wonder your events are so well attended."

"I shall let my kitchen staff know of your praise," he thanked her with a smile. "They will be pleased to hear their efforts were noticed."

Joan looked back at Hugh. "Shall we go for a walk?"

He stood, putting a hand down to her. "Absolutely," he agreed. "Lead on."

She tucked her hand in his arm and they strolled through the soft evening breezes back toward the keep. Lord Weston and Master Martin came along behind them. Joan's shoulders eased. "A perfect day," she sighed. She glanced up at Hugh. "Would you not agree?"

He smiled, nodding. "Absolutely perfect," he concurred.

Her mouth tweaked into a grin as they moved through the entry gates of the curtain wall and crossed the courtyard.

He raised an eyebrow. "What is it?" he asked with curiosity.

"So you do not regret missing the exhibition of weapons?" she asked lightly.

A hint of surprise flickered behind his eyes. "I did not think I let it show," he admitted after a moment.

"Not for most to see, perhaps," she agreed, her eyes twinkling.

They moved up the main stairs, but rather than continue up the spiral steps to the main dining hall, she pressed forward, into the lower room.

Hugh glanced ahead at the closed doors. "I am sure it is locked up for the night," he offered in a low voice. "It is fine; I am sure the other men can tell me what I missed."

Lord Weston stepped around them, pulling a key from his belt. "Or maybe you can see for yourself, without the crowds and noise," he offered with a smile.

Hugh glanced at Lord Weston, then back at Master Martin, and realization spread across his face. "You planned a personal showing for us."

Joan grinned. "I did say earlier that I enjoy private viewings," she reminded him.

Lord Weston finished with the door, then pushed it open. The large room was ringed with torches, and the walls were lined with display cases. Each held a collection of knives, swords, and other types of weapons.

Hugh's face lit up with pleasure. He moved immediately to the case on his left, his eyes running along the items within the wood frame.

"Look at this scimitar," he whispered, tracing his gaze down the curved blade. "That is stunning craftsmanship."

Joan pointed at the next case, walking ahead. "And here is a traditional Roman gladius," she called to him. "A good thrust with one of these to the midsection and your opponent goes down hard."

Hugh's eyes moved to another blade in the case. This one had an odd, almost lightning-bolt jag in its middle. "What is this?"

Master Martin came up next to them. "That is an ancient sword, a *khopesh*," he informed them. "It comes from Egypt, and that jag in it makes it ideal for hacking."

Joan chuckled. "I am more of a slasher myself," she grinned.

"That you are," Master Martin agreed with a smile.

Joan moved on to the next case – and stopped. There, lying in the center of the case, was a small dagger with a black leather grip. She knew every crease, knew every dent in its dulled blade.

Her voice was reverent. "My practice dagger."

She reached out her hand. The hilt fit into her grasp as if the weapon had never left it, as if the intervening years had vanished in the blink of an eye.

Master Martin's voice held warm amusement. "Up for a match?"

She spun eagerly, nodding, moving into the center of the room. He reached into the case and took out his own practice blade, perfectly matched to his small size. Hugh and Lord Weston looked between the two with interest, staying back at the edge of the room.

Master Martin's eyes moved down his student with interest.
"Perhaps your time in bucolic England has made you soft," he
teased Joan.

Joan's smile widened. "Perhaps not," she countered, settling
down into a guard.

He circled her, and she turned in place, her eyes watching
his. He was an absolute wizard, perfectly capable of attacking in
a direction completely opposite what his eyes might indicate.
But she had to start somewhere.

His eyes glanced to her left hip, and he lunged, but his blade
twisted at her right shoulder. She leapt back, barely drawing her
body clear of the blade. She immediately dodged back in,
sweeping low, but he spun to the side, his eyes sparkling with
delight.

"You have been keeping up with your studies," he praised
her, taking another circling step, and then he was in motion.

Joan quickly abandoned all hope of thinking three steps
ahead. He was like a master chess player, laying down attacks
that had only one possible defense, guiding her slowly but
surely toward the final hit. And then he began again.

She let go any thoughts, any plans, and simply eased herself
into the flow of motion. Soon she was turning with him,
twisting, sliding beneath his swings, leaping back, laughing
with delight.

There was a noise at the entryway to the hall. The main door
swung open and a messenger in brown stepped in.

Suddenly it was five years ago. Joan was sparring with
Master Martin in the polished-wood hall of his sword school.
The messenger had plowed in through the door, his eyes
shadowed, his face haggard.

Michael was dead ...

Master Martin was mid-swing when he saw her distraction.
He twisted to keep the blade clear of her body, but his
momentum carried him into her. She flew back against the
floor, her dagger skittering out of her hand, her dress flying up
to mid-thigh.

Joan stared up at the ceiling for a long moment, taking in deep breaths, striving to corral her roiling emotions.

Hugh was kneeling at her side in a heartbeat. "Are you hurt?" His eyes moved down to her legs and they sharpened in concern, focusing on a twisting line of red on her right thigh. "You're cut!"

She slowly shook her head. He put a hand out to touch the line and his forehead creased in realization. "An old scar," he murmured.

Master Martin's voice was rich with regret. "We were both distracted on that day, but I was the teacher; I should have been aware for both of us." He looked down at Joan. "Again, I am sorry."

She shook her head. "It was my own fault, both then and now. If I allow tragedy to distract me in a fight, then how can I protect those who depend on me? I need to be able to retain my focus no matter what surrounds me."

Hugh nodded, his eyes somber. "And yet, while you are learning that skill, you do not need to gather scars as a reminder."

She looked down at the thin line of red, absently running a finger along it. "It is all I have to remember him by," she mused softly. "If this is to be my one memento, then I will treasure it."

Hugh stood, putting out a hand, and she took it. He pulled her easily to her feet, his arm barely flexing with the effort. She walked over to the case and gently laid her dagger back into the case.

Lord Weston looked over at the messenger. "Yes?"

The man bowed his head. "M'Lord, the feast is in underway, and several of your guests are asking after you."

Lord Weston nodded. "Of course." He turned to the other three. "Come, join me."

Joan looked at the door, her heart still twisting. There would be drunken crowds upstairs, full of laughter and song. She did not have the heart to join them.

Hugh murmured at her side. "Perhaps you would prefer a quiet meal in your room?"

She nodded in gratitude, her shoulders easing. That sounded just right.

Master Martin looked to Lord Weston. "I appreciate your kind offer, but as I am leaving tomorrow afternoon, I would like to spend this last night with my student. I will have my cook send up some traditional favorites."

Lord Weston smiled, looking between the three. "As you wish. I will see you all in the morning then." He turned and walked from the room.

Hugh held out his arm. Joan slipped her hand into the crook of his elbow, moving at his side toward the spiral staircase. In a few moments the three of them were stepping into Master Martin's room.

The elderly man murmured some commands to a young servant boy, who quickly turned and hurried down the hall. Hugh brought Joan over to the plush, white rug fronting the fireplace, and she eased down onto it with a smile. She had barely settled her dress around her when he was bringing over a mug of mead. She took it with gratitude, drinking down a long swallow.

Master Martin beckoned to Hugh. "Here, come help me with this low table." The men brought it over to sit beside the rug. They then settled themselves cross-legged at its sides, preparing to dine.

Joan stared into the flickering flame, her gaze lost in the ever-changing oranges and yellows, her mind going back to that day of torment. In a single moment her world had changed completely. Her path had been forever altered.

Master Martin's voice was low. "He is gone, my student," he murmured to her.

Joan's voice was tight. "I know he is."

"And yet you still live," he continued. "Have you allowed any man to court you since that day?"

She shook her head. "I am not ready," she ground out.

"Wounds take their time to heal; we know this and accept it," he mused. "But at some point we need rise again. Otherwise the muscles atrophy."

She stared into the fire. "I will know when I am ready."

There was a movement at the door; the boy came in carrying a tray holding a collection of bowls. There were three types of olives, stuffed grape leaves, and fragrant chicken redolent with aromatic spices. Joan's mouth instantly watered, drawn back into another world with the long-missed, familiar fragrances.

The boy lay the tray down at the center of the table and turned to retreat back to the kitchens. Joan barely saw him go, she was so eagerly drawing an olive from the pile, popping it into her mouth, and sighing in pleasure.

"That is delicious," she sighed, lost in an ecstasy of texture, flavor, and aroma. Hugh's eyes eased, and he smiled at her before starting in himself.

He ate a stuffed grape leaf, then turned to Master Martin. "Your cook is superb," he praised warmly. "Perhaps you could leave him behind when you head on to London?"

The elderly man grinned. "You two will just have to visit me there," he countered. "I would not do without him."

The servant boy came and went, new courses were brought up, and by the time the dessert plates were being cleared Joan was beyond stuffed. She lounged against the side of the fireplace, her legs sprawled before her, running a hand through her hair.

"I will not eat again for a week," she vowed, patting her bulging stomach. "That was intensely good." She smiled over at Master Martin. "And now all we need is some good music while we digest."

His brow creased at that and he looked down for a moment. "My dear, you must pardon an old man. I have been selfish. It is time for me to remedy that."

Her eyebrow raised in curiosity. "Selfish? Do tell?"

He drew to his feet, moving to the side of the room to rummage through a leather bag. He withdrew a long, narrow wooden box, about the size of her practice dagger, and brought it over to the table. He placed it reverentially on the table before her.

"This is yours. I should have returned it to you years ago."

Joan leant forward with interest. She moved to kneel before the table, running her hand along the box's polished surface for a moment before lifting its hinged lid.

She stared in shock at the object that lay within on a velvet base. It was her boxwood flute, the one she had been given by her father when she was thirteen, the one she had lent to Michael when he first began leaving her on assignment. The delicate design of nightingales traced along its length.

She brought it to her lips, hesitated for a moment, then began to play. The familiar melody of an Israeli folk song drifted from the instrument. She lost herself in it, in the rich world she had left behind.

The last notes died away into silence, and Master Martin nodded at her, his face somber but proud. She turned to Hugh.

He was staring at her, dawning understanding growing on his face, his eyes moving between the flute in her hand and the woman before him.

His voice was hoarse. "That is the flute Michael played when we had spare evenings between our missions."

Her heart began tripping double-speed, but she kept her features calm. She had known this stage would come. She could only hope that he would move through it smoothly, would continue them on the path she had laid out.

He focused again on the flute. "He said that Nightingale, the courier, had lent him the flute."

She nodded, her throat tight.

He shook his head, confusion creasing his brow. "But I thought Nightingale was a man?"

She gave a half-smile. She had heard this misconception so many times that it had become a running joke between her and Master Martin. "I assure you, I am not male," she offered gently.

"I can see that," he ground out. "But the missions you were sent on; the dangers you survived, I assumed ..." He shook his head. "But I should know better than to do that," he admitted self-deprecatingly. "Every assumption should always be challenged."

He smiled wryly. "Nightingale often seemed to reach destinations in half the time it took other couriers," he commented. "Having seen your steeds, and the way you ride them, I now understand how that could be possible."

His eyes went up to hers. "It makes sense that your path never crossed mine. From our group, Michael was the only one who had contact with the base," he stated. "It was a foundation of our system. The fewer who knew – "

Joan's mouth drew into a wry grin. "The fewer could be made to talk," she finished for him. "Yes, I know."

He blinked at that, then his focus became more attentive. Realization flashed through his face. He sat back, staring at her.

"The Michael you loved – the Michael you lost – that is the same man who was my best friend for five years," he stated in shock.

It was all she could do to nod, to hold his gaze.

A roil of emotion cascaded through his face, of disbelief, and understanding, and confusion.

"But if that were true – " he began, and then he looked away for a minute, gathering his thoughts, nodding slowly. His gaze was even when he looked back to her. "Michael was a rare individual," he murmured to her. "I mourn his death with you."

"Thank you," she whispered.

A twinge of jealousy tickled her soul as she looked at Hugh. He had spent those last five years with Michael at his side, enjoying long, uninterrupted weeks of time talking with him, laughing with him. The two men had faced countless dangers side by side.

In comparison, Joan had been kept at a distance, catching only brief moments of Michael's attention. She had dreamt of a future where she and Michael could finally be together – and that future had never come.

Hugh gave his head another small shake. "Still, it seems so utterly unreal to me, that I could have been so close to him all those years and never had an inkling of his relationship with you."

Master Martin's voice eased into the mix. "If it was dangerous for general members of our intelligence community to know of each other, how much more dangerous if two of them were romantically involved? News of that must be kept as quiet as possible."

Joan looked to the elder man with a wry smile. "You refused to even allow me to visit him in Jaffa," she pointed out.

He nodded, his gaze flickering for a moment. "That I did, and for good reason," he returned.

Hugh's eyes went to Master Martin, and it appeared he had now gone beyond shock. "Nightingale was your assistant. That would mean … you were the chief of operations of our spy network?" he uttered in disbelief.

Master Martin nodded. "I am sure I do not need to emphasize that this discussion stays within these walls. But yes, now that we are disbanded, and our members scattered to relative safety, I do not mind you knowing."

Hugh looked between the two of them, shaking his head. "You were right there, in plain sight, at the center of a world-renowned sword school! You had people constantly coming and going from your facility!"

Joan's mouth quirked into a smile. "That we did," she agreed.

Hugh ran a hand through his short hair. "I had no idea," he murmured, shaking his head. "All this time I imagined a dark, shady character, tucked into the bowels of a sewer system, receiving his orders from Rome and sending them out through a tunnel network."

Master Martin's eyes twinkled. "It was a little different than that," he offered lightly.

Hugh glanced at Joan. "I can see that," he responded, an ease coming to his features.

He smiled back at Master Martin. "You must have been the one who wrote Michael with our orders for those first few months, as we got settled in. I remember him being pleased with how precise and accurate the details were. He said it saved him a great deal of time in our preparations."

Master Martin's serene face glowed. "I am glad to hear my messages were of use to your little group."

Hugh nodded. "Indeed. The arrival of those neatly blocked statements were quite a reassurance to him." He gave a low chuckle. "When you handed the message creation task off to your other assistant, he transferred the reply communication chores to me. I think he missed your personal touch."

Master Martin's eyes grew somber. "I missed him as well," he agreed in a low voice.

Joan shivered as a chill traced through her bones. She took a long drink, settling back against the side of the fireplace. Hugh was keeping his gaze on Master Martin, but she could see the wealth of questions swirling behind Hugh's eyes. She knew it was only through strict discipline that he was biting his tongue and not pressing for more information.

Her shoulders slumped; she was beyond exhausted. She could not tackle those questions tonight. Not when it was so critical for each step to follow precisely in the pattern.

She allowed a loud yawn to escape from her, and without prodding a second followed soon after.

Master Martin nodded to Hugh. In a moment the two had taken up the table and moved it to the side of the room. Hugh moved from candle to candle, cupping his hand behind each flame before blowing it out.

His voice was wry. "Time for me to head back down into the maelstrom," he offered to the others.

Joan's eyes glanced up in surprise at that. "Surely that hall is a pit of strewn food and ale by now!" she protested. "Stay up here; there is plenty of floor for all, and ours is fairly clean." A thought came to her and her eyes shadowed. "Unless, of course, you want –"

He shook his head vehemently. "I absolutely do *not* want to return to that," he responded. "But I would also not want to intrude."

Master Martin gave a warm laugh. "You forget, my lad, that we spent our lives in a sword school," he pointed out. "There were always lads coming and going, and students collapsed, exhausted, on whatever ground they could find. You are welcome."

Hugh looked over to Joan. "If you are sure …?"

She nodded, leaning over to sprawl on the soft rug, curling up with her back against the fire. "As long as I get my spot, you can sleep anywhere else you wish," she smiled sweetly at him.

The corner of his mouth turned up in a smile and he nodded. He took a pillow down from the couch, then lay lengthwise across the floor, so he was facing her. If they had both stretched out their arms, their fingertips would have just barely touched.

A serene quiet settled across the darkened room, with the flickering embers of fire sending dancing shadows of orange and gold along the walls. Hugh's eyes were steady on Joan. She found a gentle warmth stealing through her body, one having little to do with the flames behind her.

Her eyelids fluttered closed, and she drifted into a deep sleep.

Chapter 4

Peacefulness penetrated every corner of Joan's body; she gave a long stretch, relishing the feeling, before blinking her eyes open. Hugh was sitting there, leaning against the couch, his eyes steady on her own. He smiled in greeting.

"*Sabah el kheer*," he offered.

"Good morning to you too," she responded, pushing herself up to sitting and running a hand through her hair to comb it away from her face. "I imagine Master Martin is already off?"

His eyes twinkled. "Up at dawn, the man was. He certainly has an enviable amount of energy."

Joan groaned, shaking her head. "How many mornings I cursed that energy," she returned. "Did he at least leave us some breakfast?"

Hugh nudged his head at the low table, still pushed off to one side. Joan's eyes lit up with delight. A spread of hummus, fresh eggs, sausages, and other treats were waiting. In seconds she had plunked herself down next to the table and was preparing a trencher with a little of each. Hugh gave a low laugh before coming over to join her.

His voice was warm. "So, it is the last day of the exhibit – by noon Master Martin will be packing up and heading off to London. What are your plans then?" A thought occurred to him, and his smile dimmed. "Will you be going with him?"

She gave her head a shake, stuffing a nicely browned sausage into her mouth. She sighed in pleasure at its luscious spices. "Awf haf ta hep wif Uriel's thister," she reminded him.

His eyes widened for a moment, then he sat back, looking her over. "I completely forgot," he admitted in a low voice.

"This all began because you and Muriel came to ask for help in rescuing her sister, Linota." His eyes sharpened on hers with curiosity. "You clearly knew who I was."

She laughed, taking a long drink of her ale before responding. "Of course I did; why do you think I trusted you with such an important task?"

He gave a low bow at that, but then his eyes returned to hers. "Then why not tell me right out who *you* were?"

She snorted in merriment. "Oh, right," she countered. "I would have walked into that tavern's back room and introduced myself as Nightingale, the secret courier of a spy organization nobody knew you belonged to." Her eyes swept up to hold his. "And you would have said …?"

A smile stole across his face. "I imagine you are right," he conceded. "I would have been hard pressed to believe you."

"It seemed a much better plan to unfold the story slowly, in small pieces," she continued, scooping up a large serving of eggs and stuffing them into her mouth. "Essier to digess."

His eyes twinkled, but he said nothing.

* * *

It seemed all too soon they were standing in the cloudy grey of the early afternoon, horses and carts milling around them, as Master Martin bid farewell to Lord Weston and the other friends he had made during his stay. At last the elderly man turned to where Hugh and Joan waited patiently side by side.

Master Martin moved to stand before Hugh first. "I am so glad, after all these years, to finally be able to meet you in person," he stated, offering his arm. "Your work in the Holy Lands was legendary and worthy of the highest praise."

Hugh clasped his arm warmly. "And you, Master Martin. You are remarkable beyond anything I could have imagined. It was an honor to meet you. I wish you the safest of journeys."

Master Martin nodded, then turned to Joan. Her breath eased out of her, and then she tumbled into his arms, holding the frail man close, lost for a moment in his familiar, exotic fragrances.

For so many years he had been her guardian and confidant; these few days with him had made her realize just how much she missed him.

He pressed a kiss on her cheek. "Ah, my girl," he murmured against her ear. "You have so much to look forward to in life." He pulled back, gazing at her. "Tell me you will start to seek ahead, rather than behind."

She smiled tenderly into his wise eyes. "I shall try."

"You are always welcome to visit in London, for as long as you wish," he offered.

She gave a nod. "When I can make the time, I will certainly come see you," she promised.

Master Martin tenderly ran his fingers down the side of her face, then looked over to Hugh. "Will you keep an eye on her for me, until then?"

Hugh nodded, bringing his own gaze to hers. "It would be an honor."

Then Master Martin was stepping back, climbing onto his roan, and the entourage headed out. The clattering of hooves filled the courtyard and thunked across the wooden bridge. Joan strained to follow their shapes as the group moved down the well-worn path. A turn in the road, a stand of maple, and they were gone.

Lord Weston's voice called her back from her far-off gaze and thoughts. "I do not suppose I can tempt you into staying another night?"

She shook her head as she turned. "I need to get back home. Sarah has been having some trouble at the mill; I want to be nearby in case she needs assistance."

Lord Weston's brow furrowed. "Are those outlaws – those *wolves' heads* - bothering her again, trying to drive her out? I would gladly send some guards with you."

Joan smiled in appreciation. "I know you would, and you know why you cannot. I am sure Sheriff Elias is behind it all. You are already in enough trouble with that man because of me."

He responded without hesitation, his eyes gleaming. "And gladly would seek more."

"I appreciate that," she soothed him. "But for now, there is no need to exacerbate things. I will be sure to send a message if I need help."

He gave a snort. "You *never* ask for help," he countered. "You would plow into a gang of cut-throats and thieves without hesitation if you saw someone in trouble."

Hugh glanced over at her, his brows rising slightly, but he remained quiet.

Lord Weston gave a resigned shrug. "If you will be going, then I will help get you on your way. It is a long ride back to that wilderness you call home, and I would not want you riding alone after dark." He gave a wave of his hand and a young, wiry lad went running off toward the stables.

Hugh turned to her at that. "If you would allow me to, I will accompany you home. Then I could head into town from there and see if Muriel is done helping Father Picot."

Joan's heart kindled with warmth.

It might work. It just might work.

"As you wish."

* * *

Joan could not quite tell when the greyness began to seep into the world. She knew she had been full of delight when the aroma of spiced figs had filled her nose, when Master Martin's bright eyes had looked so insightfully into her own. For a moment – for a brief, shimmering moment, she had felt at home again. She had felt comforted and warmed. The world had returned to the shimmering blues and the radiant golds she had remembered.

But now, despite being back on her beloved Aquila, despite the miracle of having Hugh riding by her side, those smoky tendrils were wreathing around her chest. Perhaps things were not as ebony black as that first day, the sight of the messenger's eyes so harrowed and worn, the searing pain of the knife edge burning through her thigh. She could breathe now, after all, could move through the world, could speak.

And yet ... she pulled the reins to the left, slowing her steed to a stop by a small brook. She dismounted, looping the leather reins over a young elm tree. Behind her, she knew that Hugh mirrored her actions, but he did not speak as she moved down to the mossy banks and knelt to cup fresh water in her hands to drink.

She sat back on her heels, looking downstream to where the grey waters tumbled along a series of smooth, slate rocks. The sun seemed to have eased for the moment, hidden behind a scattering of dirty clouds.

She pushed her hair from her eyes with a weary hand. "I try to tell them," she murmured, barely aware that she was speaking aloud. "I try to explain what it was like in the Holy Land. The stunning, almost radiant sunrises when the light gilds everything in sight, making it too lovely to look on. The shimmering depths of the waters, swirling in turquoise, teal, and cerulean." Her voice caught, and she pushed away tears with the back of her hand. "The sunsets that stole your breath away; the clearest sign of God's hand on Earth that I had ever been graced with."

Hugh eased to one knee at her side, so close that she could have swayed in the wind and rested against him. His voice was a quiet murmur in the breeze. "Jerusalem was full of beauty," he agreed. "Just as every place on this Earth has its own, unique, gifts to offer." His eyes stayed steady on the stream. "Trust in me. Close your eyes."

Joan exhaled, nodded, then let her lids fall. The grays faded away. She was left with the slow, steady rumble of the water tumbling and turning over the rocks, taking the course it had followed for centuries. Her skin glowed with a soft warmth as the sun eased free of whatever cloudy wisps had held it back. A soft breeze trickled across her cheek, and she turned into it, inhaling the scent of rosemary it brought with it.

Hugh's voice moved into her awareness as a returning loved one resolves out of a morning mist. "I want you to bring to mind all those you help here," he instructed. "Young Linota, who

Muriel trusts you will bring home to her safe and sound. Sarah, at the mill, who relies on your strength to protect her. There are countless others; innocents who have nowhere else to turn. Your presence here will bring them joy. You will be the candle lit in the darkest night."

There was the gentlest of touches on her hand, just the softest caress, and yet a shiver coursed through her entire body and left her weak.

"Open your eyes."

She lifted her lids. The stream before her sparkled as if a million emeralds and diamonds had been scattered along its surface. The moss beneath her hand had taken on a velvety texture, and the rosemary scent had intensified to intoxicating levels. High above, a pair of siskins danced in the breeze, their golden bodies tracing shimmering arcs.

She soaked in the beauty of the world, her breath coming in long, full sweeps.

"It is beautiful," she stated at last.

He nodded at that, a quiet smile coming to his lips. "I understand better than you might think," he murmured. "And yet, trust in God. He has made beauty in every place; a light in every darkness."

Hugh turned to her. "Have patience, and allow it to reach you."

He drew to his feet, holding out a hand. She waited for a long moment, the tendrils of smoke still tugging at the sides of her ribs, the edges of her toes. Then, at last, she put her fingers into his, and he was drawing her up.

Chapter 5

The last vestiges of the burnt-orange sun had just drifted below the horizon as they rounded the corner and came upon her homestead. She pulled into a stop, and at her side Hugh reined in, his eyes scanning their surroundings. His mouth spread into a smile, and Joan's heart eased.

"So, you approve?" she asked, finding that there was more emotion in those few words than she would have thought.

He nodded. "Woods cut back from the outer fence, house centered within it, the stables hard aside. Your gardens are well tended, there is plenty of grass for the horses." His eyes focused on a small stone structure. "And you even have a well?"

"Yes, I do," she confirmed, smiling.

His brow furrowed. "But apparently no gate to your fence," he added.

She chuckled. "True enough," she agreed. "Be sure to follow me closely. If you were to break Accipiter's leg, I'm afraid I could not be responsible for the consequences to your health."

He smiled at that, giving a wave of his hand. "Lead on, and I shall be your shadow," he promised.

She gave a sharp nudge to her steed, and in a moment they were flying down the path, straight at the wood slats of the slat wattle fence. Aquila hardly needed a hand on the reins, he knew the way so well. In a moment they were soaring over the hurdle, turning hard right, then twisting around the oak stump. There were several dips and large rocks around her homestead, placed there to wreak havoc on unsuspecting cut-purses. But for her steeds, it was merely a last, joyous obstacle course to maneuver before their final rest of the day.

Aquila pulled up on his own as they reached the stables, and Accipiter was at his side in a heartbeat. Hugh slid down, moving to the front of the two animals, giving a fond pat to Accipiter's neck as Joan came to join him.

His voice was low. "I can stay while you stable Aquila, and then move on to town to bring Accipiter to Muriel," he offered.

Joan's heart wrenched. What if he departed now? What if he mounted, rode off, and she were left on her own, left with the suffocating isolation that blanketed her every night?

Her voice sounded shaky even to her own ears. "If you would like –"

There was movement to the right. In the growing dusk the shadowy form of a small wolf stalked toward them a step, then stopped. Its amber eyes gleamed. A heartbeat, and then a second shape joined the first.

Hugh's hand dropped to the hilt of his sword. He took a half-step before Joan, shielding her with his body.

His voice was a low command. "Get into the stables."

"But Hugh –"

The wolf on the left began a rumbling growl, deep in its throat, that set the hairs of her neck on end.

Hugh took a step forward, his eyes steadily focused on the golden gleams. "Get inside," he ordered again.

Joan shook her head, staring at the animals. "Stop it," she stated firmly.

Hugh stopped moving, but his focus did not waver. "If you think –"

Joan took a step forward to stand by his side, staring at the two wolves.

"Romulus, you stop it," she ordered again, her gaze holding the animal's eyes with focused attention. "This is a friend."

She dropped down to one knee, and the other shape bounded toward her, licking her face. She affectionately drew him in. "That's right, Remus. You show your brother."

Hugh looked between the two massive dogs. After a long moment he moved his hand from his hilt to carefully tousle Remus's head, his eyes widening. "You call these things *pets*?"

"They are mostly dog," she grinned at him, "although I admit it seems there is some wolf in there somewhere." She looked back at the second beast. "Come on, Romulus. You can trust him."

Hugh dropped to one knee beside her. After several heartbeats Romulus hesitantly took one step forward, then two. He came to Joan first, nuzzling her fondly, then stared over at Hugh.

Hugh waited without moving, one hand still resting in Remus's coat.

At last Romulus took a step toward Hugh, interjecting his body between Hugh and Remus, drawing the man's hand onto his own back.

Joan chuckled. "I figured jealousy would get the best of him in the end," she teased. "I apologize for their behavior; they are loyal defenders."

"I imagine they might get used to a visitor over time," mused Hugh, giving Romulus a scratch between his ears.

"I guess we will find out, as you are the first we have had," offered Joan with a smile.

Hugh glanced up at that, his hand stilling, and then he was giving a last rustle to Romulus before standing.

Joan glanced back at the house. "As our very first visitor, would you like the grand tour? And perhaps a drink?"

"Absolutely," agreed Hugh, and there was an ease to the tension in his shoulders. Together they moved into the stables and rubbed down the horses, hanging the tack and settling them in.

"And now, for my luxurious abode," teased Joan, moving out of the stables. "I have but two rooms – the main living area and then my bedroom." She moved along the side of the building, past a shuttered window, to the main, oak door. She reached a hand into the leather pouch at her side, withdrawing a small iron key.

"You lock it," he murmured, intrigued. "Apparently there are treasures within."

She smiled at that. "Just one. And I imagine it is only special to me, but I do treasure it." She turned the key and pushed the door wide, motioning him in.

He stepped across the threshold, and Remus and Romulus swept along either side of her to pad into the room. She drew the door closed behind them, looking across the main room as it flickered in the light of the remnants of dusk. A small, rectangular oak table stood to the right, fronted by a bench. A thick fur rug lay before the fireplace. Windows were shuttered on either side of the room. A row of unlit candles lined the mantle.

She moved to the grate, picking up the metal curve of the firesteel at the edge. She struck the stone chert next to it a few times until the sparks caught at the pile of birch bark, creating a low flame. A moment later she had taken one of the candles from the mantle and was kneeling with it. "The pitcher of mead is on the back wall, by the bedroom door," she stated, turning and handing him the lit candle. "If you could pour our drinks, I will get the rest of the room prepared."

She turned back to the fireplace, lighting another candle, then using it to move down the row. In a moment all were glowing with flickering warmth. She roused the fire, added on a medium-sized log, then moved to put a pair of candles on the small table. She turned …

Hugh was nowhere to be seen.

A flickering glow came from the entryway to her bedroom.

No. No. No.

She was not ready for him to have seen the tapestry. Not yet, not before they had time for a drink, for a conversation, for her to put in place the final pieces to span the two points in time. She was frozen in place, her eyes pinned on the entryway, wishing with all her might that she could unwind time, draw it back, hold him here in the room with her.

A long moment passed. At last she took a step forward, then another. She moved to stand in the doorway, knowing what she would find.

Hugh was standing alongside her bed, staring at the tapestry which covered most of the far wall. She knew every warp and woof of the piece, every detail of the scene it portrayed.

There, to the right, a pair of men sat at an open-air café. The marble table-top, the grey cobblestones beneath, all were exactly as she remembered them. One man was looking down at the table, his attention focused on an item there.

The second had glanced up, and was staring off to the left.

She followed his eyes, across the expanse of grey stone and turquoise waters, along the line of the wall that edged the area. There, dancing along the wall, barefoot, clothed in a tangerine, flowing dress, was a young woman with flowing auburn hair. Her mouth was lit by a smile and a seagull hovered at her side.

A sense of joy eased through Joan, as it always did when she stared at her masterpiece.

Hugh turned. For a moment she was shaken with confusion as her memories and the tapestry and his physical presence all merged and dissolved. The candle in his hand had dripped wax down his fingers, but he appeared not to notice at all.

His voice was hoarse. "The girl was you?"

She could barely nod in response, so caught she was by his gaze.

Then he was putting the candle down on her shelf, he was taking a step forward, and she had tumbled into his arms. She was kissing him. All sense of time and place was lost. He was carrying her to the bed, they were shedding clothes, and still the wonder of it all glowed within her. She laughed out loud, and he stared at her for a long moment, lost in her.

The world fell away.

* * *

Joan blinked her eyes open, the golden strands of dawn stretching through the closed shutters, sending dancing light across the tumble of man and dogs. Remus and Romulus were nestled up against Hugh, creating a warm, tumbled mound of love and comfort.

She almost could not believe that this was real. Surely it was a dream; surely another blink of her eye would dissolve the scene.

Hugh mumbled something, gave a stretch, and his hand brushed along Remus's thick fur. The animal nuzzled into him in delight. Hugh's eyes opened at a snap, going to the animal and then across to Joan. They widened in surprise, and then resolved as memory and awareness swept over him. He put out an arm.

She folded herself into his embrace wordlessly, becoming lost in the cocoon that they created.

* * *

Hugh was lying on his back, gazing up at the tapestry, while Joan sprawled contentedly across his chest. Remus and Romulus's excited barks drifted in through the closed shutter, and she knew they were tracking down the hares which lived in the eastern woods. She wished them luck in acquiring their morning meal.

Hugh's eyes sharpened as he looked closer at the two men in the weaving, and his arm drew her in against him in a reflexive action. She drew her gaze to his. "What is it?"

For a long moment it seemed as if he would not speak. Then, at last, he gave his head a soft shake. "You were *his*," he murmured.

Her cheeks reddened. "Yes, I was," she agreed softly. "Although we had never formalized it, it had been the dearest wish of our fathers since we were quite young. I took it for granted that, once his assignments were over, we would be joined."

He shook his head again, as if trying to clear a lingering fog. His voice was rough. "When I saw you in that courtyard, it was as if ..." He ran a hand through his hair, at a loss for a moment. "As if I had lost a piece of myself, and suddenly it was returned," he whispered. "I felt, for the first time in my life, complete. At home. How things should be, now and forever. And as I gazed at you, I remember saying, 'she is just right.' "

He looked at the tapestry for a long moment, taking in its weave. "Michael gave a snort – you know how he could be. But then he looked up to see. For a moment he seemed sharply annoyed, almost angry. It upset me, that he could be disturbed with such an innocent joy as yours. I was defensive and protective of you all at once, and I had never even met you."

His brow furrowed. "But then his look changed. He was accepting, almost amused, as if a beloved child had done something mischievous. And he said, 'she is quite a delight.' "

His hand clenched. "I was swept with such a rage. I had seen you first! I had been the one to connect with you. And here he was talking as if *he* would have you. It was not right! And when I turned back to you –you were gone."

Years of heartache and loss rang in his words. Joan waited, watching him relive the tumultuous emotions.

At last he turned to her, his face harrowed. "All this time I resented him for his words; I growled over how he had kept me from you. How, if only I had turned back more quickly, or he had not distracted me, I could have found you."

He gave a soft shake of his head. "But all this time, I had misunderstood the situation completely. You were his. You *were* his." He sounded as if, even now, he could not quite believe it.

"At the time, I was his," she agreed softly.

His gaze moved back to the tapestry. "I went back to that courtyard every day for a month, hoping against hope that you would return. That we could talk, could share ourselves, could connect the way I knew we would." She watched as the air left him, as the tension rippled into his face. "But I see now that you were meeting him clandestinely, so no one else would know."

Joan's throat constricted with iron bands. It took all her strength to force the word past her lips. "No."

His gaze swung to meet hers, confusion creasing his brow. "No?"

She shook her head. "That moment on the wall, with the tang of salt air and the sharp cry of a seagull in my ear, that was the last time I saw Michael alive. I turned away, and you both were gone, and then you both were *gone* …"

The tears came, hot and heavy. His strong arms embraced her, holding her close, and the pain and torment flowed out of her like a cleansing rain after a long, parching drought.

* * *

Joan stretched against Hugh on her front door step, soaking in the late afternoon sun. Remus came trotting up, a battered oak branch in his mouth, dropping it with a grin at their feet. Hugh drew his arm back and sent it sailing over a mound of tangled raspberry bushes. In a heartbeat Remus and Romulus were in hard pursuit, Romulus pushing hard to beat his brother to the prize.

Joan laughed out loud, the beauty of the moment soaking into her. Hugh's arm around her waist felt so natural. She was pleasantly full from the venison stew, and the sky was easing into crimsons and ragwort-yellows.

Hugh's voice was soft, almost hesitant in her ear. "Do you mind talking about him?"

She gave a wry smile, shaking her head. "After all these years, it is a relief," she admitted. "For so long everything was such a secret. And then, when it wasn't, there was nobody to tell, no one who would understand."

His fingers ran gently along her side, and she wondered if he was reassuring her or himself.

She forced herself to continue speaking. "Master Martin was truly a father to me. But all those years, without anyone to really understand what I was going through, without someone to confide in – I did feel lonely. I was alone with a retinue of soldiers."

He gave a wry smile. "Well, you and Agatha," he commented.

She glanced up at him. "Who?"

His grin grew wider. "I think we are past secrets," he reminded her. "When the messages changed, when the parchments metamorphosed from strong, block letters to a gentler, scrawling script, suddenly Michael foisted the duty of staying in touch with base on me." He gave a shake of his head. "There was something subtly different about the phrasing of the messages, something softer. I asked him if they were written by a woman, and at last he broke down and admitted the truth. That they were done by Agatha, an elderly nun with whom he'd had trouble in the past."

Joan could only blink at him. "Agatha?"

Hugh nodded, drawing her in against him. Remus bounded up, eyes bright with pride, bearing the branch trophy. Hugh retrieved the saliva-strewn stick and lobbed it into a copse of thin birch. The dogs were after it in a tawny streak.

Hugh's voice held amusement. "Agatha," he agreed. "Withered and hunched she might be, but her messages showed a mind as sharp as a chef's knife, and a flirtatious side as well." The corner of his mouth turned up. "I wonder if, in her dreams, she still imagined herself a young woman, seeing life's potential stretched out before her."

Joan still could not quite wrap her mind around the concept. "Agatha? A decrepit crone?"

Something in her voice finally had Hugh turn and look down at her. Awareness crept into his gaze, and his arm around her stilled.

At last his voice came, hoarse with surprise. "It was you writing us?"

She nodded mutely. It was a long moment before she could put breath behind her thoughts. "I pleaded with Master Martin to let me take over the writing. It was hard enough having Michael away for so long. At least I could be the one sending out the orders and advice. Surely it could not hurt any. After a few months he finally gave in."

She looked down for a moment. "I admit I was quite upset when it was not Michael who wrote back. I knew his writing; I knew his formal style. It was clear from that first message that he had asked you to take over. I felt rejected. Once again I had been left behind."

Hugh gave a gentle shake to his head. "He was following protocol," he stated, half in wonder. "He was keeping the distance between you two, so that the relationship could not be used against either one of you."

Joan gave a disheartened smile. "I know that logically," she agreed. "But at the time it hurt deeply. I almost asked Master Martin to take the job back. If I couldn't communicate with Michael, I didn't want to do it at all." She gave a low chuckle. "But my pride interfered. Having pleaded for the task, I wasn't going to give up without a fight. So I kept at it."

Hugh's voice took on a distance. "You were writing to me," he echoed.

She lay her head against his chest, and he drew her in closer, the setting sun's gleam gilding the edges of the birch leaves, sending a golden frosting across the meadow. "I wrote to you," she agreed, "and your responses were delightful, amused, insightful, and ..." She let out a long breath, at a loss for words. "They were just *right*," she ended finally. "Soon all I could think about was receiving your next message and memorizing it completely. Master Martin made us burn each one, of course, for security reasons." She tapped a finger to her head. "But I made sure each one was safe, for me to peruse and delight over at my leisure."

Hugh's voice was low in her ear.

"Tangerine branches were laden with opulent spheres;
Imagery blinds me undimmed by the passing of years."

She glanced up in surprise. "I wrote that about the period my family stayed in Acre," she recalled. "Even now I could almost reach out and touch the fruit, it was so fragrant and alive. The texture of each one was stunning, as if their skin held a secret message for me."

He ran a hand in wonder along her cheek. "We burned our messages, too," he murmured. "And I made sure to store each one of yours safely within my memory before that ephemeral parchment dissolved into ash."

His brow creased, and he gave a shake of his head. "But if you were writing me, how did Michael know you were coming to visit him? I don't remember any news of that in your later messages."

Her cheeks flushed, and she turned to look out at the sun's lowering orb, now resting gently on the distant forest of oak. Layers of clouds were sending waves of deep magenta toward the edges of her world.

Her voice was a whisper. "I did not go to visit Michael."

His body stilled, and it was a long moment before she felt him breathe again, before he gently turned her within his embrace so she looked up at him. And yet he waited, his eyes half-hope, half-disbelief, almost unwilling to break the silence.

She gave a soft nod, her eyes locked on his. "I came to see you," she admitted. "I knew we could not talk, not even meet, and that when I left I would have to put you out of my mind completely. I hoped that seeing you in person would dispel the fantasy I had spun and allow me to return to the life I had built."

She gave her head a shake, lost in his gaze. "But the moment I saw you, I knew. I knew in every part of my body, from the core of my heart to the depths of my soul."

He groaned, drew her in, and then they were kissing, tumbling, losing themselves in each other.

Chapter 6

Joan blinked her eyes open. The night was pitch black; only a faint, flickering glow emanated from the fireplace in the main room. Remus and Romulus were sprawled at the foot of the bed. Two pairs of eyes shone in the night, staring toward the doorway, ears swiveled to match. The blanket pulled slightly, and Joan realized that Hugh was awake, his hand carefully reaching for his sword at the side of the bed.

A sharp pounding came at the front door. Joan rolled for her weapon, coming up at the same time Hugh did. Each wrapped a robe around their body in silence. The dogs trotted at their side as they eased into the main room. She noted that they were not growling, not bristling their backs in a sign of aggression.

She put a finger to her lips before coming up against the front door. "Who goes there?"

A high, reedy voice was half-muffled by the thick wood, but she could make it out in the crisp night air. "It is Jake," called the visitor. "Sarah is in trouble!"

Joan undid the latch, pulling the door open, revealing a scrawny teen nearly her own height. His breath came in long heaves, and his flaxen hair was strewn in every direction imaginable. Even in the low light of the fireplace it was clear that his rough clothes were more mending than fabric.

She drew him in by the arm, settling him down on the long, wooden bench. Hugh placed a mug of ale down before the lad, and he gratefully drew it down before turning to Joan.

"Tobias and at least six of his wolf's heads are at Sarah's mill," he warned, his voice nearly breaking. "Sarah was hiding in the attic, last I saw, but they will find her soon enough. When they do –" His voice broke off, a look of wild panic sweeping over him.

Joan gave him a pat on the arm. "You did well," she praised him. "You get home and stay there. I will take care of everything."

He was on his feet before she finished. "I can help!"

She shook her head. "It's important for your family that you not be involved. Tobias could burn down your house with your mother and father in it. It's critical that you get home to protect them. Can you do that for me?"

He appeared torn between wanting to protect his family and wanting to ride out at Joan's side, but at last he nodded in acceptance. "You be careful too," he warned her. Then he was in motion, streaking out the door and into the black night.

Joan turned, striding back toward her bedroom. "This is not your fight," she informed Hugh, half distracted while she pulled on clothes. "You should stay here so that someone can still go after Linota."

He shook his head, taking her by the arm, turning her to face him. "If we were in my home, and Ymbert scrambled in shouting about a dangerous mission, would *you* lounge in bed until I returned from it?"

"God's teeth, no," she snapped. "But this is –"

He held her gaze steadily, and she faltered. At last she blew out a breath. "All right," she reluctantly conceded. "There is no time to argue the point. Sarah needs us."

She finished tugging on her boot, then turned to face the tapestry. With a sweep of her hand, she slid it along its wooden rail so it bunched up at the left.

Hugh shook his head in surprise. Tucked in a nook behind the tapestry was a trio of shelves. They were stacked with a variety of throwing knives, short swords, caltrops, and other weapons. "I should have known," he chuckled.

"Stock up now," advised Joan, stepping forward to select a pair of knives. She tucked one into the lining of her leather boots. Other blades eased into the back of her belt, the bracers at her wrist, and anywhere else they could get a purchase.

It seemed only seconds before Aquila and Accipiter were riding hard through the night, streaking like quicksilver beneath the sliver of moon that had risen over the horizon. Joan knew the path by heart, and Hugh stayed close at her side. She was warmed by the complete trust he put in her to guide them safely through the shadows.

It was only three miles to Sarah's mill, but to Joan it felt as if a lifetime had passed before they drew up in a stand of elm just out of sight of the structure. Long moments passed as the horses' breath eased and her heart's pounding settled into quiet. At last she could hear the soft burbling of the stream, the rustling of the wind through the birch.

She slid off Aquila, and they tethered the two steeds to a sturdy young oak. Hugh came to her side, his voice a low whisper. "What is the layout of the building?"

She picked up a stick and sketched the mill's outer walls, showing the doors on opposite walls. "Two outer doors," she explained. "The lower floor is open, with the grinding stone taking up the eastern half. The stairs up are in the center." She drew another rectangle. "Second floor has four bedrooms, and again the stairs in the center." She glanced forward, in the direction of the mill, her heart constricting. "And then there's the attic."

Hugh drew his sword. "We will get her out," he vowed.

She gave herself a shake. Her voice brooked no chance of failure. "Yes, we will."

She looked at him, and for a long moment their gazes held. She basked in the strength of his love, in the certain knowledge that, should she need him, he would be there. Then he nodded, gave a wry smile, and melted into the night.

She crept forward, moving toward the front of the building. In the daylight a grassy path might have been seen leading out into the forest on either side of the clearing. In the barely-moonlit night even the large mill building itself was only a flat shadow against the stars. There was no sign that anything was amiss in the quiet landscape.

Joan trusted in Jake's report implicitly. Tobias and his bandits were in there. Their reputation preceded them; they were some of the most feared fighters in the county. She and Hugh would have to take them out one by one - or face certain death at their blades.

Joan stood still for a long moment, closing her eyes, listening intently. If her vision could not help her, perhaps her other senses could. There was the whisper of wind through the large oak, the soft call of a fox … there! Ahead to the right; it almost blended in with the background. There was a rhythmic thrumming, as if someone were unconsciously tapping his fingers against his scabbard.

She opened her eyes again, acutely aware of every leaf, every branch which lay between her and her destination. One cautious step at a time, she crept forward. His hunched back resolved from the shadows, and she inched slowly, careful of each rolling motion of her foot.

She settled her knife firmly into her hand, then took the last step.

Her blade flashed in the moonlight, the sharp edge drawing back and right against his exposed throat. She went for the jugular, not the artery, so that the blood would not burst from the wound, only drain gently in silence. The blade neatly severed beneath his voice box, so not a sound emerged from the explosive exhale of her victim.

She pressed her body against his to support him as he sagged, carefully lowering him down into the dense grass.

She knelt by his side for a long moment, her heart pounding. To her relief there was no cry of alarm, no sense that she'd been spotted. Her breath eased out of her, and she smiled. One down.

A low cough came from the left, and she nodded in satisfaction. The team was efficient and logical. The second guard was exactly where she figured he'd be, beside the front door.

She ran her left hand along the ground, searching with her fingers for a plum-sized rock. In a minute she had just the one. She carefully crept within twenty feet of the guard, then sent the rock over to hit the wall at the far corner of the structure. He turned in alert interest at the sound, taking a few steps toward it.

In a few moments his corpse lay tucked along the outer wall of the mill, his sightless eyes pointed at the night sky.

Joan took her time, stealthily covering the ground before the mill, before she was satisfied that these were the only two guards assigned to watch the front of the building. She knew, on the back side, that Hugh was doing the same. One of their only advantages would be making sure they fought on a single front. If an opponent were allowed to get behind them, all could be lost.

Finally she moved to the window, carefully peering in. Her stomach twisted in concern, and she forced herself to take long, deep breaths. The place was a shambles. Tall wooden shelves were tipped over; leather-bound trunks sprawled open with their contents strewn about. Three rough men attentively dug through every chest and examined the contents of each. A table at the center of the room held a pile of items, from utility knives to leather belts. Candles glowed on a number of surfaces, setting a flickering sheen to the room. The mill stone, to the right, was in shadows.

Joan moved right, past the door, and over to the other window. She eased the shutters open, then hefted herself up over the sill, dropping to her feet on the other side. She knelt for a long moment, allowing her eyes to adjust, listening to every sound.

Was Hugh inside already?

There was a stuttering creak from the far side of the room, from the deep shadows behind the mill stone.

The three bandits immediately stilled in their searches, three pairs of eyes swiveling to pin the shadows with intense interest.

The hand of the grey-haired man eased to his sword. "Marcus. Go take a look."

Marcus gave a short nod, drawing his weapon. His voice was a low mutter. "Probably a cat." Yet he stepped forward cautiously. As he moved through the light Joan saw the shimmer of a scar on his right cheek. The man had been in a fight or two.

Another few steps, and he became lost in the darkness of the corner.

There was a sighing noise, and then a soft *thunk*.

The older soldier narrowed his gaze, staring after him. "Marcus?"

A low voice called out to them, tinged with awe. "I think we missed something!"

Both remaining guards glanced at each other, and the younger one's eyes glimmered with avarice. "Might be we finally earn what we're worth," he murmured to the older one.

"Don't count it until it's spent," warned the elder.

They moved steadily toward the back corner. Joan eased around to the left, positioning herself behind them. The older one was slightly ahead of the younger, and she left that man to Hugh.

Now it was a matter of careful timing. She crept forward, her knife high …

From the shadows there was a flash of silver. She dove forward, her knife driving into her man's back just as Hugh sliced his weapon across the older man's throat. Her free hand cupped the guard's mouth, cutting off his last exhale, and she eased his body to the ground.

Hugh's eyes met hers briefly, and she saw the warmth of respect in them. Then they turned as one to fix focused attention on the stairs in the center of the room.

The room fell into silence.

There were slow, steady creaks and thunks upstairs, but none came toward the stairs. Whoever was up there, they seemed oblivious to the fate of their comrades below.

After a long moment Hugh turned to her. He held up two fingers, then using both hands he pointed to the left and right sides of the ceiling.

Joan nodded. That was where she had figured the thieves were as well. Probably ransacking the bedrooms, looking for jewelry and other trinkets. She settled her knife's hilt securely in her fingers.

Hugh moved toward the stairs, looking at the open hallway above, but she put a hand on his arm. He stilled instantly. His eyes swiveled back to hers, holding a question.

She put a finger to her lips, then pointed at the stairs, then her own feet. She knew every creak and moan of those old treads. If they were going to get up them silently, he would have to follow behind her.

His gaze stilled for a long moment, and he glanced again at the ceiling, at the audible evidence of the armed men above. Then he drew his eyes back to hers for a long moment. At last he nodded.

She crept forward, every sense alert. On the first tread, she stepped to the far left. The second tread was fine all the way across, but on the third her foot needed to be slightly right. Hugh remained immediately behind her, mirroring her actions.

Joan gave a wry smile as she moved. Sarah had laughed at Joan that afternoon as she had been working out how to move silently. Joan invested hours in going up and down the stairs, examining them, teasing out their secrets. Joan was immensely glad now that she had put in the effort.

At last she reached the top, and she paused for a moment. The men were still rummaging on either side of them, apparently unaware of their presence. There was a tap on her shoulder, and she waved Hugh up to join her on the last step. His warmth next to her was nearly intoxicating, and she looked up at him, her heart pounding with a sensation which was suddenly far removed from the dangerous situation they were in. He met her gaze, his eyes smoky with passion, and it was with clear effort that he looked away, turned his head down the hallway to his right.

In a moment he was in motion, and she turned toward Sarah's bedroom. A candle's gleam shone through the half-open door. She crept carefully toward it, then peered in.

The man was built like a bull. He had Sarah's trunk open and was pawing through her clothing. He held up a pale ivory chemise and pressed the thin fabric to his face. He drew in a long inhale.

Joan's stomach turned, and she held in the urge to fling the dagger at his back, to stop him right there. Instead, she slowly crept toward the man. The long, flat curve of his back called to her, and she adjusted the angle of her blade, seeing exactly where it would slip through the ribs.

Crash!

A loud jangling noise echoed from the other room, and Joan's heart leapt in fear. Was Hugh all right? Had the bandit caught him off guard?

Then her own man was spinning, staring at her in surprise, and she found she had more immediate problems on her hands. She dove straight at him, her top priority to silence him before he could raise the alarm to Tobias. She had no doubt the leader was in the attic, and she desperately prayed that he had not yet found Sarah. There was still a chance. If she could only –

He slammed his arm from right to left, and instead of her blade drilling into his heart it only carved a gouge across his chest. His left hook instantly followed, and Joan spun left to block it, catching the blow high on her shoulder. The force of the hit flung the knife from her hand and sent her entire arm numb. As she staggered, his right arm wrapped around her neck from behind, slamming her back against his chest.

She scrambled with both hands to pull the arm lower, even a hair. It was like tugging on a massive oak.

Bright, sparkling stars danced across her vision, and she knew she only had seconds before she lost consciousness. She raised her boot and aimed a solid kick back toward his kneecap. He turned his leg as she moved, taking the kick against his calf, and her vision swam. She shifted her weight, to go for the other one. But her clawing hands were faltering, and the world shimmered out of focus. Blackness gaped before her ...

The bandit holding her coughed, staggered, and his grip on her neck eased. She fell onto all fours, desperately sucking in air. At last she turned.

Hugh was carefully lowering the muscular body onto the ground. The corpse's chest was interrupted by the bright, silver tip of a dagger protruded from a welling fountain of blood.

Hugh turned to her, putting out a hand, helping her back to her feet. He ran his fingers gently down the side of her neck, and his voice was hoarse. "Are you all right?"

She held his gaze, and it was all she could do not to fold into his arms, to show the depths of her appreciation. There would be time enough for that later. "I am fine," she reassured him. She drew another blade from her boot, then turned back to Hugh. "I assume the man you took on was not medium-height and blond?"

Hugh shook his head. "Short, bald, and quite clumsy. He dropped a box of jewelry just before I got to him. I worried the loud noise might have thrown you off, so I took him out quickly and sprinted back here."

She gave a wry smile. "Good thing you did," she murmured. Her eyes flicked to the stairs. "I asked because we still have Tobias unaccounted for. I would guess that puts him upstairs, then, where I figured he would be."

Her gaze shadowed. "He is a snake, and for some reason he has gotten even more vicious these past few months. If he has found Sarah, his latest pastime would be to gut her before our eyes, so that we had to fight him while listening to Sarah's dying screams. Whatever risks there are, we must make sure we get him away from her."

Hugh nodded, his face serious. "Let me go first this time, then."

She shook her head. "We still hold the advantage. He will think I have come alone to save Sarah. Stay behind me. You might only have one chance; use it wisely."

Hugh hesitated, but at last he nodded again. "Be careful."

She ran a hand along his arm, then turned. Once again they were moving, step by step, precisely choosing the placement of each foot on the wooden span. Joan carefully poked her head up over the level of the attic floor, looking around the cluttered room.

There were only two shuttered windows on this level, one at each end. It was nearly impossible to make anything out amongst the boxes, bales of hay, and other supplies which lay in heaps. She remained in a crouch as she stepped onto the floor.

A low chuckle sounded by the front window, and she turned. Her heart drained as her eyes adjusted to the scene.

Tobias was holding Sarah before him as a human shield, a dagger held to her throat. Sarah was a tall woman, with long, auburn hair and a navy blue dress. She practically covered Tobias from head to toe, and he had to lean his head left slightly to meet Joan's gaze.

His mouth curved up into a smile. "I figured you might be along eventually," he drawled. "That little rat-pet of yours probably went scurrying away the moment we kicked in the front door." His eyes traced down her form. "I get two for the price of one, and I have to say, you are definitely an added bonus here."

Joan settled the knife more securely in her grasp. Her world focused down to just the portion of Tobias's neck which was exposed past Sarah's body. There were mere inches to work with. Could it be done?

Tobias gave a rasping laugh. "Ah, Joan, you always did like to take risks. But keep in mind, if I kill Sarah, I still get you. If you let me kill Sarah – what do you have left? Could you live with that?"

Sarah's eyes were wild with panic. Then Tobias drew his blade slightly against her throat, creating a thin, crimson line. Sarah's shriek was cut off again by fresh pressure from the edge.

Tobias looked meaningfully from the dagger in Joan's hand to the sword which hung at her hip. "First the dagger," he instructed. "Throw it clear."

Joan looked to Sarah. She forced her tone to be steady and reassuring. "Sarah, do you remember what I told you before, when you were to hide up here? You needed to be calm and still. Perfectly still."

Sarah almost nodded, but the pressure against her neck drew her up. Instead she squeaked out, "yes."

Tobias chuckled. "Yes, dear Sarah. You remain still, while your best friend disarms herself."

Joan latched the dagger blade with her thumb, spreading her fingers wide to show she was no longer a threat. "I am throwing it away," she informed him. She took a slight step to her right, aiming at a beam to the right, sending the dagger to embed solidly into it. "Now let Sarah go."

Tobias shook his head. "The sword, too, Joan."

There was a gentle tap on her right hip, and Joan drew in a breath. Hugh was ready. Joan slowly drew her sword from its scabbard and flexed her hand along its hilt for a long moment. She held Sarah's eyes, infusing the woman with all the steadiness she could muster. Her voice was a bare whisper.

"Calm and still, Sarah."

She raised the sword high, and Tobias followed its glittering arc with satisfaction as she took a step to the right, tossing it toward the far right wall.

A flash of silver whizzed past her left ear, shaved threads off of Sarah's neckline, and embedded itself into Tobias's throat.

Joan raced forward, knocking the dagger from the falling man's hand, pulling Sarah to safety and throwing her own body over the frightened woman. Hugh's heavy footsteps behind her dove straight for Tobias, and when she was able to turn and look she found Hugh was sprawled on top of the other man, a dagger at the ready. But it was clearly not needed. The light had already faded from Tobias's marble-cold eyes.

Sarah's breath was coming in gasps. "Is he dead?"

Joan drew her into a warm hug. "He is dead," she reassured the woman, "as are the rest of them. It is all over."

Sarah burst into tears at that, her body convulsing with emotion. Joan let the shock work its way through the woman, holding her as the storm ran its course. Hugh moved alertly through the rest of the attic, checking behind boxes and bales, but at last he came over to join the two women.

Sarah's tears finally slowed, and she looked between the two in grateful relief. "How could I ever thank you," she murmured. "I can't even imagine what would have happened if you had not arrived."

Joan ran a hand fondly down Sarah's hair. "Don't imagine it," she reassured the woman. "It is all in the past. Now we need to get you to your sister's."

Sarah's face creased in confusion. "My sister's?"

Joan nodded, helping her to her feet. "First, we need to get you to your stables. Close your eyes. The less you see, the better." She glanced over to Hugh. "Maybe if you could –"

He nodded at once, stepping forward to sweep Sarah up in his arms. "I could indeed."

They made their way down the stairs and out to the stable, where a pair of quiet, aging horses waited in the stalls. Joan spoke with Sarah while Hugh placed a checkered saddle blanket on one steed and prepared its tack.

"Tell your sister that you need some time away – nothing more," she instructed the woman. "Stay there for three full days. When you get back, the mill will be as good as new, and your troubles will be over. You can go back to full production." The corner of her mouth tucked up in a smile. "You might even finally accept the suits of that nice young man. Aiden was his name, I think?"

Sarah blushed crimson, looking down at her hands. "For so long I have been living this nightmare," she murmured. "To think that it might at last be over ..."

Hugh settled the bit into the horse's mouth, then turned to them. "All ready."

Sarah climbed up onto the steed and looked down at the two. "I will never forget this."

Joan gave a wry smile. "You need to forget it all," she reminded the woman. "We were never here. Nothing happened tonight. You decided to visit your sister, and off you went."

Sarah's eyes shone with emotion, but she nodded. She gave her horse a nudge, and in a moment they were heading east down the path. A few more strides, and she had vanished from sight.

Hugh stood alongside Joan, his warmth heating more than her arm. The low rumble of his voice eased through her.

"And now what, oh guardian angel?"

She took a step forward, breaking the contact which threatened to suck her in. She raised her voice, calling out to the woods beyond the house. "Jake! You can come out now. I have another task for you."

There was a pause, a rustle, and Jake loped across the clearing toward them, his face chagrined. He drew to a stop before them, hanging his head.

"I know you told me to go back home, but I just couldn't," he insisted. "I knew you might need me."

Joan gave a wry smile. "And so we do," she assured him. "I need you to get to the Riverside Tavern as quickly as you can. Take Sarah's other horse. Go up to Greslet – only to Greslet. Tell him that Joan has ten presents for him in need of wrapping at the mill. Just that. Then take the horse home with you. You can say Sarah dropped it off on her way to her sister's, so you could care for it."

Jake didn't need a second prodding. He nodded in understanding and slipped within the stables. In a few minutes he was galloping full tilt down the road to the west.

Hugh's voice was the soft purr of a tiger, and she felt the draw of it. "And what shall you and I do while we wait?"

Joan knew if she turned that she would be caught in those eyes, would lose all sense of the outside world. The location was not secure enough for that. Not yet.

Reluctantly, she nudged with her head. "You go neaten up the back of the mill," she instructed, not changing her gaze from the far-off woods. "I will take care of this side."

She heard the amusement in his voice. "As you wish." Then, to her relief, he had gone.

Joan focused on the task at hand. The first man was near the door, so she started with him. She lifted both feet of the corpse and tugged hard.

He slid perhaps an inch.

Joan's shoulders dropped, but she took in a deep breath and began dragging him, slowly but steadily, along the path. The Sheriff could easily plan to stop by and check on his plan's progress. There could be no evidence of what had occurred.

She took her time, finally getting the first man into the building and moving to the second. Her shoulders were aching by the time he joined his friend in the shadows. Then it was the little details - gathering up the carved stick one man had dropped, checking for any larger evidence that might have been left behind. She knew the team Greslet sent would manage the rest.

There was the steady thrum of hoofbeat in the distance, and Joan stilled. Behind her the stride of footsteps preceded Hugh as he rounded the corner to come to her side. His hand rested on the hilt of his blade.

His voice was low. "Friends?"

She attentively watched the western path, running her fingers down to settle on the leather of her sword's grip. The sound drew nearer, a shape stirred in the forest –

Her shoulders eased in relief as a large, black horse came toward them, its rider reining in as he approached. The man astride was short and wiry, with curly black hair and jet-black eyes.

She smiled in welcome. "Wymon. So Greslet got the message."

He nodded, dropping lightly from the saddle and coming up to look between the two. "He did indeed. Greslet is one happy man tonight. This crew was a persistent thorn in his side. Always causing trouble in the den. Gambling, losing, and refusing to settle their debts." He glanced toward the mill. "All inside, then?"

Joan nodded. "And Sarah is safely off at her sister's. I told her to stay for three days."

"I'll be set by tomorrow, noon," he responded absently, his eyes moving from floor to floor of the mill. "Scrubbed, boiled, and clean. The sheriff won't find a trace of what happened." He glanced back down the path for a moment. "My team should be here shortly to get started." He turned to look back at Joan, then his eyes slid to Hugh, a question held in them.

Joan gave herself a shake. "Oh, of course, I'd assumed you'd met at some point. Wymon, this is Hugh. He also served in the Holy Land."

Wymon put out a hand, and the two shook. Then Wymon looked over their shoulders. "And the rest of your crew? We'll need to get alibis for the lot of you."

Joan's mouth turned up in a smile. "Nobody else. Just us two."

Wymon paused at that, blinking, staring between the two with fresh attention. "Just the two of you? Went up against Tobias and his men?"

Hugh gave a low chuckle. "If I hadn't happened to be there, Joan would have gone in solo."

Wymon blew out his breath, shaking his head. "Joan, even you know better than that. The man had no scruples at all. And his team was one of the best in the land."

Joan's eyes sparkled. "But not *the* best," she pointed out.

Wymon gave a low laugh at that, nodding his head. "Apparently not," he agreed. "But even more reason to get the two of you to where you'll be seen, and quickly. The Sheriff will be after you like a tick on a dog, and you'll want to have your story straight." He glanced to the east. "Head in to the Pickled Pear, and go around the back. The second window from the left has a diamond shape carved beneath it – climb in there. Then call out loud for Maggie. They'll do the rest."

Joan nodded obediently. "Maggie it is. And thank you for your help."

Wymon smiled at that. "Ah, lass, this is a tiny price to pay to be rid of that lot. Now you two go, and be quick about it. If the Sheriff catches you before you're safely inside, there's no telling what he might do."

In minutes Joan and Hugh were astride their steeds, flying through the night, racing against the moon.

Chapter 7

Joan pressed her back against the tavern's wall as Hugh carefully peered into the darkened window. Their horses were tethered to an elderly maple, and Joan could swear she saw two of the Sheriff's men's mounts in the stables as they crept past. Were they inside at this very minute?

Hugh finished his survey and nodded to her. She stepped forward, he made a step with his hands, and she used it to climb up and through the window. In a moment he had hoisted himself up to join her.

The room was small but neat, with a single bed against the side wall. A square table stood opposite with a stool beneath. The only item on the table was an empty iron candlestick. The door in the far wall was closed.

Hugh turned to stand before her. "We haven't had a moment to talk since the fight. I would hope, if you'd been seriously wounded, that you would have spoken up before now."

She nodded. "No real harm done; some bruises and scrapes that will heal." Her hand went to her neck. "Almost didn't make it out of that, though."

His eyes shadowed, and he brought a hand to cradle her cheek. "When I came through that door, and saw you fading –" His breath caught, and he drew her hard against him, wrapping her in his embrace. His voice was a whisper in her ear. "Next time we stay together," he murmured. "Side by side."

She smiled, touched by his concern. "As you wish," she replied in a low voice, nuzzling against his neck.

He gave a low groan, and with clear effort he took a step back, separating himself from her. "We need to establish our alibi," he reminded her in a voice rough with passion. "I need to keep you safe."

He turned, hammering at the door. "Maggie! Are you out there?"

Heavy footsteps thundered down the hall, and Hugh's hand dropped to his hilt. He nudged his head to the other side of the door, and Joan went without a word. If the Sheriff were indeed here with his men, they would need every advantage to get back out again.

The door swung in, hiding Joan behind it, and a burly man stepped through. He was middle-aged, with greying hair and a leathered face. His heavy, white apron was smeared with blood, and he wiped his hands on a less grimy portion of it as he stepped across the threshold.

"I'm Bossard, the owner here," he stated without preamble, his eyes scanning Hugh without much interest. "Haven't seen you before, so here's the drill. I go out and make comments about how you've been holed up in here for hours." He took a thin stub of a candle from his pocket, stuck it into the candleholder, and lit it. "Ten minutes from now, when this candle goes out, you come into the common room and make a fuss. Where's your ale, that sort of a thing. Then I send you back in here and we make clear over the coming hours how you are staying busy in here." He gave a low laugh. "Those drunken sots will blur the whole night together. They'll swear you were at it all night long."

He ran his eyes down Hugh again, nodding. "Bridget will be just right for you. Red-head, fiery, I bet she's just your type."

Joan's blood boiled, and hot fury filled every corner of her being. She burst out from behind the door glaring at both men. "She will *not* step foot in this room!"

Bossard shook his head as he turned. "I apologize, Sir," he grumbled. "I didn't realize you already had yourself a whore -"

The word hung in the air, and he stared at Joan in shock, his mouth hanging open. After a long moment he closed it with effort, but it took a swallow before he could speak again. "Joan?"

Joan moved to stand next to Hugh. "Hello, Bossard."

He blinked again, shook his head, and suddenly the color drained from his face. "*You* need an alibi? It's not Sarah, is it? Is she all right? Aiden will be beside himself if she's hurt. You know he thinks the world of her."

Joan smiled in reassurance. "Sarah is fine. She's at her sister's." The corner of her mouth tweaked up. "Perhaps your son could go keep her company there. I would guess she's finally ready to start thinking about her future."

Bossard's shoulders slumped with relief. "Thank the Lord," he sighed. "Aiden would have been heartbroken if anything had happened to her. He asked her repeatedly to give up on the mill, to come move in with us. But you know Sarah. Stubborn as an apple-crazed mule."

Joan grinned. "I do indeed."

Hugh held Bossard's gaze. "So, about that alibi?"

Bossard shook himself back into focus. "Yes, yes, of course. The horses are out back? We'll get them tended to. For you two, you need to wait ten minutes. You come out tousled and ..." He reddened and looked over to Joan. "If that is all right, of course. It's just what we've always done. We can instead try –"

Joan slid an arm around Hugh's waist, the warmth of his body permeating her. "Oh, we can do tousled," she reassured Bossard.

A low groan came from Hugh as her fingers wrapped along his hip, and Bossard chuckled. "Ten minutes," he reminded them, then turned and closed the door behind him.

Hugh turned in place, sliding his hands along her hips, interlacing his fingers at her back and drawing her in to him. His voice was the rumbling strength of a waterfall. "And just how tousled do you want to be?"

She brought her lips up to his neck, nibbling gently at the tender skin there. "Oh, I want to be thoroughly and completely tousled," she whispered.

He swept her up in his arms, carrying her over to the bed. "We only have ten minutes," he reminded her, his eyes smoky.

She chuckled. "Then you had better get going."

* * *

It was closer to twenty minutes before Hugh and Joan strode into the main room of the tavern, but the reaction was all she could have hoped for. A hush fell across the room as ten tables' worth of faces turned to them first in interest, then in open surprise as it became clear just who the two involved were. In a moment the room was filled with cheers and laughter, toasting mugs and shouted congratulations.

Hugh lifted Joan up in his arms, whirling her around, and the cacophony grew. The patrons began pounding on the tables, cheering, and Hugh brought Joan to face him, sweeping her into a long, passionate kiss. The room erupted into applause.

Bossard stepped forward, a pair of mugs in his hands. "All right," he joked. "Here's your mead. The last three times I came by with it, you two were, erm, occupied." He gave a meaningful wink to the crowd, handing over the tankards.

Joan swept hers up, tilted her head back, and drank down the cool liquid. She was beyond parched, and the smooth mead was exactly what she needed. She lifted the mug slowly, draining every last drop, and when she was done she slammed the mug down onto the table, sending it ringing.

A cheer echoed throughout the room, and Hugh shook his head in mock surprise. "Barkeep, another round for my woman. It's hard enough to keep her satisfied!"

Laughter erupted around them, with more toasts and whistles.

Joan scanned the group around them. Most she knew well – farmers and merchants, a stable owner and a pair of lads from the next town over. But there – she stilled for a moment. They were two of the Sheriff's men. Their faces were tight together, and one of them glanced at the door.

Hugh had followed her gaze; he nodded in understanding. He raised his voice. "Another round, in fact, for everyone! Tonight is a night for celebration!"

The cheers grew louder. Joan smiled as the Sheriff's men sat back in their seats, their eyes moving attentively to where Bossard was dutifully pouring out the fresh pitchers. Apparently the Sheriff's minions had their own priorities.

Bossard looked out at the crowd. "A celebration indeed! I think I'll get Minnie to sing us some songs, and dance for us as well! That would go nicely with the free round. What do you fine lads think?"

The room erupted in applause, with the Sheriff's men clapping harder than the rest. Joan was all smiles when Bossard bustled back over, pressing a pair of fresh mugs into their hands.

"You'll be set until after dawn, at this rate," he murmured with a wink. "Best get yourselves back into the room, though."

Joan turned in Hugh's embrace, looking up at him with innocent eyes. "Ready to take me to bed again?"

The heat in his gaze was all she could have hoped for.

* * *

Joan blinked awake, her body rich with lassitude and comfort. Hugh's arm was draped over her body, his back to the locked door. His breath came in long, even draws. The soft glow of early morning light eased through the window, sending a glistening shaft of dust motes dancing across the center of the room.

She leant forward, brushing her lips against Hugh's. He came awake instantly, his gaze softening as he saw who was before him, then becoming smoky with desire. He returned her kiss, softly at first, then with growing heat –

There was a jangle of metal from the other side of the door and a low curse. Bossard's voice came in soft apology. "My fault, Sheriff; I can be clumsy at times."

Hugh sat up in bed, blocking Joan with his body, and his dagger was in his hand by the time the door swung open. Sheriff Elias strode into the room, his two minions close behind him. The Sheriff was in his thirties, with short, dun-brown hair and a pock-marked face. He wore a crimson tunic with black leggings, and the scabbard which held his sword was intricately engraved with curling black scroll-work.

The Sheriff wrinkled his nose in disappointment. "Oh, Hugh, it's you. So your little charade with Joan didn't hold up for long. She took off already? It figures. What whore did you actually end up with for the night?"

Joan had heard enough. She wrapped the sheet around her chest, then sat up, moving to be alongside Hugh.

The Sheriff blinked in surprise, looking between the two. Then he shook his head. "She probably heard me coming and climbed back in the window," he muttered. "There's no way you two actually –"

Hugh peeled back the sheets from his own body and drew to his feet, stark naked. He settled the dagger in his grip. "There's your proof," he growled.

The Sheriff's eyes lit up in anticipation, and he turned to stare greedily at Joan.

Hugh's gaze narrowed. "If you take one step closer to Joan, then you and I will have a problem."

The Sheriff looked as if he would be half-willing to brave that, but he glanced again at the layers of muscles on Hugh's body, on the twisting scars which showed evidence of his years in the field. At last the air slid out of him, and he gave an elaborate shrug of the shoulders. "Guess I rated her too highly," he tossed out. "Seems she'll tumble anyone she comes across, in a seedy bed in the back of whatever tavern is convenient."

Joan pressed her lips together, but forced herself to remain quiet.

The Sheriff looked between the two of them. "If you had something to do with Tobias's disappearance, I'll find the evidence of it." His grin widened. "And when I do, I'll greatly enjoy handling your punishment. Personally."

Joan set her voice to hold sweet innocence. "Oh, have you lost your pet?"

The Sheriff's look darkened. "Don't you forget, my *pet* has nine minions who are loyal to him. If you have hurt him in any way, you'll not only have me to deal with, but them as well."

Joan held his gaze. "I won't forget a thing."

He nodded, then turned on his heel, the two other men scurrying after him.

Bossard waited a long moment for their footsteps to fade before turning to the two. "I'm so sorry. They got me up out of bed, and –"

Joan waved her hand. "You did the best you could, by giving us that warning. You go on back to your work; we'll be fine."

Bossard bobbed his head, looking between them. "Breakfast is ready whenever you are." He pulled the door closed behind him, and his footsteps moved away.

Joan looked up at Hugh, still standing nude by the bed. Heat eased through her at the sight. He turned, caught her gaze, and gave a low laugh.

"Not quite ready for breakfast, then?"

She put a hand up to draw him down. "Not quite yet."

* * *

It was just after noon by the time they were dressed and sitting at a corner table in the main dining area, enjoying bowls of delicious venison stew with apple and pear. Joan took a swallow of ale, leaning back in her chair.

The tavern's front door swung open, and Jake scampered over to Joan and Hugh, his thin body vibrating with energy. He blurted out his news before he came to a full stop. "Greslet wants to see you."

Hugh raised an eyebrow at Joan, and she gave him a wry smile in return. She lifted her mug, draining down the last of the liquid. "We are being summoned," she chuckled, drawing to her feet. She smiled fondly at Jake. "As always, you are a joy to see."

The boy blushed a crimson she had rarely seen in nature.

She called over to Bossard. "Could you see this boy properly fed?"

Bossard bustled up to the group, wiping his hands on his apron. "It would be my pleasure," he agreed, patting the lad on his shoulder.

She gave them both a wave, then headed out into the sunshine, Hugh at her side.

The ride west was all she could have hoped for. Fresh breezes tickled the leaves in the oaks, white clouds ambled across a cerulean sky, and Hugh's horsemanship was beyond compare. They jumped streams, dodged through dappled forests, and by the time they came up to the riverside structure Joan's heart was light with joy.

A blond man with a patch over one eye was waiting for them by the main door, and he stepped up to take the reins without a word. Joan nodded to him. "You know what they like," she murmured.

He raised one hand to gently stroke Accipiter's neck, and a smile almost came to his lips. Then he was leading the steeds around to the back of the building.

Joan stepped forward, pushing open the door.

The room fell silent. There were perhaps fifteen tables scattered around the dark, windowless room. A scattering of candles and torches shed some light, sending glistens onto the dice, cards, and other objects strewn across the tables. The men in the chairs were uniformly hard, muscular, and sharp-eyed.

Hugh took a step closer to Joan, his hand settling on his hilt.

The door swung shut behind them, Joan swept them with an even gaze, and after a moment the room wound into motion again. The dice were flung, coins were passed, the music of the gamblers.

Joan wended her way through the tables, making her way to the stairs in the back. She ascended, coming out to a hallway with a door on the right. She pushed it open. They were on an open porch now, overlooking the river, with an elegantly carved table set for four. Greslet sat at the far side of it, brushing saffron butter down a freshly baked loaf of bread. He was in his late forties, with greying hair swept back and a sturdy build which still retained a good layer of muscle on it. He wore an elegant black tunic with gold trim.

He looked up as the two stepped through the doorway and onto the porch. "Ah, welcome, welcome. Come sit. Some wine?"

A servant scurried forward to pour out the glasses before they had fully settled themselves in their seats. Greslet raised his in a toast.

"To fortuitous friendships."

They clinked all around, and then Greslet drained his down, sighing in pleasure. "Been saving this for a special occasion," he informed them. "Today absolutely qualifies."

Joan took another sip of her wine. It was quite stunning. "Thank you for your assistance with the packages."

He chuckled at that, shaking his head. "It was the least I could do. I have had people coming and going all morning long, offering their praise for what I had done." He spread his arms wide. "Of course I deny that I had anything to do with it, but for some reason they do not seem to take me at my word."

Joan grinned. "Perhaps because that is the same exact answer you give for every other action that you are in fact responsible for."

Greslet took a bite of bread. "Can I help it if I happen to work in a field which requires some discretion?" He waved a hand at the bread on the table. "Please, have some. It's quite good." He turned to the servant. "Bring that fruit platter as well." He shook his head. "The ferryman's wife brought that for me. Says after what that crew did to her husband, she is glad to see them gone."

Joan shook her head. "Word spreads quickly in these parts."

A large, wooden platter of juicy green slices of apple, golden wedges of pear, and succulent cherries was laid at the center of the table.

Greslet reached forward to pat her hand. "Not to worry, there's no notion of your involvement. They simply know that Tobias rode into the area last night, causing trouble as he always does. He nearly ran down the Chisholm girl on his way in. But nobody has seen him leave, and the Sherriff is out scouring the land for him." His mouth quirked into a grin. "They put two and two together."

Hugh held his gaze. "And if the Sheriff comes here?"

Greslet's eyes remained calm. "Then he comes here. He will find no welcome here, nor any answers that he seeks."

Hugh nodded, and his hand brushed Joan's for a moment.

Greslet blinked, looking between the two, and then his smile broadened. "Joan? Truly? I thought I would never see the day."

A flush heated Joan's cheeks, and she took up a piece of bread to cover her emotion. She busied herself spreading the fragrant butter onto it.

Greslet's gaze moved to Hugh. "You are a lucky man," he offered. "There were many here who would have gladly stood by this woman's side, despite all the trouble she manages to get herself into." His eyes grew distant for a moment. "*Many* here."

Joan looked up, her gaze softening. "You are too kind," she murmured, "but you are a powerful man, deserving of a woman who will stay at your hearth." She looked over to Hugh, and for a long moment her heart stilled. It had not quite sunk in, that he was here, finally here, and he was hers. "I will do better with a knight, where we can ride out together into the fray."

Hugh's hand closed over hers, and for a moment she was lost.

The door swung open behind them, and sturdy footsteps sounded. Lord Weston strode out onto the deck, a smile on his face, his gaze fixed on Greslet's. "Ah, Greslet, what a beautiful day," he greeted. "While we may be on opposite sides of the fence at many times, I am pleased to say that the stars have aligned perfectly this night. How you were able to –"

Greslet nudged his head at the two people sitting before him.

Lord Weston swung his gaze down to the table with casual interest. His eyes caught onto Joan's and he froze. He looked between Joan and Hugh with growing awareness; shock mingled with concern and amazement.

At last he choked out, "you two took them on alone?"

Greslet leant forward, his eyes twinkling with amusement. "Now, now, Lord Weston. You know better than that. In my den, nobody has done anything at all. Here, have a seat, and take some wine. I think you'll need it."

Lord Weston fell into his chair and drank down half of the wine in one long pull. Then he stared between the two anew, his brow furrowing. "Without support? Are you insane? Do you have any idea –"

Greslet handed over a large piece of bread. "Fresh out of the oven," he prodded. "Warm. Take a bite."

It took another moment, but Lord Weston ate a piece of the bread, washing it down with some more of the wine. At last he looked over to Hugh in resignation. "At least you were there with her," he muttered. "Lord knows she would have gone in alone, if she knew Sarah was in trouble."

Hugh's mouth quirked up into a smile. "She would have, indeed."

Lord Weston looked to Greslet. "And everything is taken care of?"

Greslet nodded contentedly, reaching forward to pick up a trio of cherries and pop them into his mouth. "Completely."

Joan looked between the two. "Sarah will be getting married soon, and the mill does need repairs, with all the mischief the Sheriff and his men have been causing."

Lord Weston brightened. "Say no more. That sounds like the perfect direction in which to aim all this outpouring of good will."

Greslet leant back in his chair. "A high quality mill, plus a man who knows how to run a tavern well? Sounds fairly ideal for our community."

Lord Weston rolled to his feet. "I'd best not stay long." He turned to look at Joan and Hugh, shaking his head. "I'd ask you to stay out of trouble, but I'm coming to think that's nigh impossible."

Joan leant forward. "But I *am* staying out of trouble! Compared with the Holy Land, this is a Sunday picnic. In my childhood I weathered sieges where we ate rats. I endured week-long marches under a broiling sun. There were protracted, bloody battles over rickety bridges, flea-encrusted churches, and small patches of land which seemed to have no redeeming value whatsoever." She turned to Hugh. "There was even that violent clash, where over a thousand soldiers were lost, all over some gemstone that looked like it had a cross within it."

Hugh nodded, sipping his wine. "The *ovum crux*. I remember that well. Lost some good men there."

She turned to Lord Weston. "See? If all I get involved with here is holding off a small group of corrupt government officials, I'm doing well!"

His gaze softened, and the corners of his lips lifted. "If this is your idea of a peaceful lifestyle, then please, stay safe."

She smiled fondly at him. "We shall," she promised.

He glanced back to Greslet. "Until next time." Then he had turned and headed back down the stairs.

Greslet popped a slice of pear into his mouth. "And as much as I'd love to converse with you all afternoon, my dear, I believe you have an appointment back in town?"

She smiled at that. "I do indeed. Your sources are as thorough as they say."

He stood and gave her a hug. "Your horses are ready for you downstairs. Stop in any time." He put a hand forward to Hugh. "And you, sir, treasure what you have."

Hugh nodded, shaking Greslet's hand. "I do, every hour."

Greslet smiled at that, then resumed his seat, taking up his wine.

Joan smiled as they headed down the stairs, through the crowded den, and back out to their horses. Hugh did not ask what the meeting was in town, and he moved at her side as naturally as if they had been together for years.

A thought occurred to her as she turned Aquila and urged him into a canter down the road. In a way, they had been together for years. They had been writing each other for four long years, sharing thoughts, a bond forged in absolute trust. Yes, Hugh had thought she was an older woman, but that had not dimmed the strength of the friendship they had shared.

And now they were coming to the final curve in the path, the moment she would find out if it was all real.

She would set him free.

Nervousness tremored through her as their horses jumped a fallen oak and streamed across an open clearing. Everything seemed so perfect when they were together. One look from him could send a flush through her body the likes she had never felt before. Up to now she had laid the stones, she had prepared the path to ease him into awareness of their history. Now he was fully informed. She had revealed everything; she had reached the end of her trail.

Now she must give him some time alone. To see if, when he had time to reflect, he came after her with the same heat, the same deep-seated desire, that had burned within her all these years.

For she knew, if he did not burn for her as she did for him, that the relationship would never sustain. She would not cajole or trick him into staying. He had to crave her presence as much as she did his.

They slowed as they approached town, and he looked around with interest as they circled the common. They approached the small church …

Joan could see when the awareness hit him, when memory connected with location. There was shock, then disbelief, and then a smoothing as all emotions were hidden from view. If she had not been watching him for the moment, she might have missed it entirely.

They reined in at the church steps. Father Picot waved, his stooped frame pale in the bright sunlight. He turned and called through the door, and in a moment Muriel stepped out, her blonde hair glistening in the sun. "Tuesday afternoon, right on time," she smiled at Joan. "You are the most dependable woman I know."

Joan grinned, sliding off Aquila and coming forward to hug Muriel. "And how was your long weekend with the Father?"

Father Picot gave a wheezing chuckle. "Ah, Muriel was a delight, as always. Such a help."

Muriel gave him a fond pat on the arm. "We had the usual - a sprained wrist, a dislocated shoulder. The patients are resting comfortably. Nothing too exciting. And you?"

Joan chuckled. "A little excitement. I'll tell you about it on the ride home."

There was a movement at her side, and Hugh came up to them. His face was quiet politeness. He nodded in greeting to Father Picot and Muriel before turning to face Joan. "I thank you for the loan of your horse and for your hospitality." His voice roughened, but his face remained even. "I treasure it immensely."

She nodded to him. "Your saddle should be repaired by now; I wish you a safe ride home." She turned to Muriel. "Speaking of which, we have to get you home as well. Ready?"

Muriel moved over to Accipiter and mounted with a smile. "For a ride with you? Absolutely. Lead on!"

Muriel was at Joan's side in a moment, and the horses wheeled in tandem. They headed out at a trot toward the west. It took every ounce of self-control Joan had not to turn, not to see if Hugh was looking after them.

Muriel rose in her saddle, twisting to wave back to Father Picot. "Take good care of my patients!" she called out. And then they were around the bend and delving into the dense wood.

Muriel leaned over, a smile on her lips. "Hugh had not moved an inch. If looks were actions, he would have reeled you back in and kept you right by his side."

Joan hadn't realized she was holding her breath until she let it out in a long, grateful exhale.

Her dreams might, after all these years, finally come true.

Chapter 8

Joan huddled behind the mulberry bush, watching the scene at the bridge with attentive interest. Hugh had arrived a full two hours ago, the first of the group. He had leant, alone, against the edge of the bridge for a long time, staring at the water. Whatever emotions he held within, they were locked tight behind a smooth face. Even as the others had arrived and attempted to draw him into conversation, he had remained silent.

Joan smoothed down her tangerine-orange dress, breathing deeply to hold off the nervousness that danced in her heart. She had to know his true intentions, and sooner was better than later. Perhaps he had been caught up in the moment earlier, willing to go along with her on a weekend of flashback and passion. But cold reality often brought a sharp end to romantic dreams. It could very well be that the time apart had allowed him to think more clearly on what had transpired. It could be, in the sober light of day, that his priorities had changed.

As Joan watched, Sybil walked up to stand behind Hugh, looking out at the water for a moment before shaking her head in amusement. "Nothing there, my friend," she grinned. "Speaking of which, maybe you'll be lucky and that meddlesome woman from Friday won't show up either. Then we can take on this mission as we always have, with just the four of us." She gave him a nudge in the ribs. "What was that you always said? *I never want a girl to slow me down?*"

Even at this distance Joan could see the tremor of emotion that rippled through him, the effort it took him to rein in his reaction. But what emotion? Was he upset at the thought? Relieved?

Joan's stomach twisted, and she shook it off. She had to know. The sun had just reached its zenith, and there was no putting it off any longer. Master Martin always said when there was something to be done, the best thing to do was to take that first step.

She stood, pressed a hand to her chest, and for a long moment she breathed in grateful thanks for all she had experienced. If that was all she were to have with Hugh, the one weekend together, it would have to be enough. It was, only five short years ago, more than she ever dreamed of.

She took the first step, then the second, moving her way down the bank.

The four people on the bridge looked up at her approach. Sybil's eyes held bright interest, glancing between Joan and Hugh. Ymbert's slender form practically glowed with glee, awaiting the reaction. Norman's lined face held a weary patience. And Hugh ...

The control over his emotions shimmered, melted, and dissolved away. Relief glowed in his face; respect shone in his eyes. He launched into a run, driving hard down the bank. As he reached her he lifted her in his arms, spinning her around, pulling her close as her feet returned to the earth.

His breath was hot against her neck as he murmured, "Don't leave me again. Do not leave me."

Her heart soared, and she raised her face to his. She ran a hand through his thick hair, lost in him. "Never."

He pulled her up into a kiss, and it was gentle and tender and heart-searingly complete. Joan knew that theirs was a sacred vow, one they would never break. It was a long moment before he stood back and looked down at her, drinking in the sight of her. "God's teeth, what you put me through last night."

She gave a wry smile. "You couldn't sleep either?"

He pulled her in against him, wrapping his arms tight. "Couldn't sleep," he groaned. "Couldn't eat, couldn't think, with a thousand different versions of new tragedies befalling you."

Joan chuckled. "I was only gone one night," she pointed out.

He ran a hand through her hair. "I know you," he reminded her. "You could find trouble within one hour."

She raised an eyebrow. "It would take me that long?" She tucked her arm into his. "Then let us go face it together."

He smiled at that, then turned, walking her up the bank toward the trio of flabbergasted eyes. As they drew to a stop, he nudged his head toward Joan. "You all remember Joan, from Friday evening," he stated calmly. "She will be by my side throughout this mission, as my partner."

Sybil's mouth was hanging open – she shut it with effort. "But you're often the one in the thick of the fight," she pointed out.

He glanced at Joan, his smile growing. "Somehow I don't think that will be a problem."

Sybil stared at Joan, speechless.

Norman leant back against the side of the bridge, rolling his shoulders. "Five it is, then. So, Ymbert, what were you able to find out?"

Ymbert's eyes showed a keen interest in learning more about the intriguing situation developing before him, but he nodded and turned to the business at hand. "Seems young women are going missing from a number of towns in the area. Always at bridges. Always in the late afternoon. The radius of these kidnappings seems to point to the base of operations being somewhere in the Spring Woods."

Hugh shook his head. "That wood is a tangle of cave and hollow," he murmured. "It would take us a year to thoroughly search it.

Ymbert spread his arms wide. "I talked with everyone I knew. I gathered a wealth of details on the girls, on the locations, on the dates and times – but nobody knows where they were taken to. I can keep at it, but it will take time."

Sybil tapped a finger to her lip. "Maybe some friendly conversation at the local taverns will help. I'm sure I could get one of their band to talk."

Ymbert shook his head. "Nobody has heard anything at all about the wolves' heads involved. Not even the slightest whisper. Whoever this band is, they're tight knit and tight-lipped. It doesn't seem they even come out of the wood. The girls are simply never seen again."

Norman nodded. "Sounds professionally run. So, ideas?"

Joan smiled. "They grab young women who are alone by the bridge in the late afternoon?"

Hugh rounded on her, his brow furrowing. "Oh, no you don't. We weren't going to separate again. I am staying by your side."

Joan arched an eyebrow. "And just what is your alternative, then?"

He pressed his lips together, turning to Ymbert. "Surely, if you dug around for a few more days, you could find out some clue to narrow down where this base is."

Ymbert glanced at Joan. "Muriel's sister, Linota, has already been in their clutches for five days," he pointed out. "We promised we would go in after her today. If we wait much longer, it could be too late."

Hugh turned to Sybil. "All right, then, we use Sybil as the bait."

She gave a tinkling laugh. "Oh, there is chivalry for you. Have you forgotten that I do not handle a sword or knife well? You made it clear that your friend here is able to take care of herself in that department. If I assume our plan is to take the kidnapper hostage ourselves, and not simply let him drag Joan along with him back to his home base, then having a victim who knows combat seems the best path to success."

Hugh growled in response.

Joan twined her fingers into his. "You know this is the right thing to do," she murmured. "We have to bring this to an end. Too many people are being hurt."

He blew out his breath and at last nodded. "I am near you every step of the way," he insisted.

She brought his hand to her lips and pressed them steadily against his skin. "Every step."

* * *

Joan stretched, looking idly at the pile of mushrooms that glistened in the last rays of sunset. She had found quite a variety of them, if she did say so herself. She wondered idly for the fortieth time if the bandits were really going to come by this location today, or if it was only an occasional spot for them to check. She knew that Linota and Beatrice had been taken on different days of the week, and that Robin's death had been on a third day altogether. Still, there could be some pattern there that she hadn't figured out yet. Or it could have been random chance. Surely the three had come and gone from the bridge on other days unmolested.

She glanced casually around her before going back to her digging. She had to hand it to the team – they were good. She hadn't seen hide nor hair of them since noon, and she felt completely alone in the woods. She knew without a doubt, though, that Hugh was nearby. She could feel the heat of his focus, sense his attentive gaze on her every movement.

There was a sound in the distance, and she perked up. At last! Perhaps luck was on her side, after all. She settled back down to dig at the mushrooms, listening as the noises grew closer. A cart, drawn by a small horse, by the sound of it. The cart came up to the far side of the bridge, and the noise turned sharper as the hooves came down on the stones. The horse was reined in as he reached her side, and she looked up with a smile.

Her shoulders slumped. It was Father Picot, hunched over in the front of the cart, looking down in recognition. "Joan, my dear, what are you up to on this fine evening?"

She stood, shaking out her dress. She gathered up a handful of the mushrooms and moved up to join him. "Collecting some mushrooms." She handed one over. "What do you think?"

He popped it into his mouth and nodded in approval. "You have a good eye, my lass. I should have you help with some of my herb gathering. Could always use a hand with that."

She chuckled. "Let me know what you're running low in, and I'll keep an eye out for you."

He turned to rummage in the cart. "Here, my lass, I have something for you, in thanks for that mushroom." He stretched to reach a brown sack further back in the cart. "Oh, could you get that for me?"

She climbed up into the cart and pulled the sack closer. "Some supplies for Muriel?"

He shook his head, drawing out a small, thumb-sized tart. "Here, one of the grateful patients made me a whole batch of these today. Tastiest little things you ever tried. What do you think of that?" He handed it over to her.

She popped it into her mouth. It had a creamy texture and a fresh, raspberry flavor to it. "That is lovely," she agreed, swallowing it down. She pulled her ale-skin off her hip and took a swallow. "Some for you?"

He shook his head, patting a skin at his own side. "I am all set, thanks."

She smiled. "Well, then, I will let you get on your –"

A strange feeling swam through her, and then her stomach twisted as if she were tumbling down a long, undulating hill. She barely got her head over the side of the cart before the contents of her stomach violently spewed into the road below.

Father Picot's eyes went wide in surprise. "My dear! Are you all right?"

Joan could not answer. She could barely breathe, so strongly had the illness seized her.

Father Picot shook his head in bewilderment. "I've had three of these without any ill effect," he protested. "Perhaps you are allergic to something in them?" He shook the reins, stirring the steed into a trot. "There's a house just up the hill. Hang in there."

Joan closed her eyes, hanging over the side of the cart, weaving between coughing and sucking in breaths. She took a swig of the ale, only to have it come right back out again. Deep velvets stretched out against the sky, but the horse seemed to know the way without any prodding, taking the turns through the wood with sure steps.

At last it seemed that her stomach had truly emptied itself, and she was left with a gnawing ache matched by a throbbing headache. She slumped down in the cart, massaging her temples, closing her eyes against the rhythmic shaking.

The world faded away.

Chapter 9

Joan blinked her eyes open in confusion. There was a regular shaking of the rough wooden floor she lay on, and the ceiling above shimmered with soft twinkling. It took a few minutes for her situation to sink into her awareness. Judging by the positions of the constellations, it was a full hour since she had fallen ill.

Father Picot was working in concert with the wolves' heads.

The certainty of it burned into Joan's soul with shock. The man could have returned to town or gone forward to three different homes in far shorter time. She saw with crystal clarity how he would have lured in the other women, how he could have gotten close to Linota's poor husband Robin without the man suspecting anything at all.

Her hand moved to her hip – and she swore under her breath. She had left her dagger on the riverbank by the mushrooms. She hadn't thought to need it for her friendly chat with Father Picot. Which left her with …

She shook her head. Normally she would have stocked up on daggers and knives in various locations. But she was acting as bait, and had not wanted to seem a spiky porcupine to the would-be kidnapper.

She ran her fingers through her hair in exasperation, then smiled. She did still have that one weapon, one which men often overlooked. Her long, silky hair stretched nearly to her waist, and when braided it was as thick and sturdy as a well-constructed rope.

Perfect.

She spent a few moments weaving it into a long plait, then settled herself back down against the edge of the cart. Maybe she could get the old codger talking a bit, to find out just what was going on. She imagined once she actually tackled him that Hugh and the others would storm from the woods and the chance of quiet conversation would be long gone.

She gave a low moan, as if she were just waking up. Father Picot glanced back in surprise, and she saw the crafty calculation in his gaze which was quickly overlaid with a mask of worried concern.

"There you are, my lass. We're almost there. Are you feeling a bit better?"

Joan feebly moved a hand to her stomach. "Not really," she groaned. "What did you feed me?"

"You must have had a reaction to one of the ingredients," he mused. "Not to worry. My friends will know exactly what to do with you."

Joan fell back against the cart as if thoroughly exhausted. "We are long past the farmers' homes," she countered weakly. "I know you poisoned me, and I know you are working with the wolves' heads. Just tell me what fate awaits me, now that I have fallen into your trap. Will you kill me?"

He looked as if he might deny the charge, but after a moment his eyes lit up with pleasure. His voice grew sharp. "The townsfolk are always treating me like a simpleton. As if my furrowed face and spotted hands mean my mind has turned to gruel." He spat off the side of the wagon. "Catching you girls is like gathering up petunias on a summer's day. Just there for the taking."

Joan pitched her voice to hold resignation. "So you *are* going to kill me."

He gave a barking laugh. "Kill ya? How much would you be worth dead? Nah, they pay me and the other collectors a pretty penny for our efforts." His mouth grew into a twisted grin. "And I'm sure they send you off to nice, new homes, where your – ah – assets are well appreciated."

Joan slumped further, her face drooping in despair. "Which of the locals would do such a thing to me? Maybe the blacksmith?"

Father Picot shook his head. "Locals? If they sold ya local, you'd be fetched back too easily. Nah, Burt gathers up a tassel of you and others like you. Tossed into a cart, loaded onto a ship." He gave a low laugh. "Hope you don't get seasick."

He glanced up ahead. "Not too far, now. Just over that hill and –"

Joan didn't wait for him to finish. She lunged forward, swinging the loop of her hair up and around his neck. She pulled him backwards, hard, and he flailed as he came, grabbing for the edges of the cart. He was stronger than she had thought, much stronger, and he nearly pulled himself back up before she gave a sharp twist that landed him face down against the floor of the cart. His gasps became heaves, and at last he slumped unconscious before her.

There was a bound of movement at her side, and Hugh was there, his dagger in his hand, his face creased with worry. "Are you all right?"

She unwrapped her hair from Father Picot's neck, nodding as she looked down at him. "I'm sure whatever he fed me will be out of my system soon enough. I can't imagine they would permanently want to '*damage the goods*'."

Sybil gave a bright grin from the side of the cart. "See? Told ya she was fine. She seemed a woman who could take care of herself."

Ymbert scrambled into the cart with them, digging a hand into the rumpled brown sack. He came out with a handful of the small tarts. "So, what'd'ya think are in them?" He broke one open, staring at its insides with interest.

Joan peered at the substance. "Maybe aloe. While the juice is good for fighting nausea, the outside skin has the opposite effect. Plus heaven knows what else, thrown in for good measure."

Norman leant against the side of the cart, his eyes glancing forward for a moment. "So, did you learn anything about your destination?"

She nodded. "Just over the hill, apparently. Father Picot here is just one of several *collectors* who bring in the captured women. They get carted to the coast and then shipped out somewhere overseas, as prostitutes it would seem. Someone named Burt seems to be running everything."

Ymbert wrinkled his forehead, putting the tarts back into the bag and wiping his hand off on one leg. "Burt? I did hear a name mentioned when I was over in Carthage. Umberto of Meccini. He is a visiting priest."

Joan stilled. "I know that name. It was mentioned in several of our reports. He rented out women from his string of *stews* and aggressively expanded his territory. He liked to use women as madams to manage his houses of ill repute. Said they were better at keeping the workers under control."

Sybil perked up. "He liked to work with women? Perfect!"

Joan swung to look at her. "The man is a monster."

Sybil barked a harsh laugh. "As if I haven't had to deal with that type many times over," she assured Joan. "This is ideal; just leave everything to me. I will waltz in and explain that I have a regular supply of pure, young women available to me. That rather than ship the girls overseas, we could open business right here."

Joan shook her head. "I don't think that's a good idea. Father Picot said they avoided local operations, because -"

Sybil's gaze darkened. "You had your fun. You played with the elderly priest. Now it's my turn. This is what I do, and I'm superb at it." She glanced up the road. "Or would you rather we send Hugh in to fight who knows how many guards, on the hope that we figure out where the girls are before they are slain to destroy any evidence?"

Joan looked to Ymbert. "We could send in -"

Sybil cut her off. "You are a visitor here," she snapped. "We do things our way, and I say I am going in." She climbed to the front of the cart. "You four wait on this side of the hill for me to return." Her grin widened. "I am sure I will have everything we need to prove their guilt by that point."

Ymbert hopped off the edge of the cart, landing lightly on his feet.

Hugh looked over to Norman. "Surely you aren't agreeing with this?"

Norman rested a hand on the edge of the cart. "We don't know the layout, and we don't know how many men we face," he pointed out. "Sybil is talented at getting men to trust in her. If this Umberto likes to work with women, all the better. She'll chat him up and get what we need. Then we can sneak in, free the women, and be out before they know it."

Joan pressed her lips together, saying nothing, and allowed Hugh to help her down from the cart. She had said her piece, and further arguments would only fix Sybil in her position. But there was no way in Hell she would leave Linota and the other women to depend on Sybil's wheedling to rescue them.

The cart rolled down the road, turned a corner, and vanished from sight. The moment it did, Joan glanced at Hugh and nudged her head left. His eyes serious, he nodded in agreement. The two of them eased silently into the woods, making their way up the long slope.

There was no need for words between them. They navigated the terrain slowly, cautiously, attentive to even the slightest sound or sign of motion. Each foot-fall was carefully placed. They crested the hill and looked down into a small, enclosed hollow. The only entrance was the narrow path which Sybil and her cart were currently traversing.

Joan eased her way east along the ridge, getting a better view of the structures below in the strong moonlight. The main building was three stories high, with a flat roof and small arrow-slits for windows. A low rectangle lay alongside it – stables, judging by the large shapes she saw moving within. Beside that lay a sealed warehouse of some kind, its front door securely locked. All three were backed up against a sheer cliff some fifty feet high. Trees overhung from the top edge, adding even more disguising cover for the buildings below.

Joan carefully made a note of where the various guards stood amongst the many flickering torches and lamps. Three came forward as the cart slowed, helping Sybil down from her seat and talking with her. The distance was too far to hear their low voices, but they seemed more welcoming than hostile.

Hugh's voice was a murmur. "She could pull it off."

Joan continued to assess their defenses. Two more guards stood in front of the larger building, there were three walking patrols, and another two moved about within the stables. She had no doubt there were a matching number inside the main structure, and some out watching the entry path as well. Far too many to easily take on.

Joan shook her head. She had read the reports on Umberto over the years, and she knew what the man was capable of. He and his right-hand-woman, Cecily, had been responsible for countless deaths and abductions. They were beyond ruthless. In one report, he had been moving in to take over a rival's territory. Umberto had captured the wife of the rival and brought her to the top of a building. He held her at the very corner of the roof, threatening to drop her, until the panicked rival gave in and agreed to all the terms of surrender. Umberto had pushed the woman off anyway, to send a message.

One of the guards led the steed and cart into the stables, while the other two escorted Sybil to the door of the main building. She gave them a friendly wave, then sauntered inside.

Joan dropped to one knee, preparing for the wait. It could be two minutes or two hours before the woman came out again. She would be ready.

Hugh moved a hand to the back of his belt, and to her relief he handed over her crossbow. "Thought you might need this," he offered in a low voice. A handful of bolts followed. "Just in case."

She smiled at him, turning the crank and laying a bolt in its channel. "You are a wise man." She drew the weapon up in her hands, sighting down it at the stables, then the main door, then the corners of the roof. The moon's full light gave sharp relief to the scene. *One thing finally falling in her favor.* She spoke as she aimed toward one of the burlier guards. "Better to be prepared for anything, with Umberto involved."

Hugh's voice was a soft growl. "That is for sure."

She glanced over at him. "I suppose he was operating near your area. Did you have any dealings with him?"

His face grew distant, and he stared toward the large building. "Yes, some."

She blinked in surprise, turning to him. "You didn't mention that in any of your messages," she mused. "What did you –"

He cut her off, low and urgent. "The roof!"

Joan spun back to look. To her shock, a tall, aquiline man with jet-black hair, wearing emerald green, was climbing out of a hatch at the far end of the roof. He dragged up an arm, and in a moment Sybil was beside him, her slouched figure showing clearly her defeated state of mind. Umberto pulled her along with him to the front corner of the building. He forced her to the point, and then raised his head, looking out at the woods.

His yell carried easily up out of the hollow to them. "Hugh! I know you're out there, watching. This blonde harlot would never have come traipsing in on her own. Answer me, or she loses some of her pale beauty in an untimely encounter with the ground below."

Hugh turned to whisper to Joan. "Get away to the west. Once I call out, they'll know to converge on my position."

Joan resolutely shook her head. "Side by side, remember?"

His voice was tight. "And then you went and climbed into that cart with Father –"

Umberto's voice carried an edge to it. "Not there? Guess I'll just have to toss –"

Hugh stepped forward to the overlook, throwing his arms wide. "I am here, Umberto. You have me. Now let the woman go."

Umberto smiled widely at that. "Let Sybil go? When she has such talents? I hardly think that is in my best interest. And I would guess that your other two gang-members are back down the path, waiting in safety for the return of your silver-tongued seductress. So it is just you and I. Perhaps we can have a little chat."

Hugh's voice was steady. "Let her go and we can talk all you want."

Umberto chuckled. "It sounds like some of Michael did rub off on you, after all. That was his way. Talk and banter, bargain and manipulate. You were always the man of action. I imagine it was why you two made such a great team." He shrugged. "Pity it had to end the way it did. But, you know, Cecily was always a bit ... *impetuous.*"

Joan froze in shock. Master Martin had told her it was an accident; Michael had stumbled and fallen to his death over the wall of the patio. It had happened just a month after her visit there. She had seen those sheer cliffs herself, had seen the jagged rocks which lay fifty feet below. The scene had haunted her dreams for months afterwards.

Why would Master Martin have lied to her?

Umberto's lips curled up into a grin. "Then again, you know how these lover's quarrels can be."

Chapter 10

Joan shook her head in confusion. Surely she had not heard Umberto correctly. He almost seemed to be implying that Michael – *her* Michael – had been involved with this Cecily woman. The thought was ludicrous. They had been practically engaged since she was eight. She had followed him to sword class, had watched patiently while he trained, and had agreed without complaint to the long separations while he went away on missions. She had put her entire life on hold to wait for him to return to her.

And he had spent that time betraying her?

She drew her gaze to Hugh's form. She could see the tension in his shoulders, the iron will it took for him to keep his focus on the man before him, not to turn to her and say something. Anything.

It was true.

The knowledge sunk deep within her. Here she had done everything she could to fight against her attraction to Hugh. She had traveled the long distance from Jerusalem to Jaffa to shake loose her fantasy visions. She had taken every step possible to break the hold he had over her. When that hadn't worked, she had ruthlessly cut off all contact, turning over all communication back to Master Martin. And while she was as cloistered as a nun, Michael had been –

Umberto's voice rang out into the dark night. "What was best of all was that that naïve girl of his never knew the truth of what he was up to. She thought he was an upright man, all she could ever dream of. To think he was spending his nights rutting

with his passionate paramour. I wonder if he even thought of his
fiancé while he thrust –"

Joan could not take any more. She launched to her feet,
preparing to stride out alongside Hugh and shout her fury to the
world.

Hugh flashed his left hand down at his side, fingers spread
wide.

Trap.

Joan froze, her mind reeling. Did they truly know she was
here? Was this dialogue aimed to draw her out into the open,
and for what reason?

Umberto's voice rolled out over the open space, describing
in lurid detail just how Michael had enjoyed Cecily's curves,
and as Joan examined the situation clinically she realized that it
was carefully constructed to push her past her limits. It was
clearly not aimed at Hugh. Hugh showed no sign of jealousy or
anger over the litany. He seemed to accept it for truth, a fact she
filed away for later discussion with him. For now, though, she
carefully crept forward, scanning the ground below for the
threat.

Ah, there he was. At the corner of the stables, a man with a
long plait of blond hair held a longbow. His eyes were
attentively scanning the ridge of the forest, watching and
waiting.

Joan pitched her voice low. "Hugh. Archer. Stables, front
corner."

He gave the slightest of nods. Then, in a louder voice, he
shouted, "Are you done with your romantic tales for the
evening, or are you next going to share Troilus and Criseyde
with me and your guards?"

Disappointment showed on Umberto's face as he scanned
the forest behind Hugh. "And here I'd hoped for a larger prize,
but I guess tonight was not the night." He shrugged. "Still, I will
enjoy this being the last sight you see before you, too, fall. You
have been a thorn in my side for long enough, Hugh."

The world stalled into slow motion. Hugh's voice shouted in
helpless frustration, "Sybil!" Umberto's hand swung forward at

Sybil's body as Joan's arms swung up to aim the crossbow. She fired just as the sight came to Umberto's chest. The whistling of the bolt was echoed by another whistling, and Hugh dove at her, driving her to the ground as an arrow slammed into a nearby oak.

She rolled onto her stomach, sliding forward to peer over the edge of the ridge. Umberto was splayed back on the roof, blood pooling around his chest and shimmering in the moonlight. Sybil clung to the edge of the roof with both hands, screaming. A guard poked his head up through the hatch, took in the scene, and vanished.

Hugh set off at a run, and Joan was right on his heels, leaping a rotting trunk, dodging around a rocky ravine. She knew well the orders left for any of Umberto's locations which were breached. She could see the flames licking from the arrow slots as they came down to the floor of the ravine. The guards streamed away down the road, abandoning their camp.

Hugh raced to the door of the structure, but smoke billowed from it, and he shook his head in frustration. He looked up the three stories to the woman dangling above him.

"Hang on, Sybil!"

Joan sprinted into the stables. Only the priest's elderly horse waited patiently in a stall at the far end, with the cart tucked in the opposite corner. Besides that, there were random rakes, hoes, buckets ... ah! Joan spotted a coil of thin rope and grabbed it off the low bench. It might just do the trick.

She raced back out to the side of the larger structure. Hugh was attempting to scale the outside of the building, but the construction was not providing hand-holds for him. He lunged for a sill, missed, and fell the eight feet back to the ground with a crash. He groaned as he pushed back up to standing, his eyes scanning for another route.

Joan dropped to one knee and began cranking as fast as the gears would work. With the crossbow set, she tied the rope to the lead end of the bolt. The weight would greatly impede its ability to fly straight, but she wasn't looking for precision on this pass. Just the ability to launch the rope.

She slid the bolt, with its rope attachment, into its channel, and pointed it nearly straight up. Above her, jutting out from the cliff-face top, was an ancient, gnarled oak, its roots delving deep into the rock. Its main branch was thicker than a man's waist. She only hoped it would be strong enough.

She aimed carefully, drew in a breath, and let it out in a long sigh. Then she squeezed the trigger.

The bolt arced up, higher, slowed, and drifted just over the top of the branch before falling back down toward earth.

Relief coursed through Joan. She dropped the crossbow, grabbed the loose end of the rope, and carefully lowered the bolt down on the other side. When it reached her she had a loop of rope going up, over the branch, and down again.

Hugh was at her side, staring at the rope in confusion, where it now hung looped over the outstretched trunk. "That rope is a good twenty feet from Sybil," he protested. "She'll never jump that far!"

Joan grabbed up the crossbow and again furiously cranked. "She won't need to," she muttered, all her attention focused on the turning of the handle. She knew, with every passing second, that Sybil's hands were slipping. She had to get a lifeline to her.

She took up the bolt, which still had one end of the rope tied to it. She carefully slid the bolt into the channel, willing her pulse to slow. She blocked out all else from her awareness – the groan of the building as something within it collapsed, the crackling of the fire reaching out from the arrow slots, the thick billowing of black smoke. The pounding of horse hooves as Norman and Ymbert galloped down the path, the three other horses trailing behind them.

Hugh's eyes widened in understanding, and he leapt for the free end of the rope, wrapping it around his waist, then looping the upward end several times around his right arm for good measure. He set himself up in a braced position, his eyes moving from the pivot point over the branch to where Sybil clung desperately to the ledge.

His voice was low and determined. "I'm ready."

Joan's world narrowed down into a pinpoint focus on the terrified woman. She had seen how the bolt had flown, how it had angled to the right, how the drag caused a truncated arc. If she misjudged this … she put the thought out of her head. She visualized the bolt flying true to its destination; it had to.

Each beat of her heart sounded like a bass drum; her breath coming in was the sweet whisper of wind through fall foliage. A meteor glistened gold, streaking across the sky.

Ymbert stared at the crossbow, followed its aim into the night sky, and his eyes landed on Sybil's helpless form. He screamed in unbelieving fury and launched himself at Joan.

She let the bolt fly.

Ymbert's impact threw the crossbow from her hands, toppled her over, and her breath blew out of her in one long *whoof*. Then there was the sharp edge of cold steel at her throat, and she went as still as death.

Ymbert's eyes blazed fury. "You traitor," he snarled. "Shooting at Sybil when she was as helpless as a babe! I will make you pay. And if you think Hugh will save you after –"

Hugh's voice was hoarse with focus, carrying over the whoosh of the fire and the whinnying of the horses. "God's Teeth, Ymbert, let her up and come help me!"

Ymbert looked up in shock, then his eyes widened as he took in the scene. Hugh held one end of the rope. It looped up over the tree-trunk and headed straight for the main structure. The bolt with the other end had embedded itself into the building ten feet to Sybil's right, and down about three feet. She was carefully working her way over to it.

Sybil glanced back over her shoulder at Hugh, her eyes wide with panic.

"Don't drop me!"

Ymbert dove to hold onto Hugh's waist, and in a moment Norman was there as well. Joan brought a hand to her neck, and her fingers became wet with the thin line of blood welling there. She sucked air into her lungs. All of her focus was on the scene above.

Sybil gathered herself up, coiled, and sprung for the rope.

The bolt yanked loose from the wall as she landed on the rope. The men hauled in on their end of the rope as she swung, keeping her high, and she arced toward the cliff face the tree jutted out from. She put out her legs, using them as shock absorbers. The upward motion of the rope helped to lessen the impact. Then she swung away again, out toward the center of the valley.

Slowly, carefully, Hugh and the other two fed the rope out, lowering Sybil until she collapsed onto the ground. She held her hands in against her chest, moaning in pain.

Ymbert was at her side in a minute, pouring some ale into her mouth. "Her hands are ripped raw!"

Joan pushed herself to her feet, her back and shoulders aching from the rough tumble Ymbert had given her. She trotted into the stables, moving to the shelf with the ointments and tinctures. She found the scrape mixture – honey with chamomile, and grabbed up the pottery jar. She was back by Ymbert's side in a moment, handing over the fist-sized container.

He took it without a word, all attention focused on Sybil, and carefully layered the goop on her bloody palms and fingers. "I need bandages," he added.

Joan's hand went automatically to her hip, and she cursed as her fingers swept open air. *Really?* There was a movement at her side, and Hugh pressed the hilt of her dagger into her palm. She dropped to one knee and cut away the bottom of her tangerine dress, first one long swath, then another. She handed both to Ymbert without comment, and he carefully wrapped each hand in colorful swaddling.

At last both hands were mittened and he breathed out a sigh of relief. He looked up to Joan and blinked as if seeing her for the first time. His gaze moved from the bottom of her dress to the wound at her neck, and his shoulders slumped. He pushed himself to his feet.

"I'm … I'm sorry, Joan," he mumbled. "When I saw Sybil in trouble, and you pointing your crossbow at her, I'm afraid I lost control for a moment." He glanced back down at Sybil, where

Norman was helping her to her feet. "I owe you an apology. You saved her life."

Joan held his gaze. "I have an idea how you could repay me."

His eyes brightened. "Oh? Anything!"

She nudged her head to the warehouse building on the other side of the stable. "Can you pick that lock?"

He stared at the building as if it had sprung out of the ether, and then his gaze narrowed. In a second he was sprinting toward its door, his hand moving to the leather bag at his hip. By the time Joan and Hugh came up behind him, he was kneeling before the heavy, iron padlock, carefully working the tumblers with a pair of delicate metal picks.

There was a snapping noise, and Ymbert cursed under his breath. "Good quality lock," he muttered. He reached into his bag, drawing out another pick. "Needs a lover's touch."

His words brought back to Joan the interchange with Umberto as he challenged them from the rooftop.

Had Michael been cheating on her with Umberto's partner, Cecily? Had Hugh known about it?

She glanced at Hugh, and by his shadowed gaze she knew his thoughts had gone in the same direction. When they finally had a spare moment beyond this chaos, she would demand that he tell her the truth.

There was a soft click, Ymbert gave a chortle of glee, and the heavy, iron lock opened. He disengaged the lock from the two rings it had held together, then stepped back. He drew his dagger from his hip, staring at the door.

Hugh nodded, moving forward to the right hand door. After one final glance at Joan and Ymbert, he pulled the door open.

The interior of the building was pitch black. There were no candles or torches lit within, and no windows to let in the soft moonlight. Not a hint of sound emanated from the shadowy depths.

Hugh shifted to take a step forward, and Joan put out a hand. He froze in place, glancing between her and the blackness before them.

Joan lowered her dagger. She pitched her voice to be calm and reassuring.

"Linota, it is all right. It's me, Joan. It's the fifth day. I've come for you with Hugh and his team, just as we planned."

There was a long pause, with the only noise the crackling of the fire which now had fully engulfed the main building. Then there was a movement, and Linota came warily into the opening, blinking her eyes. Her auburn hair was now a short bob, barely below her ears, and in her hands she held a thick braid. It was nearly three feet in length, thick, knotted at the end. Joan had no doubt that it would be a formidable weapon.

Linota's eyes relaxed in relief as she came into the light, and she drew Joan into a grateful hug. "Thank the Lord, it really is you." She turned to look behind her. "It is all right, you are safe now. Come out, my friends."

In slow, staggering motion, another twenty women slowly emerged from the shadowy depths, all of their hair short, all of them holding a braid of varying thicknesses and lengths.

Joan smiled, tousling Linota's short hair. "You really did have them well prepared," she praised.

Linota's grin sparkled in the firelight. "The soldiers would never have known what hit them," she agreed. She looked over, taking in the inferno for the first time. "Looks like you didn't go for the stealth option."

Joan chuckled. "Well, we did, but it didn't work out quite as planned. Still, I think this branch of their operation is permanently out of business."

Linota's gaze darkened. "And what of Father Picot?"

Joan nodded. "We have him. I'm sure that Lord Weston will be quite happy to deal with him for us."

Linota looked into the roaring flames. "There was a boss here, in charge of the operations. Ruthless as a viper. Seemed Italian."

Joan nudged her head toward the roof. "Umberto. Yes, we met him. I'm afraid he met his demise at the pointy end of one of my bolts. He won't be causing trouble any more."

Linota shivered with cold, and Joan became aware of the hollowness in the women's eyes. "There'll be plenty of time later for us to catch up on what went on here," she reassured the woman. "Let's get you safely home."

In a few minutes Father Picot's horse was hooked back up to the cart. Joan and Hugh helped the rescued women climb into its back, and Ymbert lifted Sybil up to join them. Joan then passed around stable blankets to ward off the evening chill.

Norman returned, prodding Father Picot in front of him. The rope which had helped Sybil down to safety was now put to good use, tying Father Picot to the back of the cart.

In a moment the rest of the group had mounted. They started the long trek back to civilization, the moon shining their way home.

Joan took the back of the group, her eyes attentively roaming the woods and the path behind, ever alert for danger. But occasionally they came to rest on Linota, and on Hugh, where he rode at the head of the group.

Just what would she learn, when the truth was finally revealed?

Chapter 11

Joan groaned into life from what seemed a full day's slumber. Every part of her body either ached or throbbed. There was a welt on the back of her shoulder, a grinding pain digging into her left calf, and her throat felt as if someone had tried to strangle her with a wet cat. She wearily blinked, rolling herself into a seated position.

Someone pressed a metal mug into her hands. She drank down the rich ale, relishing the flavor, draining the mug fully before handing it back. Finally her eyes came open.

The room was completely unknown to her.

It was a comfortably sized room, sparsely furnished, burnished by the warm glow of the late morning sun. The dark wood floors were polished until they gleamed. The one large window gazed into the green branches of nearby maple trees – she was on the second floor. A low table had a pair of tangerine cushions before it, and a set of shelves held metal mugs, pottery bowls, and a trio of wooden spoons. The thick blanket on top of her was the rich swirling colors of sunset.

Hugh's voice at her side was low, almost hesitant. "Welcome to my home."

Memories came back to her now. How exhausted she had been by the time they returned to the tavern, how Hugh had caught her in his arms as she practically fell from her horse. The tavern had blossomed into a celebration of homecoming for the kidnapped women, but Hugh had carried her up the long, external steps behind the tavern, bringing her to his apartment on the second floor, overlooking the back woods.

He gave an apologetic shrug. "Makes it easier for me to work with clients, if I live just upstairs," he explained. "They always know where to find me in an emergency."

She turned to sit sideways on the bed – and stopped. Behind her, hanging on the wall behind the pillows, was a large, carved round of oak. In its center was the form of a soaring seagull.

She reached out a hand, tracing its curled wingtips, the bright gleam in its eye. For a moment she could hear the call of the sea, breathe in the rich, salty air.

"It's gorgeous," she murmured.

He gave a wry smile. "It's the only thing I brought back with me from the Holy Land. I found a talented wood carver who lived near the courtyard and paid him to sit there studying the seagulls." His eyes held hers. "I had a faint hope that perhaps, just perhaps, he would end up carving his form based on the one you had been dancing with on that ledge by the sea."

She put a hand up to him, he came down at her gentle pressure, and for a long while the aches and bruisings became a distant memory.

* * *

Joan leant over the large, round table in the tavern's back room, eagerly taking another spoonful of the venison stew. She was starving, and despite its disreputable appearance the place did have a talented cook working in its kitchens. Ada moved around the table, refilling mugs of ale from a pitcher. The late afternoon sun sent golden streaks across the room, and candles glimmered from several sconces.

Hugh looked over to Norman. "So are most of the women safely returned to their homes?"

Norman nodded his head. "Lord Weston's guards are arriving at a steady rate. There will be quite a number of celebrations going on tonight, and enough church candles lit in gratitude to illuminate the entire county."

Sybil was raising her mug to her lips with two mittened hands, and Ymbert gave it a gentle lift from below to assist. She nodded her thanks to him. When she put the mug back down, she commented, "I think Linota was going to come by in a little while to share what she knew of the wolves' heads. While we might have killed the leader, it would still be good to bring the remaining fiends to justice."

Ada shouldered the door open and glanced back at the group. "Here she is now," she called out. Her mouth spread into a smile. "She looks a bit peaked after last night's festivities."

Indeed, there were dark shadows around Linota's eyes, but her face lit up with pleasure as she came into the room. She moved around to each person, offering them a warm hug, before settling down in the empty chair. In a moment Ada was back, placing a fresh mug of ale before her.

Linota raised up her mug, and the rest mirrored her action.

"To clearing out the vermin," offered Linota in a clear voice.

Mugs clinked together, and they all drew down a long swallow of the amber liquid.

Hugh ran his eye over her. "So, you are all right? No injuries from your ordeal?"

She shook her head. "They were careful with us," she explained. "I imagine they wanted their merchandise to remain as healthy as possible to fetch the highest price."

He nodded in understanding. "What happened when you arrived at their camp?"

"Father Picot took me as far as the stables, and then a pair of guards escorted me into the main building. On the ground floor was a room with a ring of lamps and an X painted in the center of the room. I was told to stand on the X, and they circled around me, looking me over. I was worried that they might force me to undress, but apparently they have this down to a science and had no need for that. They simply made some notes in a book, asked me a few questions about my background, and that was that."

She pursed her lips. "I assume that investigations of a more … intimate nature are done further along in the process. I almost got the sense that they did not want to tempt the guards in any way. By leaving us unseen for now, they reduced the risk their wares would be spoiled."

Joan tucked the last bite of the venison in her mouth and washed it down with some ale. Her stomach bulged with comfortable fullness, and she leant against Hugh. His arm came up around her as if it had always belonged there.

Linota looked around the group. "It was eerie. I almost got the sense that I was being looked out for. I was spoken to kindly. They asked if I wanted anything in particular. The guards treated me as if I were their sister. I could see how some of the women began to relax and become friendly with the guards."

Sybil scowled. "Well, I found Umberto to be anything but friendly," she grumbled.

Linota glanced over in surprise. "Oh, Umberto wasn't running the camp," she corrected. "I'm not sure what he got called in to do. Cecily was the one handling everything."

A jolt of electricity ran down Joan's spine, and Hugh's arm tensed around her hip. Joan leant forward. "A woman named Cecily was there?"

Linota nodded. "She had to leave yesterday morning for some reason, but before then she was running the camp. She had this way of talking with the women, convincing them that this was all in their best interest." She pressed her lips together. "I think some of the women half-believed it."

Joan's throat went dry. "Did you get a sense of where Cecily was from? Was she local?"

Linota shook her head. "She said she was from the Holy Land, and her voice had a trace of an accent."

Hugh's brow creased in confusion. "What in the world is she doing out here?"

Linota shrugged her shoulders. "Apparently she had a man she loved back in Jaffa, but an ex-girlfriend caused all sorts of trouble for her and –"

Joan's voice burst out before she could rein it in. "*Ex-*girlfriend?"

Linota looked up in surprise, her face paling at the emotion she saw on Joan's face. "I'm so sorry, I had no idea."

Joan turned to Hugh, the events of that night in the ravine swirling back in on her. She took in a deep breath. "I need to know what happened to Michael."

Hugh's eyes were shadowed. "Maybe now is not the best time to –"

She shook her head, holding his gaze with focused intensity. "Linota certainly deserves to know, if it's in any way related to her husband being slain and her sister-in-law being kidnapped. The rest might as well hear, if we're going to be going after Cecily."

Hugh seemed to go within himself for a moment. At last he nodded. He leant back from her, taking both her hands in his.

"After the day I saw you in the open air courtyard, I became convinced we would cross paths again," he explained. "I went back there every afternoon, hoping against hope that you would show up. Every day for a month I sat at that same table, watching the seagulls soar." His gaze shadowed. "And every day I went home alone."

He ran a thumb over her fingers. "Then there was a day that a courier I had to meet with ran late. I remember being frustrated with him, sure that this would be the one day you arrived. When we were finally done with the transaction, I raced as quickly as I could to get to the courtyard. It was past dark by then, and the square was almost deserted."

He looked down at her hands. "I saw Michael at the far end of the plaza, by the stone wall overlooking the cliffs. He was arguing with a woman, and at that distance I thought it was you."

Tension rippled through his shoulders. "Fury burst through me when I saw him. I was in a rage that he had somehow managed to steal you away from me."

He looked up and gave a wry smile. "At the time you *were* his, which makes my anger even less appropriate. But I remember even now the power of it, how it took every ounce of my self-control to remain in place, to not storm over and challenge him."

Joan's chest constricted into a smaller and smaller ball; it was all she could do to draw a breath. "What were they saying?"

His brow furrowed in concern, but after a moment he continued. "The woman was screaming at him, saying she was … was sick of the delays. That she needed a decision from him. And at last he turned away as if he'd had enough. He told her that he had made his decision, and that he was ending their affair."

A thread of hope tingled in Joan's soul, and she looked up. "He was going to end it?"

Hugh nodded somberly. "He told the woman that he couldn't take the lying any more, and that he was going to go back to you. That when he finished with his current job, he was going to go home and marry his childhood sweetheart."

Joan's eyes misted. "He did care for me, in the end."

Hugh dropped his eyes. "The woman was infuriated by that and gave him a solid push in the chest. 'Go, then,' she snapped. I think she just meant to push him away, but somehow his foot must have caught on a rock. Instead of falling back, he spun to the side. The woman cried in panic and reached for him, but it was too late. He went over the edge."

The table went silent for a long moment. Joan remembered clearly the deep cliffs, the jagged rocks down below.

Hugh's gaze was far away. "I raced toward the wall, desperately hoping that he was still alive. The woman fled to the south, and that is when I realized it was Cecily. But I had no thought of chasing her at the time. All my focus was on Michael." He shook his head. "When I got to the wall, though, it was clear that the fall had done him in. His broken body lay on the jagged rocks below. And then the tide dragged him out before I could reach him. I could only watch as he drifted into the dark night."

Joan shook her head. "Why didn't Master Martin tell me?"

Hugh ran a hand tenderly along her cheek. "I wrote to Master Martin in a message for his eyes only. At the time I was simply concerned about keeping an agent's death a secret." His gaze held hers. "However, I can imagine why he then did not tell you the full details. Michael had been loyal at the end. Why taint your memories of better times with the truth, when nothing could be done about it? In a way, the accident story was true. I don't think Cecily meant for him to die. If anything, she probably hoped he would change his mind and return to her. She seemed quite distraught over his death."

Norman leant forward. "Distraught enough to seek revenge?"

Hugh looked up at that, then slowly nodded. "Umberto's actions on the rooftop did seem gauged to prod Joan into action, rather than me," he agreed. "I would not have been jealous at all about Michael being with Cecily. There was no reason to go on at length about it for my benefit. He must have known, somehow, that Joan would be near."

Joan looked over at him. "But why would Cecily have left, if a trap was being set? Surely she would have wanted to be there for my capture?"

Hugh pondered that for a moment. "Perhaps she was not certain of the outcome and wanted to play it safe. This way you could be brought to her if things went well and she would be elsewhere if things went poorly." His mouth quirked up. "Which they did."

Joan turned to Linota. "Did you have any sense of where they were going to take you?"

Linota pursed her lips, considering. "I remember something about a mermaid."

Ymbert raised an eyebrow. "Could be the Drifting Mermaid tavern, out in Ravenscar."

Hugh nodded in agreement. "It could be, indeed. Kidnapping seems exactly the kind of mischief that establishment's crew would be into."

Norman took another drink of his ale. "Lord Weston is eager to lend a hand in this, and Greslet has offered to send along some of his men as well. I think we should take tomorrow to make our plans and then head out as a group the next day. That way, even if the bandits have a larger force waiting for us, we are prepared."

Joan looked with concern at Hugh. "What if Cecily makes a run for it?"

He shook his head. "If that woman was one thing, she was tenacious. She built her reputation on pursuing her goals like a determined badger." His eyes held hers with concern. "If she is focused on getting to you, the last thing she would do is leave."

She smiled at that, leaning against him. "Not to worry," she assured him. "Together, I am sure we can defeat her."

* * *

Joan blinked her eyes awake; the room was pitch dark. Hugh was gently snoring, lying alongside her, his arm resting across her stomach. Only the faintest of starlight gave edges to the low table across the room, to the door which led to the outside stairs.

There was a quiet knock.

Hugh was awake instantly, reaching for the sword at the side of the bed. Joan took up her own, then pulled the blanket to cover her chest.

Hugh stalked, naked, over to the side of the door. "Who's there?"

Ada's voice eased through the wood. "I'm sorry to bother you at such a late hour, but it's Linota. She's come back from Muriel's, just as I was heading to bed, and she seems upset. She wants to talk with Joan, alone. Seems it's about something that happened to her while she was captured."

Hugh looked over to Joan, his eyes shadowing. "I had wondered if there was more to what she said," he murmured. "I can imagine she didn't want to reveal the full details in front of the group."

Joan nodded, returning her sword to its place. She slid out of bed, quickly pulling on a tunic and slipping on boots. She came up alongside Hugh and gave him a gentle kiss. "I might be a while."

He tenderly ran a hand down her cheek. "Take all the time you need," he answered. "Linota is a brave woman. If she needs a friend tonight, she couldn't ask for better."

Joan nudged her head, and Hugh glanced down at his bare skin. He moved to stand behind the door, and Joan pulled it open just far enough to slip out. Ada stood there waiting. "I'm sorry about this," she said again.

Joan shook her head. "Linota deserves our support," she pointed out. "I am more than glad to spend the night talking with her, if that will help her."

Ada led the way down the stairs. "I lit a candle in the back room," she explained. "Figured you two could talk in private in there."

"That was thoughtful of you. Some ale might help as well."

"Of course. I have two mugs set out and a full pitcher."

Joan smiled. "You have thought of everything." She came up to the door and pressed it open. "Linota? How can I be of assistance?"

A lone candle flickered on the round table, sending shadows across a ring of empty chairs.

A solid blow landed on the back of her head, and the world cascaded into black.

Chapter 12

Joan groaned into life. It seemed that she had bruises on her bruises, and the back of her head ached with a throbbing pain. Her world was jarring, thudding, and it took a long moment before she connected the sensations together. She was on horseback. A warm body sat behind her, a thick wood surrounded her, and a bright sun was shining against her half-open eyelids, twisting her headache to epic proportions.

The sequence of events resurfaced in her memory. Confusion swept over her. Who had taken her?

She twisted in the saddle, looking back.

Ada sat there, a relaxed smile on her lips. She reined in to a stop. "About time you woke up," she commented. "We need to start moving a bit faster if we want to get to Cecily in time." Behind her, a second horse was trailing along on a rope.

Joan threw herself from the horse, grunting in pain as she landed on her side on the hard-packed dirt. Scrambling, she made her way over to the second horse, sure that at any second Ada would be behind her, pressing a knife to her back.

She reached the saddle, turned, and stopped in surprise.

Ada was exactly where she had been before. She sat quietly on her saddle, one eyebrow cocked, watching Joan with amusement. "Did you enjoy that?"

Joan put her hand on the saddle, fresh aches hammering at her, and she stared at Ada in confusion. "Aren't you taking me hostage?"

Ada returned her gaze evenly. "Isn't a hostage being taken somewhere she doesn't want to go? I thought you wanted to go see Cecily."

Joan's hand dropped to her hip, and she gave a low curse as it swept empty air. She had nothing with her – only the thin clothing and boots she had yanked on in order to talk with Linota.

Still, perhaps she could overpower Ada on her own. She took a step toward her. "So you know where Cecily is?"

Ada grinned. "Attacking me won't get you what you want," she calmly stated. "I only know the next town to go to. If you and I arrive there together, someone will approach me and let me know where to go after that. If you have me tied up, nobody shows. I don't know who to look for, and the trail goes cold."

Joan glanced back at the horse. "I could go back for help."

Ada shrugged. "Sure, and Cecily will vanish. Believe me, she's taken her time with this. She is more than happy to wait another year or two until the next opportunity presents itself. You will never find her by tracking her down."

Joan pursed her lips. "You seem to know Cecily well."

"As well as anybody could know her," mused Ada. "I've worked with her for four years now.

Joan's leg buckled, and she stumbled back against the horse. Ada grinned. "You might not even make it back in one piece," she pointed out. "Especially with your little group all eagerly heading out in the opposite direction, toward Ravenscar."

Joan's heart chilled. "Is Linota in on it as well?"

Ada laughed. "Not even Cecily can turn someone that quickly," she teased. "No, Cecily just made sure to drop some misdirectional clues in Linota's hearing. I'm surprised that's the only one the woman picked up on, but she was under a lot of stress at the time."

She drummed her fingers along her reins. "So, what will it be? Do you want to have a chat with Cecily and find out what really happened between her and Michael?"

"How do I know she won't just kill me?"

Ada raised her eyebrows. "Kill you? If she'd wanted you dead, you'd be lying in a pool of blood back in that hell-hole of a tavern, and I'd be done with my babysitting duty."

Joan held her gaze. "Maybe she wants to do it herself."

Ada's laughter was rich, echoing through the forest. "You really don't know Cecily very well, do you," she teased. "Cecily, do something like that herself?"

"Maybe she wants to watch, then."

Ada shook her head. "She just wants to talk with you. She has a lot of respect for you, you know. Your training, your experiences."

A glimmer of insight arose within Joan. Perhaps Cecily had been using Michael, trying to gain knowledge of his operations. Joan had been at the center of the spider's web, handling messages and information from all over. Certainly it was several years ago – but undoubtedly there was information she knew that Cecily would find quite useful.

And, beyond that, Cecily seemed to take pride in turning people to her cause. Maybe she felt that, with a little time and patience, she could even convince Joan to join her.

If Joan went along with the plan, and left enough breadcrumbs behind her, eventually Hugh and the others would realize that the Mermaid clue was a false one. They would return, track her down, and be led straight to Cecily.

Joan put her foot in the stirrup, took in a deep breath, then hoisted herself up into the saddle. She held in a groan of pain as she settled down into position. She gave one last, long look to the road behind her.

Hugh would be furious.

She knew it with every fiber of her being, and she almost turned, almost headed back to him. But she knew Ada was right. If she left now, Cecily would vanish into the mist. And then in a year, or two, or five, the same thing would happen. Joan would somehow be caught off guard, would be given a chance, and she might be even less well prepared than she was now.

She had to find out what Cecily knew.

Nodding in resolution, she kneed her horse into motion, coming alongside Ada. "I am ready."

Ada grinned in delight. "Then we're off!"

Chapter 13

Joan groaned in pain as they approached the sixth small, remote village in what seemed like a never-ending chain. Ada hadn't been joking about Cecily's attention to detail. It seemed like the entire village had been paid to stay quiet, and the one person who sought them out only knew the next location in the path. Twice they were provided with fresh horses, and each stop offered ale and some quick supplies. But Joan hadn't slept properly in several days, and her head was throbbing in a steady rhythm.

Ada smiled cheerfully at her. "You might be in luck," she commented. "I see a wagon over by that farmer's house." She kicked her horse into a trot, moving over to drop to the ground by the surly man. He glanced at Joan for a moment, then nodded.

Joan reined in next to the two, holding onto the saddle as she carefully slid to the ground. Her body ached as if she'd gone over a waterfall in full spring flood. She didn't even ask where they were going next, as she had at previous stops. Ada would never answer, and it really didn't matter much. She had no idea if the seagulls she scratched into the ground with her heel at every stop would ever be seen. For all she knew, a rainstorm would sweep through tomorrow and wash them all away.

Ada nodded her head at the wagon. "All right, then, we both get in and he drives us for a while. Gives us a chance to catch up on sleep."

Joan didn't argue. She was beyond exhausted. She climbed into the low wagon, nestling in amongst the bags of grain. There were a pair of blankets to one side, and she pulled one over her.

In a moment Ada was up next to her, taking the other blanket. She closed her eyes, and in moments she was softly snoring.

Joan had the thought that now was her chance. But for what? Ada had no idea where they were going. Indeed, Ada had made it clear that Joan could turn back at any time. But Joan had no intention of doing that. For now, it seemed, she would have to let the dark-haired farmer bring them further toward their destination.

Heaviness pulled her down, she closed her eyes, and the world swam away.

* * *

Joan was getting tired of waking up in strange surroundings. Just once she would like to wake in her own bed, with Remus and Romulus nestled at her side, the familiar warp and woof of the tapestry hanging before her. Instead she was bumping along in a stained wagon, a crimson sunset streaking the sky above her, and Ada snoring like a river in full flood.

She pushed herself up to a sitting position, taking up the ale skin and drinking down a long swallow.

The driver turned his head. "Nearly there," he commented with a disinterested look on his face.

The woods were still thick around them, and the path the horse trod was barely wide enough for the wagon to pass. Joan wondered just what sort of a place they were going to. She rubbed wearily at the aching lump at the back of her head. Despite having slept the day half away, she still felt exhausted.

The trees opened up before her, and she sat up in surprise. The ocean stretched wide before her in a plain of dusty blue, the shoreline a rocky cliff high above it. Before them was a walled keep perched over the crashing waves. The treeline had been trimmed back a good fifty feet around the outer wall, and the wagon made its way steadily toward the main gate. Alert guards manned the wall, watching them approach, and the heavy doors were pulled open.

Ada made a groaning noise, then shook herself awake. "Finally," she said, stretching. "Thought this old cart would never get there."

The wagon pulled into a large courtyard which was neat and well maintained. The stables, kitchens, and other buildings were clean and organized. Ada leapt down from the wagon, then put up a hand to help guide Joan down. Joan's legs still felt wobbly, but she bit back the cry of pain that threatened to emerge from her as her feet met the cobblestones. She had to do her best to present a strong front.

Ada turned toward the main keep. "C'mon. You and I need a bath, after all we've been through. Then we'll head in to dinner with Cecily."

Joan was eager to meet Cecily, to get all this over with, but the idea of a bath called to her with a strength she hadn't thought possible. She followed along after Ada as they went through the main doors of the keep, then up a set of spiral stairs. The second floor seemed to offer several bedrooms evenly spaced down a long hallway. Ada stopped at one of the doors. "This one's yours," she commented. "Mine's the next one on the right. Take your time, and come get me when you're ready. I'm sure everything you need is there."

Joan pushed open the door, stepped through, and closed it behind her. She slid the bar across its channel, and her shoulders slumped in relief. For the moment, at least, she was safe. Then she turned to survey the room.

It was elegantly furnished, with crimson curtains and beddings, and a low fire in the fireplace. Candles shone on several surfaces, providing a counterpoint to the glowing colors of sunset outside the window. A wooden wardrobe in one corner stood open; several dresses in various shades of crimson hung within. Before the fireplace was a large wooden half-barrel, nearly full of steaming water. A small table alongside it held a towel, a small pottery urn of wood ash soap, and a variety of brushes and combs.

Joan glanced back at the barred door, then forward at the large windows overlooking the distant ocean. It seemed perfectly safe here, and she couldn't remember the last time she had a proper bath.

She stripped down, easing herself into the warm liquid, sighing in pleasure as the various aches and bruises over the past week met the soothing water. It was a long while before she roused herself to scrub off the layers of dirt and sweat. The process was luxurious. Her fingers and toes were thoroughly wrinkled by the time she finally, reluctantly, drew herself out of the water and toweled herself dry. She carefully inspected her injuries to ensure none needed further attention.

That done, she slipped on a chemise, then chose one of the dresses; it fit perfectly. She brushed out her hair until it shone. At last she was ready to face whatever lay below.

Her stomach growled, and she chuckled. Perhaps it was a good thing that food was the next item on the list.

She slid aside the bar, then walked down the hall to the next door. She gave a sharp rap.

Ada pulled the door open promptly, nodding a smile at her. The woman was wearing an elegant crimson tunic and looked less the tavern wench, more the noble lady. "Feels good to be clean and properly dressed," she commented with a chuckle. "Let's get some food into us. Cecily's cooks are some of the best I've met."

They went down the stairs together, stepping into the main hall. The lower tables were full of soldiers and other keep staff. Joan didn't recognize any from the camp she had raided two days ago. She looked up ahead to the main table, set cross-wise against the end of the hall.

Cecily sat at the center of the table, waving in welcome. She was a woman of rich curves, her auburn hair shining in the candlelight. She wore a dark crimson tunic with gold embroidery along its hems. She motioned to the seat on her right, and Joan took it. Ada sat down on Joan's other side.

Cecily's voice was warm. "Welcome to my home," she offered. "You must be famished." She looked up. "Ah, here comes Catharine."

A maid stopped by with a pitcher of mead, filling their mugs. Joan took a sip, relishing the delicious flavor as it traced its way down her throat. Then plates were laid out with roast ham, fragrant duck, stewed turnips, candied apples, and a myriad of other dishes Joan could not name.

All thought of talking fled her mind. She filled her trencher, immersed herself in the delicious offerings, and she had finished up thirds before she had become so full that she could not attempt one more bite.

Cecily leant back in her chair. "If you want to talk now, Joan, I am quite at your leisure. But I might advise we wait until morning, when you are fresh. I can only imagine that you have not had a proper night's sleep in quite a while."

Joan knew that she should begin the questioning immediately. She should find out what was going on and get safely out again. Hugh and the others were undoubtedly scouring the countryside for her.

But her mind could just not focus on the task. The warm bath, the delicious food, and the rich mead had all conspired to make the thought of that luxurious bed a clarion call in her mind. There was no way she could attend well to an important discussion right now.

Her eyes drooped.

Cecily gave a knowing chuckle. "Bed it is, I think," she commented, looking over at Ada. "I shall see you both in the morning?"

Ada nodded, standing, putting a hand down for Joan. "Come on," she prodded. "Cecily will be here in the morning, and you can talk with her as long as you wish. That is why you're here, after all. First, you need that sleep."

Joan pushed to her feet, following along behind Ada through the throng and back up to her room. Again there was no sense of threat or trouble as she stepped in and barred the door. The bath had been removed, the blanket turned down, and she barely got the dress stripped off of her before she had tumbled into the bed.

The mattress was pure bliss, and she drifted off into a relaxed sleep.

Chapter 14

Joan stretched her arms wide, more alert than she had in weeks. She took in the luxurious surroundings of her bedroom with a wry grin. If she were to wake somewhere different every day, at least today's choice was quite a treat. Cecily must be doing pretty well for herself to be able to afford such a home.

She rose and opened the curtains, looking out on the rolling ocean. The day was sunny, and the water glistened with gold edges to the waves. Seagulls flew high above, calling out, and Joan smiled. The fresh tang of salt air awakened her further. It was a good sign.

She went to the wardrobe, finding that today's selection included a range of tangerine dresses. She wondered if there would be color themes to the days. She chose one, pulling it on over her chemise, then brushed out her hair.

There was no answer to her knocks on Ada's door, so at last she made her way down the stairs and into the great hall. The room was mostly empty; apparently most of the keep had already eaten and started in with their daily tasks. Cecily and Ada were sitting at the far table, talking relaxedly with each other, and they looked up with smiles as Joan approached.

"There you are," welcomed Ada, sliding a seat down so Joan could sit between them. "Come, the cooks kept your food warm for you. I imagine you must be famished."

Indeed, Joan's stomach had begun to rumble again. The moment the eggs, bacon, and other items were placed before her, she dug into them voraciously. The two women waited patiently while she ate, talking across her about general keep business.

Finally Joan was finished, and Cecily lifted her glass. "Come, let us sit by the fire. It'll be easier to talk there." The three women relocated to a trio of chairs by the large, carved fireplace. A low pile of embers glowed within the grate, offering a gentle offset to the late spring weather.

Cecily leant back, taking a sip of her mead. "And here we are, Joan. I imagine you have countless questions for me. So, ask away."

It was all so different than Joan had imagined. She had thought Cecily would be a hard, sharp-edged woman who ran her stews with an iron fist. The woman before her was smiling, pleasant, with healthy curves and a wide smile. The maids and servants had seemed contented and well cared for.

Joan's mind went back to the intelligence she had processed with Master Martin on Cecily and Umberto, on the range of activities the two had been involved with.

"You worked with Umberto in the Holy Land?"

Cecily nodded in agreement. "Yes, indeed. When I was young, my father decided he had too many mouths to feed. As soon as I turned thirteen he sold me to a local stew." Her eyes shadowed. "It was a Hell on earth. The girls were beaten regularly, the clients were abusive, and the conditions were beyond filthy. After three years I managed to escape, but I found myself starving on the street. I only knew of one way to earn my bread, but this time I found a better employer. I worked my way up through the ranks. I was recruited by another madam, and under her care I realized that a woman could do quite nicely for herself. It all depended on the environment she was in."

She took a sip of her mead. "Eventually I was in charge of a five-room brothel in Jaffa. Small, but with some of the most talented women in the region. The men flocked to our doors. Our women were happy, and that shone through in everything they did. The men were willing to pay top dollar for their tender ministrations."

Joan leant forward. "So where did Umberto come into this?"

Cecily gave an elegant shrug. "I wanted to expand my business, and Umberto had both the financing and the knowledge of the area. It seemed a good fit at the time. Yes, I knew he had an unsavory side to him, but don't all men? I figured I could manage that aspect of the relationship. Over time I had three locations, and then eight. My empire's reputation was known from Rome to Paris."

Joan looked down at the plate at her side, making a show of selecting from amongst the various wedges of cheese laying there. Cecily was working hard to present herself as an honest businesswoman, pulling herself up by her own bootstraps, earning respectability for herself through hard work and diligent effort.

Joan could see how women would be drawn into this story, would want to be a part of the world Cecily had created. Indeed, for many women, the independence she seemed to promise was all they could dream of. For women in poverty, the elegant furnishings and delicious meals would seem a Heaven on earth.

However, Joan had seen the reports. She had talked with Master Martin long into the night about how the various intelligence reports linked together. Cecily was far from a beneficent guardian angel. Yes, a select few women had been able to live a life of luxury – for the scant months or years that they were at the top of their form. Then they were demoted to lesser quality stews, eventually ending up in flea-bitten locations that were not far off from the hellhole Cecily had started her poignant story with.

And if Umberto was ruthless with burning down locations rather than seeing them be taken, Cecily was not far behind. She had been known to scar the faces of women who left her so that they could not work anywhere else.[1]

Joan arranged her face into a docile, enraptured smile before looking up again. "This cheddar is delicious," she murmured. "The food here is the best I have ever sampled."

Cecily smiled. "That means a lot, coming from you," she offered. "You have seen much of the world and know the variety it presents to us." She looked around the room. "As you can see, hard work presents its rewards. It is a message I offer to women every day. They do not need to slave and toil at the beck and call of a man barely worthy to wash their feet. They can take charge of their own destiny and make their own fortune."

Joan wondered just how much of the fortune the women were allowed to keep and how much went into bolstering Cecily's wealth.

Cecily leant forward with a smile, by all appearances a magnanimous hostess with an honored guest. "So, what else would you like to know about?"

Joan raised an eyebrow. Time to ease into it slowly. "Your empire sounds magnificent, indeed," she praised. "What is my part in all of this?"

Cecily smiled widely. "Seeing the appeal of my world, are you? Of course you are. You are intelligent and talented. Your skills have been wasted for years. You were little more than a servant of men, being forced to scurry around, following their orders. You are ready for something more suited to your abilities."

She nodded her head to Ada. "You can see that I employ able women in positions of authority. I have heard much about you over the years, and I have long had my eye on you."

Joan allowed an expression of doubt to creep over her face. She could not seem *too* gullible. "To run a stew, like the one you were setting up in the woods?"

Cecily gave a tinkling laugh. "Oh, my girl, no, no. Those women were not there to be whores!"

Joan raised an eyebrow. "They were not?"

Cecily shook her head. "I can get whores anywhere," she countered. "I do not need to track them down. They come to me." She took a drink of her mead. "No, those women were singled out to be recruited for my management team. Each one was unmarried and had shown her talent in a variety of ways. I distributed a list of names to my collectors, and if one of the women was found alone, she was brought in for discussion."

Joan's brow furrowed. "But why kidnap them, then?"

Cecily spread her hands wide. "I'm afraid that my line of business is considered disreputable by many. A woman who simply announces to family and friends that 'I am going to go run a bordello now' would be ostracized." Her smile grew. "However, if the poor girl was taken against her will, put into that position, and then made a thriving success of it, the perception would be different. Now she had made the best she could out of what life had given her. For whatever reason, that is considered a better outcome."

Joan brought a brightness of understanding to her eyes. "So you were helping those women."

Cecily's wide smile showed bright white teeth. "Absolutely. Half of the women were ready to accept before they had even been brought to me. The other half would have been joining them within a day or two. I have never had anyone leave my employ. They are spoiled by me and have no desire to go back to a man's world."

Joan thought there was an entirely different reason that no woman ever escaped Cecily's clutches, but she kept that idea to herself.

She brought hesitance to her voice. "So that is why you had Ada take me?"

Cecily nodded, looking fondly over at Ada for a moment. "The moment I realized who you were, I knew you had to be a part of our organization. Ada said she could handle the collection process, and sure enough, here you are with us now."

She gave a slight shrug. "It could have been difficult for you, as you well know, if you announced that you voluntarily joined an organization that promoted prostitution. It has such a negative connotation to it." She smiled and looked around her. "But as you can see, we are about empowering women. Men – and some women they have brainwashed - are strongly against any system that allows females to flourish and prosper independently. So, by providing the cover of a kidnapping, we create a cover story for how this process took place."

Joan looked up with large eyes. "You are kind to go through all of this for me."

Cecily patted her hands. "You are worth it, my dear," she vowed. "Believe in yourself the way I believe in you. Together, we can reach the stars."

Joan looked down again. Cecily's skill with her recruitment pitch was impressive. She could see how single women might fall for the story. Especially with the shortage of men caused by the Crusades, many women faced a nunnery or spinsterhood as their only two options in life. Cecily was dangling a powerful lure that would be hard to resist.

She modulated her tone to have what she hoped was just the right amount of interest and concern. "Is it all right if I think this over for a little while?"

Cecily sat back, contented. Her eyes almost glowed with satisfaction. "Of course, my dear, I would expect no less from you," she murmured. "You take all the time you need." She smiled, nudging her head to the left. "Through that door is our back patio courtyard. It overlooks the ocean. There are bowls of fruit and pitchers of ale. Go and sit for a while. Soak in the beauty of it all."

Joan nodded to the two women, then stood and made her way over to the far door. The sun was brilliant as she stepped through to the large patio, and she moved forward to the edge wall, giving her eyes time to adjust to the sun's glare, looking out over the vastness of the ocean. White clouds skittered high above, foam danced on the tips of the curling waves, and a trio of fishing boats drifted offshore. She drew in a long, deep breath of the salty air.

Whatever else Cecily had done, she had chosen a perfect keep for her home. Joan wondered what crusader had died in order for Cecily to slide in to his family estate.

At last she turned to look down the length of the patio. There were a scattering of empty chairs looking out over the ocean, and a long table against the back wall held several wooden bowls of apples and pears, along with a trio of pewter pitchers of ale. A row of pottery mugs lay alongside them. And against the far side of the patio was a table with –

Joan's breath caught, time slowed down, then ran backwards. Her tangerine dress rippled around her, caught by the ocean breeze. A seagull soared up next to her, his white wingtips deftly catching the movement of the air. The scent of the sea and gentle roar of the ocean filled her senses.

Michael sat at the far table, his gaze steady on her, his short, dark brown hair ruffling in the breeze, fully alive.

Chapter 15

Joan's feet were in motion before she gave it conscious thought. Suddenly she was back in Master Martin's training room, there was a movement at the door, and it was not the messenger with news that would shatter her world. Instead it was Michael – *Michael* – and he was home to her, safe and sound. Her heart blossomed with overwhelming joy and relief which threatened to drown her.

He stood as she approached, and she flung herself at him, wrapped her arms around him, her breath coming in long, staggering heaves.

But he was stiff within her embrace, as he always had been. He had the wooden quality of a man who was resigned to put up with the overenthusiastic actions of a spoiled child. His frame held the weary patience of someone who hoped this kind of unnecessary behavior would end soon so he could get on with more important things in life.

It swept back in on Joan all at once how Michael had always been this way with her. How he would allow her a short hug on his returns, then go off with friends to spend the evening regaling them with tales. She had forced herself to take it in stride. He was a busy man. He had many obligations to juggle. She needed to act more like him – more distant, more cool.

Then another vision filled her mind – that of the banks of the river, when she had stepped out into the sunshine to walk toward Hugh. She had seen the glow of relief and welcome in his eyes, and then he had run to her, had swept her up and spun her around in unbridled joy.

The feeling burst through her with unwavering certainty. Hugh was the man she needed in her life. She missed him, craved him, with every fiber of her being.

Michael firmly pressed her away from him, and smiled when he looked down in her eyes. "You did miss me," he chuckled. "I can see it in your face."

The current situation came crashing down on Joan. A thousand questions blared in her mind, each louder than the next. The words that ended up blurting out of her were, "Where have you been?"

He settled himself back down into the wooden chair, stretching his shoulders in relaxation. "It is a story, indeed," he stated. "Go fetch us a pair of mugs and a pitcher of ale like a good girl and I'll catch you up."

A bristle of annoyance ran down her spine, but she held the smile on her face. Amidst the confusion and relief was reemerging the core thought that she was here with a purpose. Clearly Michael and Cecily had something planned for her, and she had to find out what. She had to lure them into thinking that whatever schemes they had developed were working on her.

She dutifully moved to the long, back table, looping two mug handles through one hand and picking up a large, metal pitcher with the other. She carried all back to the round table and set them out. When she sat down in the chair next to him, she could still see over the low wall of the patio, to the trio of fishing boats floating on the water, going about their business as they had done every day for centuries.

Michael followed her eyes. "It could be the Holy Land," he commented. "The ships would have a leaner shape, and the sky would have that richer color, but so many things are the same." His eyes drew back to the mugs. "Something you forgot?"

Joan blinked, then leant forward to fill each mug. Michael picked his up, holding it in a toast. "To new beginnings," he offered. Joan clinked her mug against his, then drew down the fragrant liquid. She finished half the mug in one long swallow. She had a feeling she would need its strength.

She turned to Michael, to the face she knew so well. "You didn't die," she commented, her mind settling down to more logical thought.

His eyes twinkled at that. "Certainly not," he agreed. "A simple matter of a rope securely attached on the far side of the wall. I rolled over the stones and grabbed a hold of that, flattening myself against the dark shadows. Hugh never had an inkling of the switch. He simply saw, as he expected to see, a broken form at the bottom of a long drop. Once his eyes had pinned on that, no other solution presented itself." He took down a long drink of his brew, smiling. "He was always simple like that."

Joan held in the stream of anger which coursed through her. She knew that Michael was good at what he did, would notice the minute changes in her face and breathing, so she added, "It nearly killed me when I heard you had died."

He put a hand out to gently pat hers for a moment. "I heard about that incident at Master Martin's school. A shame, but you should know better than that. You have to be able to work through any emotion and keep your focus on the task at hand. It's the only way to succeed in life."

The advice seemed exactly what she needed as she faced him, and she nodded. "You are right, as always."

He smiled, stretching his arms above his head, looking around the patio contentedly. "So, I suppose you want to hear what this was all about."

Joan wondered suddenly if he was imagining a larger crowd, imagining he was telling this tale to his room full of buddies at the tavern, and not just her, not just the woman he had pledged himself to once, long ago.

She nodded. "I would, indeed."

"Well," he began, settling himself in, "it all started during a series of investigations I was making into a ring of corrupt officials. A great deal of money was changing hands, and I knew the web had to stretch into fairly high places. The further I delved into it, the more I realized just how much the acquisition of intelligence factored into their activities. They were buying and selling knowledge, and making quite a profit at it."

"So you told Master Martin?"

Michael glanced at her in annoyance, and she sat back in her chair. "My apologies," she murmured. "Please, go on."

"So I decided I should go under cover," he stated, his emphasis making clear that he felt his way was far better than her feeble offering. "Soon I had the group trusting me thoroughly. I moved up quickly through the ranks. Praise was heaped on me from all sides for my effectiveness and talents."

Joan nodded silently.

His brow furrowed in concern. "And then I came across news that was troubling indeed. Hugh was on the payroll. And, not only that, but he was acting as a guard for one of the most notorious stews in the city."

Joan's heart went still, and she stared at him in disbelief. He could not be serious. Not the Hugh she knew, not the one who had tended with such gentle care to the women they had rescued.

Michael's eyes shone with contentment at her focused attention. "It was then I talked with Master Martin," he continued. "I laid out my plan of the fake death. It would have been impossible for me to investigate Hugh if we remained a team. He would expect to know where I was going and what I was doing. Once I 'died', I could see how he acted when he believed he was free and clear."

He was lying to her.

It was suddenly so clear, so perfectly etched, and yet her brain could not quite connect the pieces together. He was looking at her with complete earnestness, and once upon a time she would have sworn on her life that he was telling the truth. She would have stepped before a loaded crossbow, pointed it at her chest, and vowed that every word Michael had said was honesty itself.

But she knew it was not. She had seen Master Martin's face when the news came of Michael's death. She had seen him in the following days and months as he mourned the loss of a favorite student. That was no act put on for her benefit. That was the snuffing of hope in an aging man.

Michael's eyes narrowed. "Is something wrong?"

She looked down, running a hand through her hair. "It is just so much to take in," she honestly stated. "To think you have been alive this whole time? That Master Martin was lying to me?"

His suspicion eased, and he patted her hand again. His tone became lofty. "You'll find, my dear, that in our business, few people can be trusted. You have to always look out for yourself, to question the motives of everyone around you."

He took a drink of his ale. "Take Hugh, for example. That stew he worked for crammed four women into each room, with barely a flattened mat to sleep on. Half of them were diseased, and the other half bore scars from their attempts to escape. That grated main door only opened for the customers – either lowborn who could afford no better, or those with more coin who wanted to engage in activities that the higher-end stews would forbid."

Joan wondered how he was so intimately aware of the stew's offerings, but she held her tongue.

Michael leant toward her, holding her gaze. She could see the small gold flecks in the green, the sure curve of his chin, and it came to her suddenly, strongly. She had loved this man once. She had adored him, had longed for him, had prayed every day for him to come back to her so they could settle down and raise a family together. It had been all she had ever wanted.

Michael smiled, seeing the look in her eyes, and nodded in satisfaction. "I am back to you now," he stated. "I know all about your little dalliance with Hugh. No need to feel ashamed; it happens to all of us. But that is over with. You thought I was dead, and after a few years your resistance crumbled." His eyes grew serious. "But now I am here, and you are mine. Things will go back to the way they were."

Joan could only nod. She did not trust herself to speak.

Michael drained down the rest of his ale, then set the mug on the table with a sharp ring. "Good, that's settled. Let's get you inside and into proper clothes for dinner. I hear the cook's making roast lamb tonight."

Things were moving quickly, and Joan felt as if she needed a moment to breathe or she would be overrun. "I just need a few minutes to look out at the ocean," she murmured. "It has been so long since I've seen it."

He shrugged. "Just don't be late for dinner," he warned, then he turned to stride to the far door. In a moment Joan was alone on the patio.

She walked to the edge of the patio, looking out over the ocean, the edges of her tangerine dress catching in the salty breeze. Her world was being sliced into a thousand pieces by the curved blade of a *khopesh*, was falling and rearranging into a pattern which barely made sense. She felt like a mouse who had been mesmerized by a snake and was somehow barely able to shake free of the spell.

Just how many of her past conversations with Michael had been lies? She was still stunned with the ease with which falsehoods streamed from his mouth, with no indication at all that the words he was speaking were untrue. How many other stories had been complete fictions? What had the man been up to all those years?

And what part did he expect her to play in all of this?

Crimson and golden streaks were painting the sky, and the fishing boats were slowly gliding back to shore. She stared at them, at the normalcy they represented. Then she set her lips into a line, and she turned.

She would find out what was going on here, no matter what it took.

Chapter 16

Joan sat between Cecily and Michael, taking another bite of the fragrant roast lamb. Michael had not been lying about one thing – the dish was every bit as good as he had promised. She washed it down with a mouthful of mead, then bit into the roast turnips sprinkled with rosemary.

Divine.

Cecily smiled at her enjoyment. "You could eat like this every day," she prompted. "While we move from location to location for obvious reasons, we þring our retainers with us. This cook has been with me for several years now. We have her whipped into shape."

Michael stabbed a piece of meat with his knife and plunked it into his mouth. "She *will* eat like this every day," he corrected Cecily. "Of course Joan will be staying with me."

Cecily's smile widened, and she turned to Joan. "So it is all decided?"

Joan forced her face to hold a smile. "Of course," she murmured. "My Michael is back with me again. I would be no place else."

Michael skewered another piece. "No place else, indeed," he agreed. "You were made mine years ago. Your father practically gave you to me."

Joan pitched her voice to be dutiful and meek. "I will never leave your side again."

Michael shook his head. "You will be heading out tomorrow morning," he corrected.

Joan's pulse quickened. Finally, they were getting to something. "Oh? But I just found you!"

That look of weary annoyance she knew so well flitted across his face, quickly replaced by an attentive smile. "Ah, my dear, I know you miss me. But this is important. It has to do with that blackguard, Hugh."

The sound of his name on Michael's lips stilled her breath. What would they want from Hugh?

Michael tapped the table with one finger. "When we shared an apartment in the Holy Land, Hugh knew that one of my personal items held special meaning to me. It was a silly thing, a wooden salad bowl, but it always reminded me of my mother. I had often joked with Hugh that, should there be a fire, the one thing I would want to save was that salad bowl."

He gave a soft shrug. "When Hugh thought that I had died, apparently he kept it with him. Probably to celebrate his ability to outlive me." His eyes sharpened. "I want it back."

Ada leant over from her place on Michael's other side. "I've been through Hugh's apartment at the tavern," she commented. "He's got several pottery bowls there, but that's it. I don't know where he's put it."

Joan looked between them. "Maybe he threw it out or gave it away at some point," she mused. "It's been five years, after all."

Michael shook his head, his face glowing with certainty. "I know Hugh. He is a simpleton about things like honor and duty. He has that bowl, and I want it back. It belongs to me."

Joan stilled, suddenly remembering the morning she lay in Hugh's bed. She had looked up over her shoulder and seen the wooden circle with the soaring seagull carved into it. There had been a convex curve to the wood surface, a roundness to the shape.

She kept her voice even. "So you will send me, alone, back to fetch this bowl?"

Michael gave a harsh laugh. "Absolutely not! I would not risk having that man get a hold of you." He nudged his head to the side. "Ada will be with you every moment. For every breath. When you have met your objective, she will guide you back to our new location, the same as last time."

Joan's heart thumped in her chest. "It might be better if I went alone, so that –"

Michael cut her off. "This is my plan, and we do it my way," he stated. "Ada will never leave your side."

Joan dropped her gaze. "As you wish."

Michael put a hand beneath her chin, and raised her head to look into his eyes. "You always were a good, obedient girl," he reminded her. "Do not let me down in this."

She held her voice to a meek murmur. "I won't."

"Good," he stated, and then he was standing, calling out to the men sitting at the lower tables. "And now, who is ready for some gambling?"

A roar of approval echoed back to him, and he was lost in the swirl of bodies.

Joan drew herself to her feet. "I am afraid that I am worn down from the day's events," she apologized. "I will call it an early night."

"Of course," agreed Cecily with a smile. "Just be sure to be ready by noon tomorrow. You and Ada have a long ride before you."

Joan nodded, then made her way through the hall, up the stairs, and into her room. She slid the bar into place across the door, then crossed to the window, looking out at the glistening ocean. The moon was high in the sky, sending pearlescent shimmers over the waves. A lone fishing boat was plying its trade, a small lantern adding its soft, golden glow to the scene.

Joan sat on the sill, closing her eyes for a long moment. The events of the day were still nearly too much to take in. Her memories of Michael were becoming tangled and skewed, as if someone had taken a beautiful tapestry and begun pulling randomly on its strings.

And what was the true story about the bowl? Joan doubted Michael was sentimental. Was it that he was jealous of Hugh, that Michael bristled at the thought of Hugh having anything that rightfully belonged to him? Or was there something intrinsically valuable about the bowl? Surely a carved piece of wood could not hold much worth. But Michael had seemed insistent on getting it back, and when Ada's investigations had failed, he felt this was his next best chance.

Iron bands constricted around Joan's chest as she thought about the task that lay before her. Ada would be watching her every move, her every glance, and would report back to Cecily and Michael if one action went awry. Joan would have to pretend that she was over Hugh, that she was fully back in love with Michael. She would have to deceive Hugh and somehow get her hands on that seagull-carved bowl.

Then she would bring the bowl back to Cecily and Michael, to see what the true story was. Maybe, then, they would trust her enough to reveal their involvement in the kidnappings and smuggling activities. Joan had no doubt that the empire was far less beneficent than Cecily purported it to be.

She took one last look at the fishing boat before her, then pulled the curtains closed. It was time to get some rest. Tomorrow she would start one of the most challenging tasks of her life.

Chapter 17

Joan nervously glanced at the closed main gates of the curtain wall, then back to the trio who stood before her. Ada, like her, was dressed for travel with a light cloak and sturdy boots. Both wore a long, crimson dress over a white chemise. Cecily and Michael were more elegantly outfitted, with embroidery dancing at their cuffs and gold piping around their neckline.

Cecily stepped forward first, giving both women a warm hug. "I have the utmost faith in you," she offered them. "You will do what needs to be done and return to us. Then will have a celebration the likes of which has never been seen."

Michael was cooler, first touching Ada on the cheek, then turning to Joan. He ran his eyes down her body, then nodded in satisfaction. "You are fully mine," he reminded her. "See that you do not disgrace me while you are outside these walls. Your temporary fling with Hugh was understandable, but it is over."

She looked down. She kept her voice to a low murmur. "Of course."

Satisfied, he nodded, then held his arm out for Cecily. She hooked hers into his, and together the two returned to the main keep.

Ada's eyes lit up in anticipation, and she turned, striding toward the main doors leading out into the wood. Joan followed along behind her in confusion, glancing back to the stables. "But surely we will be taking horses?"

Ada shook her head with conviction. "Not necessary."

The large, wooden doors were pulled open before them, and Joan's heart fell. It would take them a week, if not more, to walk the distance back to town. She held in her complaints. If, for whatever reason, this was Michael's plan, then she would not cause waves. Not when they felt she was under their spell.

Ada stepped through the gap, and Joan followed her, the midday sun shining down over the clearing. A rutted dirt path headed across the opening and into the depths of the shadowed woods. The two women stepped quietly along the trail. Behind them, there was the soft thunk as the gates sealed the keep.

The oaks and birch closed in around them, a coolness settled over her shoulders as the shadows grew dense, and a shiver ran down Joan's spine. Her hand moved to her hip – and swept through open air. *She still had no sword.* The loss of it wore at her, so used to it had she become. Both she and Ada wore knives, of course, but what use could they be if bandits were to attack? Little better than a kitten's nails against a hungry badger.

There was a creak behind them, and Joan's heart leapt. Ada seemed oblivious, and Joan wondered if the woman had nerves of steel or simply had not noticed the sound. There was a shimmer before them …

Hugh stood in the center of the road, his face in shadows, his stance still.

Every ounce of Joan's being called her to race to him, to wrap herself in his arms, to press her face against his neck, and to know that everything would be all right. It was only through the greatest self-control that she held herself in place, drawing in a deep breath and soaking in the sight of him.

There was a long moment where it seemed the world held its breath. At last he took one step toward them, then two. His gaze flicked to Ada for a moment before returning to hold hers.

Joan could barely speak his name. "Hugh …"

Ada stepped forward into the gap. "We are so relieved to see you," she stated brightly. "We are fortunate that Cecily did not find any use for us. Her wolves' heads have freed us, and we can now return back home to where we belong."

Hugh held Joan's eyes with steady regard. "Cecily had no use for you?"

Joan flinched. She could see, now that he had stepped forward from the shadows, how the mask of steadiness overlay depths of passion, of desire – and of keen hesitation.

His voice, when it came again, was rough. "And was Cecily the only person in the keep?"

He knew.

The image of the fishing boats sprang to Joan's mind, and suddenly she knew with absolute certainty that he had been on one of those vessels. He had seen her run into Michael's arms. He had watched as they talked together at length on the cobblestone patio.

Ada gave a tinkling laugh. "Of course there were others *at* the keep," she teased him. "But none of note." She began walking forward. "If we are going to go on foot, we should get moving. It's a long way home."

Hugh's eyes were still on Joan, but he gave a soft, clucking noise. Two large forms moved in the woods, and in a moment Accipiter and Aquila stepped into the open path.

Ada's eyes lit up with delight, and instantly she was at Aquila's side, running a hand down his dark brow. "I had heard of them, of course, but to see them in person!" She wound her fingers through his mane. "Joan, you and I should ride on this one. Hugh can take the other."

Hugh glanced over at that. "I thought I might ride with Joan."

Ada shook her head in determination. "I will stay by Joan's side until I get her to safety," she stated, brooking no discussion. "The woman has been through a lot, and I will not leave her alone. Not for one moment."

Understanding lit Hugh's eyes, and when he brought his gaze back to Joan there was a softer edge to it, a gentling of his focus. "Are you all right?"

She nodded, not trusting herself yet to speak.

Ada vaulted onto her horse's back. "Come on, Joan," she urged. "The faster we move, the more quickly we get this all done with."

Joan moved over to her horse's side, and Hugh went with her. He put out a hand, and she folded hers into it.

Electricity shimmered through her at his touch. Despite her best intentions she glanced up into his eyes, passion and desire warring within her.

She wanted him. She craved him with every particle of her being.

He drew in a breath, stilling for a long moment, and there was an easing of his shoulders. He gave her a boost, and then she was sitting before Ada. He mounted Accipiter and drew alongside them.

Ada urged Aquila into motion, and they were in flight.

* * *

Joan watched for an opportunity, a space, even the briefest of pauses in which she could talk with Hugh alone. Ada was clearly on guard for such an event. She stuck stubbornly by Joan's side, watching every word, every glance that passed between the two. They rode and rested, pacing the horses, and Joan would have guessed that they were halfway back before Hugh called for a halt. He had steadfastly avoided every village along the way, and they now made camp in a quiet clearing by a trickling brook.

He took the crossbow off his saddle, slipped into the woods, and a short while later returned with a plump rabbit. Ada set up a spit over the small fire they had built, and the fragrant smell of roasted meat soon set all of their stomachs rumbling. Hugh passed around the ale skin, and the rabbit was soon being shared as well.

He looked between the two women. "I imagine we will return to the tavern about dusk tomorrow. Is that where you both want to go?"

Ada nodded in agreement, tearing off a bit of flesh with her teeth. "That would be perfect. If you wouldn't mind letting us use your apartment, I think Joan and I would sleep best there. Just for the first night, of course. To get over the shock of it all."

Hugh nodded without inflection. "Of course."

The words burst out of Joan before she could reel them in. "I want to go home."

Both turned to look at her in surprise. Ada spoke first. "But Joan, my dear, I think it would be best if we took advantage of Hugh's kind hospitality."

Hugh's eyes held hers as if they were searching for something. "Why do you want to go home?"

An intense longing carved its way through Joan's heart. Why? Because home was safe. Home was where the tapestry hung, where she could sort through all the chaos which had invaded her world, twisted her memories, and made her unsure of what to believe. Home was where she had curled against Hugh, with Remus and Romulus snuggled at their feet, and the world was whole and complete.

Ada's eyes narrowed, and Joan was brought swiftly back to the present. She could not falter now.

"I … I want to check on my dogs," she murmured.

Ada raised an eyebrow. "You have dogs?"

Joan nodded. "Two of them. I haven't been home for days, and I just want to make sure they are all right."

Ada relaxed back against an old oak stump, taking another bite of the rabbit. "I'm sure they're fine," she soothed. "What are their names?"

A thought suddenly struck Joan, and she drew in a breath. Perhaps she wouldn't be able to converse with Hugh without Ada listening in – but that didn't mean they could not share information.

She held his eyes. "Apate and Dolos."

He stilled, all attention on her.

Ada gave a tinkling laugh. "What kinds of silly names are those?"

Hugh's voice was low, considering. "They are Greek gods," he explained. "They came from Pandora's box. Apate was the goddess of deceit."

Joan nodded. "And Dolos was the god of trickery."

Ada shook her head. "What kinds of names are those to give to pets?"

Joan's voice was hoarse. *This might just work.* "Oh, the names seemed quite appropriate at the time," she murmured. She gave herself a shake, turning to Ada. She put on a warmer smile. "They were quite mischievous as puppies," she explained.

Hugh's voice was steady, and his eyes were fixed on Joan. "I enjoy stories, especially by a campfire. What would the young pups do?"

Joan knew she had to be careful. Ada was no dullard; she would catch on if they spoke too openly. "Dolos, especially, loved to play fetch."

He sat back for a moment, his brow creased in confusion. "Fetch?"

Ada laughed in delight, taking a long swig on her ale. "Did you never have dogs as a child, out there in your father's camp?"

"I grew up here in England," he replied absently, his focus still on Joan. "I only went out to Jerusalem when I turned eighteen."

Ada belched. "Oh, right," she agreed. "It was –" She stopped abruptly and took another long swallow to cover the halt. Then she wiped her mouth with the back of her hand. "It was someone else," she finished up.

Joan looked into Hugh's eyes. "Fetch is a game where one player wants an item, and the other one goes and finds it, then brings it back."

Ada leant forward. "Dogs *love* to play fetch," she informed Hugh. "They could play it for hours and hours."

Hugh held Joan's gaze. "And what did Dolos like to play fetch with?"

Joan's mind raced through the options. Ada clearly knew what they were actually looking for, and she would be alert to any mention of it. But if it were seemingly innocent …

Her eyes lit up. "I started him with a wooden stick, when he was young," she explained. "But that quickly got to be too easy for him. So I made for him a wooden discus, like they used in the Greek competitions. I could throw it much further, and that absolutely was his favorite toy. That is what he would want me to fetch."

Ada nodded in approval. "Smart puppy."

Hugh's brow furrowed. "A discus? Of wood?"

Then, suddenly, awareness sharpened his eyes, and he sat back. He let out a long breath. "Of course."

Ada nudged Joan in the ribs. "See, he's starting to get why dogs are so much fun," she teased. "Soon he'll want one or two of his very own."

Hugh's gaze was even more attentive now. "At least, when you needed to get the discus back from him at the end of the day, you could simply go to his doghouse."

Joan shook her head. "Apate and Dolos were wild puppies. They didn't like to stay in the same place for long. I'd have to track them down each time to see where they were holed up."

Ada giggled. "One night in the stables, the next in the shed!"

Joan nodded. "Exactly right, Ada. Sounds like you had some puppies of your own."

"Oh, we had loads of them," agreed Ada. "A bundle of terror, sometimes. You never knew what those rascals would get into. Tearing holes in clothing, chewing the life out of shoes."

Hugh's voice was tight. "How did Dolos feel about snakes?"

Joan could see the pain hidden in his eyes, the tightness in his shoulders, and she could hear the question as clearly as if he had asked it out loud.

Was the man you met really Michael?

The reference to the Archangel Michael and his legendary battles with snakes clearly went right over Ada's head. She laughed. "Dogs hate snakes," she informed Hugh. "I imagine Dolos despised them."

Joan barely moved, knowing how much Hugh must be going through with this revelation. She herself had barely begun to absorb it. "Yes," she murmured. "Dolos was quite the snake-wrangler. I do believe, even if dragons had come to my home, that Dolos would be the one to slay them."

Ada chuckled, taking down another swig of ale. "Dragons. Don't think we'll get many of those in these parts."

Joan drew a smile onto her face. "You are so right, Ada. I suppose Dolos will be safe, then."

Hugh shook his head, and Joan could see the turmoil that swirled behind his carefully neutral face. When he spoke, his voice was tight. "We should get to sleep. We have a long ride ahead of us tomorrow, in order to reach the tavern before dark."

Ada took one last, long draw on her ale, then moved to her place immediately beside Joan. "We will be fine," she assured Hugh. "You sleep on the other side of the fire, please."

He nodded, his eyes going to Joan. "*Lailah tov.*"

She smiled at that, the familiar words rolling over her like a gentle surf on a moonlit night. "Good night," she answered him.

Ada gave a soft chortle as she settled down between them. "Snakes and dragons. Tomorrow it'll be three-headed horses."

Joan barely heard her. It was as if Hugh had reached over and wrapped his arms around her, reassuring her that everything would be all right.

Her eyes closed, and she faded into sleep.

* * *

The horses were walking along side by side, and Joan was again in front of Ada, when Hugh suddenly spoke up.

"Did you have swallows in your home, when Dolos was a rambunctious pup?"

Ada rolled her eyes. "And the menagerie grows."

Joan's mind searched through the permutations. Swallows ... birds ... martins! Martins were closely related to the swallow. "We had an elderly one," she responded, her heart tripping with nervousness. "He was still fairly sprightly, though."

The corner of his mouth tweaked up. "I bet he was," he agreed. "How did the bird behave around Dolos? Were the two close?"

He wanted to know if Master Martin knew about Michael's faked death.

"Oh, Dolos lived up to his reputation for trickery," explained Joan. "The puppy would sprawl in the middle of the dirt, pretending to be dead. The poor bird had no idea."

Ada's eyes lit up with delight. "I bet the bird would swoop down to take a look," she urged. "And then I bet that swallow got the surprise of his life when he realized Dolos was alive!"

Joan nodded, her eyes holding Hugh's. "The surprise of his life," she agreed.

Hugh's shoulders eased slightly, and Joan could see the relief shimmer into his gaze. She had felt the same way, knowing that Master Martin had not been a part of all of this.

Hugh looked down for a moment, and when he brought his gaze up again there was a new seriousness in it. "And did Dolos have any playmates? A best friend, perhaps?"

Joan took in a deep breath, a shadow falling over her heart. Hugh wanted to know if Michael had said anything about him. As much as she wanted to shield him from Michael's lies, she knew it was important to tell him everything she knew. Something she found unimportant might be meaningful to him.

Ada leant forward with a smile. "Dolos had Apate," she pointed out. "I bet they got into all sorts of trouble together."

Joan kept her gaze on Hugh and gave him a low nod. "While Dolos and Apate were close, there was another male pup in the mix for a while. Dolos and he were nearly inseparable."

Ada's eyes sparkled. "Let me guess - his name was Dionysus."

Joan shook her head. "No, this one was Stuart."

Hugh gave a nod in appreciation. "The name means *guardian*."

She gave a soft smile. "It does indeed."

His masked eased for a moment; warmth flickered along the edges for her alone to see. Longing spread through her. He was right there. She could just reach out her hand and touch him. She could ...

She pushed the thoughts away with determination. She had to find out what Cecily and Michael were up to, and bring an end to their activities once and for all. Otherwise, who knew how many other innocents would be hurt?

Ada prodded her from behind. "You said for a while. What happened to the two pups to break up this beautiful friendship?"

Blackness seeped into Joan's vision, and she drew in a long breath. She knew Hugh would be upset with what Michael had said about him, but she had to let him know. Every piece of information she shared would help them prepare for what was to come.

"Dolos discovered that Stuart was guarding more than just his family farm."

Hugh's face stilled, and he watched Joan closely. "What did Dolos find?"

Ada nudged her in the ribs. "Yes, do tell. What did Dolos discover about the rascally Stuart?"

Joan's face flushed with heat, and she was thankful that Ada sat behind her, unable to read her expressions. She focused on keeping her voice even. "Dolos led me to ... to see ... what Stuart was keeping watch over."

Hugh's face was a mask of stillness. "What was he guarding?"

Joan's throat went dry, and she swallowed. "It was a ... a poorly kept, run-down kennel. Within it were countless mangy female dogs. If one of them would try to escape, Stuart would ..." She looked down. "He would bite them in the face."

There was a long silence. When Joan looked up, she saw the deep shock on Hugh's face. His voice was hoarse when he spoke. "Dolos showed you that?"

She found she could only nod.

Ada's voice was harsh. "Well, I hope you put an end to that!"

Joan nodded in resolution, steel easing along her spine. "Absolutely."

Hugh's jaw gained an edge, and she saw, shining in his eyes, the same conviction.

Ada gave a shake of the reins. "Shall we run for a while? The sooner we get home, the sooner this is all over with."

Hugh wrapped his hands around the reins, nodded, and then they were in motion, Accipiter and Aquila flew down the path, the miles disappearing beneath their blurred hooves.

Joan wondered just what would happen after she returned to Cecily and Michael with the wooden bowl in hand. She knew one thing. She wanted to look into Michael's eyes when she finally brought him to justice.

Chapter 18

Dusk's violet shadows stretched across the town common as the two horses were reined in to a stop by the tavern. Hugh was beneath her in an instant. Joan was grateful for his sturdy hands supporting her as she eased off the saddle. Her entire body ached from toe to crown with countless reminders of the long journey.

She turned in his arms, and her moan of pain stilled. She could see clearly in his eyes that he had not slept for days, that what he had endured had been far, far worse than her time away. And yet his gaze held only gratitude, a sweeping relief that she had been brought safely home.

A loud cheer went up from the tavern. Suddenly a crowd swarmed the trio, congratulating them, patting them on the back, offering hugs and laughter. Lord Weston was there with several of his soldiers. Sarah had come in from the mill, Aiden close at her side, beaming.

Sybil came up to Joan, supported by Ymbert, and the blonde put forward her arms for a hug. The bandages were no longer on her hands, and Joan could see the healing scars. Sybil's voice was gruff. "Knew you would get through this just fine," she commented. "Especially with Hugh hot on your trail. In all the time I've worked with him, I've never seen him so fiercely dedicated to a task."

A way parted through the crowd for Greslet, and he gave Hugh a hearty clap on the shoulder before stepping forward to embrace Joan. "I would have come after you myself," he vowed, "if Hugh had not sworn that it would do more harm than good. He felt a single person could follow the trail more surely than a larger group. He vowed to us that he would reach you within a day and a night."

Ada stepped into the center of the crowd, raising her arms high. "And he was," she proclaimed, smiling at Hugh. "By the morning after our arrival, Cecily informed me that Hugh was in the woods surrounding the keep." She glanced back at him. "I told her it was impossible. How could anybody find us that quickly? But she was quite right. He has some sort of a sixth sense."

Norman stood in the doorway, looking evenly between Ada and Joan. "So, just what *did* happen?"

Ada hooked her arm into Joan's. "Pour us some drinks, and I'll give you every last detail!"

There was a roar of delight from the assembled crowd, and Joan was drawn into the main room, pulled down at Ada's right, and a mug was pressed into her hand.

Hugh moved to sit on Joan's other side, and Ada immediately shook her head. "No, no," she insisted. "Come sit on my other side. That way I can confer with you if I need to clarify any details. The crowd must have their story!"

Hugh's eyes shuttered, and he glanced briefly at Joan before nodding. "Of course, as you wish," he murmured, taking the indicated seat.

The hours seemed to roll on without end. Ada held court with delight, covering every aspect of the escapade in a modified telling that Joan found fascinating to hear. Somehow they had been taken away by bandits who had watched their every move. The gates had been guarded at all times. So had their rooms. Joan and Ada had been petrified throughout the ordeal, but thankfully Cecily had finally released them.

Joan knew this prevarication was a necessary part of the process. She did her best to nod, smile, and raise toasts at the appropriate moments. Still, at last she was beyond exhausted. Her head jerked awake, inches away from splashing into her fifth mug of ale.

Hugh murmured something into Ada's ear, and she turned in surprise. "Oh, look at you, poor duck! Let us get you up to bed!" She turned to the assembled crowd. "We can continue with this tomorrow evening," she promised them. "I'm afraid my friend needs to recuperate from her ordeal!"

A warm wave of cheers and well wishes followed them as they headed out the back door. Hugh's footsteps mirrored theirs as they walked the flight up to his apartment. Hugh reached over to unlock the door for them, and they headed in.

Joan could barely keep her eyes open. She stumbled for the bed, tumbling into it fully clothed.

Ada turned to Hugh. "I will keep her company for the night," she promised. "But I think, with all she has been through, that it's best we stay in here alone. Would you grant us that?"

Hugh's eyes moved to Joan's for a moment, and then he nodded. "Of course. Rest well." His eyes held Joan's. "If you need anything at all, I will be right outside."

Ada's face sharpened with a look of fierce disapproval before the pleasant mask was back in place. "It is a sweet offer, but that will not be necessary," she intoned sweetly. "I'm sure Ymbert would be happy to share his room."

Hugh's eyes had not moved from Joan's. "I prefer to sleep outside the door. It is no hardship; it would be an honor to protect you after you have clearly been through so much."

Ada tapped her fingers along the doorframe for a long moment. Then her gaze brightened. "Oh! Joan! Those dogs of yours, that you were so worried about. You had wanted to go back to them this very night, you were so concerned." She snared Hugh with her stare. "Joan would be so grateful if you would go and stay at her home tonight, to ensure the dogs are all right. You could return tomorrow at noon. I'm sure that would give the dogs enough time with human companionship around."

Joan's heart thundered in her chest. He could not leave her. Not now, not when she had just returned to him again. Not with all the chaos and confusion still whirling through her mind.

He had to stay.

He held her gaze for a long moment, his face carefully neutral, and then he nodded.

"I shall do as Joan wishes," he murmured.

Ada smiled widely. "Tomorrow at noon it is," she called out, ushering him out of the doorway. "We will bar the door. With all the folks in town, we will be quite safe here. Travel safely!"

Hugh nodded, first to Ada, then to Joan, and then he was gone.

Ada stepped forward to slide the bar, and she turned with a sharp movement. "Thank God that's all done with," she snapped. "I don't think I could take another moment of playing the bubble-headed maid." She rolled her eyes. "Poor me this, and I'm so thankful that! The men treat us like we're three years old and incapable of independent thought or action!"

She turned to Joan, and her eyes lit up. "Although, I have to say, your going on and on about your animal menagerie was simply brilliant. Hugh ate it up. You could have told him about your pet fish and darling spiders and he would have nodded to every word." She grinned in satisfaction. "You note how, on our ride back, he forgot completely to ask us about our capture or our time in the keep? You distracted him completely. You are quite a master at this type of deception."

Joan was still staring at the door, at the last place Hugh's face had been. She dragged her gaze away, settling to nestle her head into the pillow. It was impossibly soft, and deep lethargy pulled at her. She forced herself to focus on the task at hand, to soothe any of Ada's suspicions.

"You did your part brilliantly," she praised. "You played along with the stories, and gave it just the right air of simple fascination. I am sure Hugh was thoroughly taken in."

Ada took a look around the dark room, then shrugged and came over to lay down next to Joan. "I have been doing that for years," she pointed out. "Men are stupid. All we women have to do is pitch our voices high, speak on foolish topics, and the men think we are being perfectly natural. They dismiss us as 'little girls' and put our conversation on a lower level." She chuckled. "Heck, we could be talking about fairies and elves, and they would nod and smile. They think that's all our heads can hold."

Joan rolled over to hold her gaze. "So, what's the plan?"

Ada glanced at the shadowed room. "It's far too dark to rummage around tonight, and we need the rest. Tomorrow morning, when our senses are primed, we can begin a thorough search."

Joan nodded in understanding. Her mouth went dry, but she pressed on. "And Hugh?"

Ada's grin widened. "You did an incredible job with your dog stories," she pointed out. "By the time he returns, we have either found the bowl here, or we know it's simply not in his room." Her eyes lit up. "In that case, you begin using other techniques to get the information out of him."

Joan held her face steady. From the glee in Ada's face, the woman had used this approach many times in the past.

She forced her tone to stay even. "And once we find this wooden bowl?"

Ada's eyes glowed in satisfaction. "Then we escape this hell hole once and for all. We get to Flamborough, vanish into the mists, and put everyone here in our past – forever."

* * *

Joan stirred awake. The room was pitch black. Her lids still drooped with exhaustion, and she could not say what it was that had dragged her from her dreamless stupor. However, now that she was awake, she would not pass up this opportunity to slip from Ada's side, at least for a few minutes.

She carefully pushed the blanket off her body.

Ada stirred, scratching idly at one ear. Her voice was a sluggish murmur. "Where ya goin'?"

Joan pitched her voice to be apologetic. "I'm sorry for waking you. I need to go down to the outhouse."

"Chamber pot in the corner."

Joan glanced there and nodded. She moved a hand to her stomach. "I'm feeling sick, though. I thought you might appreciate it if –"

Ada sighed and made a rolling motion with her hand. "Go, go. Just be quick." She pulled the blanket up over her head.

Joan held in the smile of relief, then moved quickly to the door. She slid the bar free, slipping around the door and half-running down the stairs. The area around the tavern was absolutely deserted; clouds covered the sky, blocking out the moon and stars. Only a lone lamp hanging on the side of the stable cast a faint light across the ground.

Joan crossed to the small wooden structure and threw the door wide, making a show of striding into it just in case Ada was watching. She then slammed the door shut, submerged in darkness. Her heart pounded against her ribs. It was only a guess, of course. Hugh could very well have taken Ada at her word and ridden off. He could be miles away.

Carefully, Joan creaked open the door, just enough to allow her to slip through, and she curled herself around the side of the building, out of sight of the tavern. Now if only –

A hand clamped down over her mouth, a strong arm pulled her back into the wood, and she was pressed up against the rippled bark of an oak.

Her pulse escalated into near panic, and she looked up –

Hugh.

She dove forward at him, his arms came up around her, and they were embracing as if they had been parted for years. Tears of relief slid down Joan's face, and she could feel the tenderness of his lips on her forehead. She clung to him as if she were drowning in a flood, and he was all that held her in safety.

His voice was a low murmur in her ear. "It's all right," he assured her. "Everything's all right." His hand gently stroked her hair, soothing her.

It was a long while before she was able to step back and look into his eyes. Her voice burst from her in a hush. "Michael's alive."

He nodded, his gaze steady but lined with weariness. "I nearly thought it a trick of the light when I saw you both on the patio," he admitted, "but your confirmation on the ride here put that out of my mind. Somehow he and Cecily faked his death."

"Ropes tied to the wall," Joan explained.

"Sounds like I was getting too close for comfort," pondered Hugh. "This way they simply move on to another location, and we're none the wiser."

Joan glanced back up toward the dark window. "I can't stay long."

He ran a hand tenderly down the side of her face. "I know." He hesitated for a moment, then asked, "what do you want to do about the bowl?"

She had known the question would be coming. "Ada will be sure to realize what it is in the morning," she pointed out. "I think I should go with her to return it to Michael, to find out exactly what all the fuss is about. Now that you know how this relay works, you can follow me with the full force." She smiled in contentment, looking up at him. "I have no doubt you all will find me and bring the two to justice, along with all of the wolves' heads. We will bring their entire group to an end."

Hugh's eyes shadowed. "I hate to send you back into the lion's den."

"Linota risked far worse," Joan pointed out. "I am treated quite well. Michael has made it plain that he wants to keep me alive."

At Michael's name, Hugh's face shuttered.

Joan reached forward a hand, twining it into his. "The Michael I cared for as a child is truly dead," she promised him. "It will take me some time to decide if the transformation came over a long time, and I simply never saw it, or if something happened to him while he was on some mission. But, whatever it was, the man he is now is abhorrent to me. I would never stay with him."

Hugh's hand traced her cheek, and there was a slight tremble to his movements. "Still, to think of you under his control …"

She smiled at that, moving forward to nestle in his arms. Hugh's embrace was strong, steady, and seemed as if it could protect her against any force known on earth.

At last she gently unraveled herself from his warmth, giving him a tender kiss on the lips. "I do need to go," she stated. "Ada said our first stop tomorrow will be Flamborough. If you gather the forces to watch for us there, you should be able to trail us without a problem."

He nodded, his eyes darkening in determination. "Flamborough it is. I will make sure everybody is ready."

She smiled tenderly. "And get some sleep."

The sharp lines of his jaw eased at that, and he gave a soft chuckle. "I will try," he agreed.

She drank in one last look of him, then turned, climbing the stairs in the inky night.

Ada still had the blankets pulled over her head as Joan slid the bar closed on the door, but her voice rumbled from beneath the covers. "Done with your puking, I hope? If I wake up to find the room smelling of –"

"I'm done," assured Joan, slipping beneath the covers. "Just too much mead, I think."

"You need to build up your tolerance," groused Ada, her voice sinking back down into a growl. "But first, we need to get some rest."

Joan did not argue that point. A moment later she was adrift in a dreamless sleep.

Chapter 19

The faintest tinges of grey dawn were tickling the edges of the window when Joan was shaken awake.

Ada's voice was sharp. "C'mon, lazy bones. We have until noon to get this place searched. We need to get started."

A loud rumble of thunder sounded, and Ada tossed her head at the window. "And as if we didn't have enough to handle today, we also need to beat this storm."

Joan nodded wearily, pushing herself to sit up. Ada turned and strode over to the far wall, starting at the right-hand corner by the door. With the attention of a world class architect she began moving inch by inch along the wall. She sounded each board, tested each peg, and checked every slight protuberance for loose construction or levers to activate.

Joan climbed to her feet and moved to the opposite diagonal, on her left. Satisfaction welled within her. Ada had inadvertently set up the search so that she, herself, would be the one to get to the bowl. However, she would have to go through the entire exterior wall first, and then half of the back wall, before she reached it. That would give Hugh even more time to prepare the troops and be ready to give chase.

Joan poured all of her attention into the task at hand. It was almost fun, this careful attention to every aspect of a wall. She'd never given masonry this much scrutiny before. There was a knot-hole in a beam which almost looked like a whirlpool. The main stretches of the wall were the traditional combination of wattle and daub – woven willow sticks coated over in a whitish, hardened goo of mud, clay, and horsehair. One swirl looked like a cloud high over a distant horizon. Another could be the twirl of a young girl's hair.

She had just turned the corner to the far wall with the shelves of kitchen supplies when Ada cried out in delight. "The decorative hanging!"

Joan turned, preparing her face for the look of surprise and admiration she knew Ada would expect. Indeed, Ada was holding up the wooden circle as if it were the Ark of the Covenant. "It was here in plain sight all along! But look!" She flipped it over in her hands, showing the curved interior. "It clearly is the bowl Michael is after. Funny, he never mentioned the seagull carved into its base. That would have made it much easier for us to find."

Joan shrugged. "You know how men are."

Ada's brow furrowed. "I do indeed. Idiots." Her face brightened. "Still, we have the prize, and it's an hour or more from noon. Plenty of time for us to make our escape."

Joan allowed her gaze to shadow in confusion. "We are going to just ride out of here? Surely someone will ask where we're going, with it being so soon after our last capture."

Ada strode over to stand before her. "There's a small chapel just a half-mile east. We'll tell them we want to go pray there, alone, in thanks to the Holy Mary for her role in protecting us. With the storm about to release, we'll want to stay there all afternoon." Her grin grew. "They'll expect us to pray in thanks for our safe return," she pointed out.

Joan tapped a finger to her lips. "They might want to send an escort with us.

Ada shook her head. "We need to do this alone, to show our gratitude." Her eyes held sharp focus. "It's only a half-mile. They would think we are quite safe in that distance and agree without much fuss. And then we simply keep riding."

Ada seemed enormously pleased with herself as the stable hands prepared Accipiter and Aquila without a complaint. She grinned as the cook waved farewell to them. She took it in stride that the other men were sleeping off the excesses of the previous evening's festivities, and that her excuse of going to the chapel was accepted without a squeak of protest.

Joan held in a smile, running a fond hand down Aquila's mane, then climbing into the saddle. Where Ada saw the execution of a brilliant plan, Joan saw the sure, deft hand of Hugh preparing the way for them, allowing their travels to start smoothly and unhindered. And, even better, her sword had been in Hugh's room, right where she had left it. Ada had not complained as she strapped the scabbard at her waist. If anything, Ada seemed to take it for granted that they were now a team.

Ada glanced around at the empty courtyard, and her voice was a crow of triumph. "I told you! These simpletons can't think past their next meal." She gave a shake to Accipiter's reins, then looked up at the billowing clouds. "Might be our last chance for a proper run. Race you to the chapel!"

Joan's eyes lit up in delight. No reason that the ride to Flamborough should be boring. "You're on!"

The two burst into a gallop.

They were laughing by the time they drew in at the side of the small stone chapel. A billowing of forget-me-nots lined one end of the building, shimmering in soft blues and delicate white. A strong breeze shook them into brighter life, and a few errant drops plunked down from the sky.

Ada slipped down from her steed, smiling up at Joan. "Seems like the storm is finally here," she commented. "I'll just make sure nobody is here, and then we'll be on our way."

Joan's brow wrinkled. "What if someone *is* here?"

Ada shrugged. "We take them hostage with us until the first stage, and let the people there deal with it," she answered easily. "It'll give us enough time to slip the net." Her grin widened. "And this time, with the torrent about to deluge us, there's no way in Hell that Hugh will be able to track us."

A nervous tremor shot through Joan, but she pushed it away. Hugh would find them. No matter what it took, he would stay with them, from the moment they arrived in Flamborough until the instant they crossed into whatever new keep Cecily and Michael had commandeered.

Ada approached the front door of the chapel. "Hallooo," she called out in a friendly tone. "Anybody around today?" She came up to the arched wooden door and pressed it inward.

Creak.

Whoosh.

Ada staggered backward, a crossbow bolt standing straight out from the center of her chest like a mast on a ship. Then she timbered back, blood welled from around the wound, and she slammed hard to the ground.

Thunder growled immediately overhead, and lightning flashed a split-second later into the depths of the wood. Heavy raindrops hammered the earth, the flowers, and Ada's motionless body. The blonde stared blankly up into the dense clouds, the crimson of her blood mixing with the rivulets of water, and she did not move again.

Joan's heart thundered; she swept up the reins, preparing for a gallop to the woods. At that instant Michael stepped through the door, a crossbow held casually couched across one arm, his eyes sweeping from the fallen woman to hold hers. "No need to fear," he calmed her. "Just cleaning up some loose ends."

Cecily strode through the opening behind him, standing over Ada's body and staring down at her. "Good riddance," she snapped. "Still can't believe she would turn on us like that, but there you have it. Hard to trust anyone these days."

Joan's hand twitched at the reins; it took her a long moment before she lowered them. She looked between the corpse and the other two in surprise. "Ada betrayed you?"

Michael gave a soft shrug, his eyes still on her. "We had our suspicions, with how cozy she had become with Hugh's group. So, when we sent her back with you, we told her the first stop would be Flamborough. It wasn't true, of course, and nobody else knew of that location."

He ran a hand down the center strut of the crossbow, almost caressing it. "Next thing we hear from our contact in Lord Weston's stables, the soldiers there are gearing up to head out to

Flamborough. Oh, the soldiers were coy enough about their destination, and it took some doing, but the information was reliable. So it seems Ada was playing both sides of the fence."

Joan pressed her lips together. Hugh, Lord Weston, and all the rest were now camped out near Flamborough, awaiting her arrival. And apparently that town was a completely false trail.

Michael's gaze dropped to land on the bowl tied to the back of her saddle. A grin spread on his face. "And everything works out just as it should," he murmured.

A blast of thunder sounded directly overhead, the lightning crackled at the exact same time, and Accipiter reared up in panic. Joan turned in surprise. Both steeds were battle trained. Indeed, Aquila stood as quiet as could be beneath her. But Accipiter was now streaming toward the woods in full gallop.

Her eyes narrowed. Was that the hint of a thin hand she saw clutching the saddle, as if a thin, teenage boy were clinging to the far side, allowing the steed's body to shield his own?

Michael's voice was sharp. "I thought you had trained these steeds properly."

She couched her face in disappointment before turning back to him. "I thought I had, too," she admitted.

He looked after the disappearing horse for a moment, then shrugged. He turned to glance down dismissively at the corpse. "Cecily, get that inside," he ordered. "Then bring the steeds."

It was only a few moments before Michael pulled up alongside her. By then she had composed her face into a mask of contentment. "Just like old times," she murmured.

A softness edged his gaze for a moment, and he nodded. "That was a long time ago," he commented.

Cecily drew up on her other side, her hood pulled low over her eyes. "This storm is only going to get worse," she pointed out. "Let's get going!"

Michael nodded, and in a moment the three were in motion, submerging themselves in the depths of the wood's shadows.

Chapter 20

Joan carefully steered Aquila along the mud-drenched river which had once been a trail. Ahead of her, Michael cursed in exasperation as his horse tripped for the ninth time on a hidden root. The torrential rain hammered their heads and backs, the steady noise a drone which reverberated the air around them. Occasionally a ground-shaking rumble of thunder jarred them, accompanied by a blinding flash of light.

Joan wondered if any part of her body would ever be dry again. She was so thoroughly soaked she could almost feel her fingers and toes pruning.

There was a clearing up ahead, and Michael steered toward it. Joan could see movement, and her hand dropped to her hilt, but Michael plowed forward without concern. As Joan emerged from the shadows, she could see why. Sheriff Elias waited there with ten wolves' heads. They seemed as a whole thoroughly sullen and miserable. Joan scanned the faces beneath the hoods. She thought she recognized a few from the camp she had raided a few days ago with Hugh, but the two men of the Sheriff's from the morning at the tavern were nowhere to be seen.

Michael pulled to a stop before the Sheriff. "No problems?"

The sheriff shook his head. "None at all. I sent my two men to follow along after the crew from Lord Weston's keep. If the group tries to turn and ambush us, we'll get advance warning."

Michael nodded in satisfaction. "Good. With any luck they'll just watch over Flamborough for the night and assume the women were delayed because of this storm. By the time they realize their mistake, our trail will be thoroughly washed away."

He gave the side of his cloak a shake, fruitlessly trying to release some of the water. "Either that or we'll all be drowned."

He glanced around at the group. "C'mon. I'll get us some shelter for the night. Maybe the worst of it will be over by dawn and we can make proper speed."

A murmur of relief swept through the group. Michael crossed to the opposite side of the clearing, starting in on a trail that seemed vaguely familiar to Joan. She set after him, pondering it, while the others fell in line behind them.

It wasn't until they passed a greying stump, speckled with fungus, that the pieces clicked in Joan's mind. She shook her reins, moving to ride alongside Michael.

She strove to keep her voice even. "Where are we going?"

He gave a barking laugh. "You know well where we're going, or has the darkness and rain gotten you thoroughly turned around?"

Joan's pulse quickened. She forced herself to take a long, steady breath. There had to be some way to keep Michael away from there. It was her sanctuary, her private retreat. "But surely they might look for me at my own house."

Michael shook his head. "It's the last place they'd look for you, once they realize Ada is dead and you are missing. So it's actually the safest place to be." He shrugged. "Besides, that's assuming they even leave Flamborough tonight. My bet is on them sitting watch over there at least until tomorrow night." He gave a wry smile. "If Hugh is anything, he is determined when he sets his mind to something."

Joan nodded in acceptance, allowing Michael to pull forward in front of her. If she resisted more strenuously, Michael would undoubtedly get suspicious and only want even more avidly to go to her home. She could get through this. Although it had been her sanctuary, it was only a structure of wood and mud.

She wasn't feeling so sure of herself an hour later when they finally pulled up, soggy and bedraggled, at the fence which surrounded her property. Michael swung his eyes left and right down its length. At last he turned to her in grumpy confusion.

"Where's the gate?"

She shrugged apologetically. "I didn't get around to building one yet."

"Fine," he snapped. He pointed to the Sheriff. "Get one of those sections torn down."

The Sheriff looked as if he might object, but there was another crash of thunder immediately overhead, and he slid in resignation from his saddle. He waved over two of the bandits, and together they leaned on one of the poles until it separated from the surrounding fence. In short order they had opened up a small but serviceable path through.

Michael waved a hand. "Joan, lead the way."

Joan was half-tempted to gallop through the path, but she knew that, with the drenching rain, Aquila would be lucky to escape without a broken leg. She took the route at a slow, careful pace. Even so Aquila slipped several times before they made it to the safety of the stables.

Michael pulled in beside her. "Put the four main horses in here," he ordered. "The rest can set up beneath that stand of oaks. It should give them some shelter, at least."

Cecily slid off her horse and turned to the bandits. "Once the horses are settled, set up three watches. Make sure both the outer perimeter and inner area are covered thoroughly. Whoever's sleeping first can stay here in the stables with the steeds."

The men nodded in resigned acceptance.

Michael turned to Joan. "Leave your sword here. The men can sharpen it for you while they're on watch."

A knot formed in Joan's stomach. "It might be better if –"

Michael's eyes sharpened. "- if you followed my orders."

Joan pressed her lips into a line and nodded. She still had her knife on her. It was best if she played along for now.

The stables had four stalls; each of them led their steed into one. Joan hated to leave Aquila in the hands of hired help, but at least it was the leader, the blond from the camp with the long plait down his back, who came over to take care of her steed. He nodded to her, his gaze going with admiration to the horse. She knew he would take good care. It could instead have been the two giants, easily six-foot-five, who seemed to provide in brawn what they lacked in brains. They were gathering up the reins of the other steeds and leading them to the woods.

There was a soft scratching noise, almost lost in the pummeling of the rain, and Joan moved to the doorway. A pair of amber eyes glowed from the darkness.

Her heart stopped. If the bandits saw the dogs, she had no doubt what would happen. Target practice, and a brutal death for both animals.

She made a flicking motion with her hand. She pitched her voice low but stern. "Go!"

The eyes blinked, then vanished.

Michael came up to her shoulder. "What was that?"

She looked over. "I said, we should go. Get inside out of this rain."

He nodded. He lifted the bowl from her saddle with an easy move, then turned. "Cecily, Elias, hurry it up."

In a moment the others were with them, carrying various sacks and supplies. Together the group raced through the downpour to her front door.

Joan slipped her hand into the small leather bag at her side, running her fingers over the key for a long moment. Every instinct in her body was screaming for her to stop, to run, to keep her sanctuary safe from these bandits. But she knew she could not. She had them all gathered, now. They were neatly wrapped up with bows. Now all she had to do was keep them in place until Hugh and the others arrived. She had no doubt that it had been Jake on the horse and that he had reached Flamborough by now. Even if the men had to take the return ride at a slow pace because of the rain, they would still be here before dawn.

And then this long nightmare would finally be drawn to a close.

She put the key into the lock, turned it, and pressed open the door.

With all that had happened over the past few days, she almost expected her home to be radically different. There should be overturned stools, sliced up curtains, and walls stained with who knew what. But the room looked as it had always looked – comforting, warm, and safe.

She stepped forward to the fireplace, which was long since cold. It took her a few minutes to get a fresh fire going and to then move around with a candle to get the rest of the room lit. By then Michael had poured out mugs of mead and passed them around.

Cecily left her cloak in a sodden puddle by the door, groaning in misery as she stood as close to the fire as she dared without setting herself alight. "One of the most miserable rides I've had in ages," she grumbled.

The Sheriff shook his head, looking at the wooden bowl which Michael had placed on the table. "All that grief for a stupid wooden bowl," he snapped. "Surely you could have just bought another one." He had a pair of bags draped over his shoulder, and when he eased them to the ground they echoed with a heavy, jingling noise. "At least the things *I* choose to carry with me have some value," he added.

Michael looked up at Cecily with shuttered eyes. He held her gaze for a long moment. She nodded, then turned brightly to the Sheriff.

"Is your shoulder acting up again, you poor duck?"

He nodded, his face easing a bit. "It is, with all this rain," he admitted.

Cecily came over next to him. "Let me help you out of your jerkin, and I'll give you a proper back massage."

He didn't need to be asked twice. He put his hands up in the air, giving her access to the ties and stays. In a minute she was lifting the leather up over his head and laying it on top of her cloak by the front door.

She moved around to stand behind him. "There you go. Now just lean over a bit." He obliged. She stood for a minute, staring at the thin white shirt he wore, as if wondering where to begin.

The Sheriff's look soured. "Well, then, get on with it already!"

A grin grew across Cecily's face. "As you wish!"

She drew the dagger from her belt and plunged it deep into his back, the blade driving straight into his heart from behind.

The Sheriff half-stood, turned with a gurgling noise, and then slithered to the floor. His mouth remained open as his body gave a final shake and lay still.

Michael barely looked at the body as he went to refill his mead mug. "Push him a bit closer to the door, to help block it," he instructed Cecily. "We'll have a story for the others by morning, and it'll give us some peace until then."

He glanced over at Joan, who was standing motionless by the fire, her mug of mead forgotten in her hand. "Well, then, don't just stand there," he ordered. "Surely you have some food in this place?"

She nodded mutely, going to the cupboard in the back corner and fetching out cheese, dried apples, and some chicken jerky. She passed them around to Michael and Cecily before settling down before the fire to eat her own. She kept her gaze on the apple slices before her, blocking the sight of the pool of blood which was steadily growing by her front door.

Her home had been violated.

Joan wondered how much scrubbing it would take before it finally felt clean again.

Cecily held up a piece of the jerky, wrinkling her nose. "Not quite the same as the food in that seaside keep, is it?" she sighed. "Still, I've had worse. Only a few more days and life will be back to normal again."

Michael smiled at the wooden bowl which still sat on the table. "Better than ever," he corrected.

Cecily raised an eyebrow. "Oh? And just what is the magic in that little piece of tree, anyway?"

Michael looked between them, apparently relishing the attention. "Would you like to see the secret?"

Joan found herself intrigued. "Yes," she answered honestly.

He grinned at that, putting down his mug and taking up the plate with two hands. He made a show of examining it from several angles, as if to demonstrate that it was just a normal wooden bowl. His brow creased as he ran his fingers over the seagull carving.

"Hugh never knew when to leave well enough alone," he muttered. Then he looked up at Joan. "I assume you have an axe?"

She nodded her head. "I'll go get it." She moved to the back closet, grabbed the hand tool, and brought it out to him.

He laid the bowl curved side up on the table, then took a step back from it. "Ceiling's too low for a proper swing," he grumbled, and positioned himself at a side angle.

He swung the axe hard, nearly parallel with the floor, then twisted at the end to drive the blade into the bowl. The bowl shattered. The axe's blade dug deep into the table itself, embedding there. Pieces of wood flew all over the room in a maelstrom of splinters and chunks.

Cecily looked around the room, shaking her head in amusement. "Never could do things the simple way, could you, Michael?" she admonished. "And just what –"

Her eyes brightened in fascination as she bent over toward a shadow, and her face suddenly shone with avarice.

Chapter 21

Cecily turned and held the stone up in the candlelight, cupped between her hands. It was about the size of a seagull's egg. Its color was a translucent shade of light brown which reminded Joan of a dusting of cinnamon on a fragrant oatmeal pudding. The oval glistened with a shimmer that almost seemed to make it glow. Visible within the center of the shape lay an internal fracture of some sort – an oak-brown formation in the shape of a cross.

Joan's hand moved to her chest in awe. It was the stone. Michael had somehow found the *ovum crux*.

Cecily was spinning around in a circle with glee, laughing, holding the stone out to Michael. "And you had it this entire time! I should have known. If anybody could get his hands on this, you could. Do you know how much this hunk of rock is worth?"

He took it from her with a chuckle, holding it up before one of the candles to peer through it. "Absolutely," he agreed. "Enough that those bags of gold the Sheriff was so proud of are like grains of sand in comparison. This will be enough to set up our empire for life, with an eternally renewing stock of *employees*."

He looked up to Joan, and his eyes brightened at the look on her face. "Not expecting this, were you, my sweet?" he asked as he stepped over to her. "Call it my little insurance policy." He tucked the egg into a pouch at his side. "And with Hugh good enough to follow my instructions, keeping an eye on that bowl over all else, the egg is now safely ours again. Nothing will hold us back from achieving our every dream."

Joan nodded mutely, every ounce of her energy directed at keeping her face calm and full of admiration. Her soul screamed out for justice for all those who had died in the needless wars over that holy relic, the antipathy which even now tainted the Holy Land as a result. She pushed that down with firm resolve.

Later. That could all be handled later.

For now she had to simply hold out until sunrise – until Hugh and his forces could reach her. Then all would be resolved.

Michael raised his mug of mead, Cecily and Joan brought theirs together in a toast, and Joan drained hers down. The candlelight flickered evenly across the Sheriff's dead body, still leaking his vital fluids in a stream across her floor. It shimmered on the blade of the axe embedded in her dining table. It glistened on the shards of the beautifully carven seagull, now burst into tiny fragments all over her home.

A deep rumble of thunder shuddered through the house, and Michael finished off his mead. "We have a long day ahead of us," he pointed out. "We'll need every moment of sleep we can get."

Joan's eyes went to the flickering fire. "I'll sleep out here," she offered instantly. If she was lucky, they'd fall asleep in her room without looking closely at the tapestry. By morning, it wouldn't matter any more.

Michael's smile widened into a grin. "That is what I always loved about you, Joan," he offered. "You are so predictable. And simple. I remember how you used to sleep by the fire at the sword school while I was practicing. Haven't changed a bit, have you?"

She gave a wry smile. "Not one bit," she agreed. "I like it there."

He stepped up to her, snagging her arm. "Well, we will break you of that childish habit soon enough," he stated calmly. "You are with me, again, and we can't have you sprawled on the dirt like a maid-servant. I saw a glimpse of a bed in that back room. You and I will be taking that." He looked up at Cecily. "You'll be fine out here on the couch, I imagine."

A surly look crossed Cecily's lips, but she nodded. "Soon we won't have need for such rough surroundings," she murmured, half to herself.

Michael smiled magnanimously. "Soon we will be living as kings and queens," he promised. "Gold chased plateware and solid silver knives. All of our meals will be spiced with saffron and cloves."

Cecily nearly glowed. She nodded in contentment, settling down onto the couch with a sigh.

Michael tugged at Joan, then picked up a candle in the other hand. "And now to see our room."

Joan forced her breathing to be even. One step at a time. One moment at a time. She could get through this. It must be – what – approaching midnight? If she could convince Michael that any amorous activities were best put off until they had the luxury of enjoying them, he might simply go to sleep and wake to his deserved justice.

As they stepped through the doorway to her bedroom she quickly moved to the side of the bed, drawing his eyes there. "I normally sleep on the side closest to the door," she explained. "But if you would rather –"

He cut her off sharply, looking down at the floor. "What is this?"

Joan glanced over. She froze as he bent down to pick up a bronze cloak clasp from the ground. She knew at an instant whose it was. Hugh must have dropped it when they were racing off to save Sarah – and she must not have seen it during her brief night home on the subsequent evening. It all seemed so long ago.

"That is –"

"I know whose it is," he snapped. "And I thought we were done with reminders of that brief, meaningless dalliance of yours." He strode over to the shuttered windows and unlocked them, flinging them open to the stormy night. He flung the clasp hard into the darkness.

As he turned back to the room, the candle light flickered against the walls, and he drew to a stop, transfixed by the tapestry. The harsh lines on his face softened as he took a few steps to stand before it.

"Ah, but Joan, it looks as if you did miss me after all," he murmured. "I still remember that day when you were so foolish, so stupid to come out to see me." He gave a wry laugh. "And yet that was always part of your charm. You simply did things because you felt strongly about them. No matter how idiotic they were."

He shook his head. "Even then, that dolt Hugh was entranced by you. You should have seen the look on his face. The bastard didn't even realize that you belonged to me." He snorted. "I bet he realizes it now. I bet tomorrow, when the knowledge hits him of how thoroughly he's been fooled, that he rails against his misfortune for the rest of his dying days." His eyes drew down Joan's form, and heat grew within them. "He had you right in the palm of his hand, and he let you slip away."

Joan nodded encouragingly. "He is in the past," she agreed. "Now we should get some sleep if we are going to make good our escape in the morning."

He put the candle down on the table by the tapestry, his eyes not leaving hers. "You are mine now, just as you always have been," he stated with growing strength. "It's about time you were reminded of that fact."

She put her hands up before her. "I know it well," she insisted. "I am yours, and you are mine. When we are safely away, free of all this grime and blood, we can be together properly. Right now we need –"

He slammed her into the wall, his body pressing against her. His lips were only a breath away from hers. "What I need," he corrected, "is to feel your total submission to me. I have waited far too long for this. I will not wait another moment."

His lips descended on hers.

Every cell of Joan's body rebelled against the contact. She flung her head to the side, pushing her hands up against his chest. *Not this.* She was willing to pretend to be one of their group, to hold her tongue when they spoke out against those she loved – but this was too much. She would break if she allowed Michael to go any further.

Michael's gaze turned to steel. His fingers curled into a fist. Joan desperately sought for a way to salvage the situation.

"It is just too soon – I thought you were dead!" she pleaded. "There have been long years since I have last felt your touch. Please offer me just a few more days, just a chance for us to reconnect at the level we once did. Then I am sure I can –"

He snarled at her, raising the fist at his side. "Then you will be sure to finally grant to me the favors you have been throwing at Hugh these past days?" His eyes bored into hers. "Were you missing me tragically while he mounted you in this very room, while he took *my property* beneath the tapestry which represented your eternal vow to me?" He spat on the ground. "How long did you honor that vow, I wonder. Did you wait a whole day before you made yourself available to him?"

The unjustness of the charge shook her to her core. "I stayed absolutely pure for you," she shot back. "Yes, I saw Hugh that one time in the courtyard – and then I cut all contact with him. Less than thirty days later, you were dead! I still bear the scar on my leg from that day. I mourned you for months. I did not think about another man for years. It was only a few days ago that I saw Hugh again."

The truth of it hit her, staggering her. So few days did they have together. She could count them on two hands. And yet, their years of correspondence had drawn them so closely together that she could imagine no other in her life.

Michael's eyes narrowed. Then without warning he hit her soundly across the temple. She staggered back against the wall, her hand darting for her knife. He kicked at her forearm, and the blade went spinning across the room.

"So you're not free of him yet, are you," he accused. "No matter. After I'm through with you, there will be no thought of any other in your brain. The only name which will be seared on your soul is mine. You belong to me!"

Her breath caught in her throat. She looked into his eyes, desperate for even the slightest glimpse of the boy she had once cared for, the lad who had ridden with her side by side through her father's camps. "Michael, please, don't do this."

His smile stretched into a grin. "That's right, beg me."

Her stomach twisted, but she forced the words through her lips. "I beg you, Michael, let's just get some sleep for the night. In the morning –"

He gave a harsh, barking laugh. "What, in the morning you'll open your legs to me like a good little girl? You'll finally realize your proper place in life?" His hand shot out to grip her neck, squeezing. "You'll learn it now, girl, and on my terms."

Her hands went to her neck, clawing at his fingers, but he had a grip of iron. She could barely draw in breath. The word came out as a soft hiss. "Michael –"

His voice was a low growl. "Michael, what? Michael, I love you? Michael, I need you? Michael, I never should have given myself to that bastard, Hugh? Michael, I am a whore? I deserve to be put in the lowest of the stews, in with the diseased, and if I try to escape, my face will be marked, because that is all I deserve?"

Joan tried to shake her head, but the hand at her neck grew tighter. Her throat burned.

His other hand went to his hip, and he drew up his dagger, his eyes glittering with emotion. "You did try to escape, didn't you?" he challenged. "You went to Hugh. I think we shall have to mark you, to parade your shame to the world. Let's start with –"

A clap of thunder shook the entire building, rattling the candle along the table. The simultaneous blast of lighting blinded them, and the smell of charred wood and ozone swept in through the open window. Joan blinked her eyes, frantically trying to bring them back into focus.

There, in front of the window, stood Hugh. His sword was out in his hand, water poured off of every inch of him, and his attention was focused on Michael's hand on Joan's throat.

Hugh's voice was a low hiss of command, one which sent goosebumps down Joan's body.

"If she is not released in five seconds, I will carve your God-cursed name over every square inch of your body."

Chapter 22

Michael slowly turned to face Hugh, his hand still clutching Joan's throat. Joan's vision danced with brilliant sparkles of light. The edges of the room thrummed in waves of darkness.

Then, suddenly, he threw her down on the bed, drawing his sword at the same moment.

Joan landed on her side, gasping for air. Her hands flew to her throat, to the deep ache that gnawed at the flesh there. She cupped her fingers there in a protective ward, rolling to sit up against the back wall, to stare at the two men who now faced each other at the end of her bed.

Michael nudged his head at the tapestry which hung on the wall. "Take a long look, old friend," he jeered at Hugh. "You might have had her for an hour or two, but I am the one she sought in her dreams every night. I am the one she awoke to each morning. You are but the flitting of an insect. You are about to be consumed by the flame."

Hugh's gaze did not waver. With his eyes attentive on Michael's every move, he asked, "Joan, are you all right? Did he seriously hurt you?"

Joan went to shake her head, but her neck ached at the mere start of the motion. "I am fine," she assured him with a hoarse rasp. "My throat will heal."

Michael's voice took on a sing-song lilt. "She is fine," he mimicked. He threw his shoulders back. "She is my property, and I will use her however I wish," he snapped. "Perhaps your ghost can hang around and watch me in action, once I disconnect it from your corporeal being."

Hugh's voice was steady. "The first time you died, it was a cause for great sorrow. This time, it will be a triumph of justice."

Michael raised his sword higher, keeping the point aimed between Hugh's eyes.

Hugh settled deeper into his stance, watching, waiting ...

Michael sprung, but not at Hugh. Instead, he swept his blade right, catching the candle with the motion, driving it full into the center of the tapestry. The thick fabric flared into a blossom of flame, billowing with heat and light.

Michael dodged back, reversing his swing, catching the engulfed fabric on the tip of his sword. He swept straight at Joan. The tapestry, glowing incandescently, cascaded down on top of her.

Her scream echoed off the walls; the pain went on for an eternity.

A strong pair of arms swept her up, she was launching through the air, there was the splintering sound of wood, and then she had landed hard on top of him in a cacophony of noise. He rolled on top of her, and then beneath her. The pounding rain and deep, muddy puddles beneath them quickly extinguished the pieces of ember-laden tapestry which clung to her.

She lay on top of Hugh, struggling to draw in breaths between the pelting rain, the smoke rising from their bodies, and the throbbing pain still echoing from Michael's strangle-hold.

He looked up at her in concern. "Are you badly burnt?"

She shook her head, gazing down at her body. Her hands were blistered and red, but it seemed that no more serious damage had been done. "Are you all right?"

He rolled so that she could sit up, and he quickly checked himself over. "I will heal," he responded.

There was a sharp crackling noise from the house, one that pushed past the thrumming of the rain all around them, and a bright burst of light flared from her bedroom. Then flames were licking out the windows and along the edges of her roof.

Joan could not take it in. Her voice was barely a whisper. "My home ... it's ..."

A loud whinny sounded. Michael burst from the stables on his horse, closely followed by Cecily. Joan watched in hollow shock as he exactly followed the course she had led him in on, vaulting the fence at the end. The remaining bandits scrambled for their horses and streamed out after him.

Joan roused herself, pushing herself to her feet while her home blazed into light behind her.

"Where are the others?"

Hugh nodded his head east. "About an hour out. They could not keep up." He gave a wry grin. "I had Accipiter beneath me, after all."

She smiled at that. "Then, my love, let us set after the blackguards and lead the way for our friends."

He was sprinting for the stables before the words had finished leaving her lips.

* * *

It was the deepest part of the night, perhaps two a.m., and while Joan had not thought it possible, the storm had worsened. Now the thunder and lightning seemed nearly continuous, and she would swear the rain was coming in sideways. There had been times that the trail seemed lost, but always they had been able to find a hoof print in the mud, or a bent branch, and their way had been made clear again.

Now it seemed that they were lost in a sodden world of mud and waterfalls. She could not tell where her soaked clothing ended and the eternal deluge in the air began. Joan had to trust in Aquila's keen balance, for she had no idea what lay on the trail ahead.

The woods parted on either side, and Hugh drew to a sudden halt. She stilled beside him, straining in the dark, in the torrential waterfall which was their air, for any sense of what lay ahead.

The crack of lightning nearly burst her ears. She threw her hands over them to protect them from the sound. In the brief flash of light she saw a sight which froze her breath.

Her breath was a bare whisper. "It can't be."

Hugh nodded, drawing his sword from its sheath. "It's Sarah's mill."

Joan blinked again. It was a dream. Surely it was a dream. She could not be here, again, dismounting from her horse, tying him alongside his brother. She was not crouching, again, behind a large gorse bush, scanning to see where the threat lay.

Joan's throat ached. It was all she could do to put voice to the words. "If he should hurt Sarah –"

Hugh's response was a low rumble. "He will not."

He glanced behind for a moment, looking back up the trail they had followed. "We should have help within an hour."

She sharply shook her head. "Sarah does not have an hour," she stated with certainty. "In the state Michael is in, I will be surprised if she has ten minutes."

He turned to hold her gaze. "With all you have been through over the last days, are you sure you are ready for this? If we go in and fail –"

She shook her head again, her grip on her sword turning to steel. "We will not fail Sarah," she vowed. "For if we fail Sarah, we doom thousands of others to the same fate. Michael, Cecily, and all of their scheming ends here. Tonight."

He looked at her for a long moment, and at last he leant forward, pressing his lips to hers. An ache of desire filled her heart, twining around her soul, blossoming out to fill every corner of her being.

Then he had released her and was kneeling before her. He raised one hand to tenderly trace the edge of her cheek.

His voice was low, but it carried clearly to her through the pounding rain.

"I love you, Joan. We built that love while we corresponded, and I knew it for a truth the moment I realized all you were, by your tapestry. Whatever happens, I will treasure this time we have had together."

She smiled, then, a joy filling her that was beyond any she had experienced before. She knew that everything in her life had led her up to this one moment.

"I love you, Hugh," she sighed, running a hand through his hair. "I fought the connection we forged. I struggled to put it aside. In the end it has been the one truth in my life. It has been the one commitment I can be wholly proud of."

The corner of his mouth turned up, and he held her gaze for a heartbeat longer. Then he drew to his feet, gave her a last nod, and vanished into the thrumming darkness.

Joan stared at the empty space for a long moment, the hollow ache resounding in her heart. Then she turned resolutely toward the front of the mill.

Ten men, Joan reminded herself as she crept steadily toward the front of the building. If she assumed there were five soldiers inside, that still left five skilled swordsmen guarding the exterior. Two would be waiting for Hugh in the back. Another two were undoubtedly in place for her here in the front.

Which would leave the remaining wolf's head ... where?

She shook her head, pushing the thought aside. One step at a time. One man at a time. The previous assault had been challenging enough, and those had simply been local men recruited by the Sheriff. She had no doubt that Michael's men would be an order of magnitude worse.

There – the faintest glimmer of a sword blade in a hollow by a white birch tree. The thrumming of raindrop on sodden earth was deafening, and she focused on placing each foot on solid ground as she approached him. The combination of mud and wet clay underfoot made the process nearly impossible.

Just a few more steps ...

She placed down her right foot, it slid sideways in the ice-like substrate, and she let out a yelp. The soldier spun in a low crouch, his eyes seeking the source of the sound. His sword was out in his hand, the edge glittering.

Then, to Joan's immense surprise, Jake stepped out before the bandit. His young face shone bright with innocence; his lanky, teenage body dripped with rain from every seam. His voice was tight with nervousness, but clear.

"Excuse me, but could you tell me where –"

The bandit spun toward Jake, his sword out. The wolf's head growled in exasperation, spinning his sword in his grasp before raising it high to cut Jake down.

Joan dove forward with her dagger, slicing it forward and down across the guard's throat. She split his carotid artery in two. The man collapsed instantly, his hands flailing at his throat, his voice a mere gurgle before he stilled.

Jake ran up to stand before her, his eyes wide as saucers.

She put a fond hand on his shoulder. "You were perfect," she praised him. "Where are the others?"

He nudged his head to the east. "Still behind me. Hugh traded me Accipiter for his steed, and while he then left me behind after that, his steed must be a half-brother of yours. I outdistanced the others in minutes."

She smiled at him. "Go bring your horse with ours, and make sure you catch each incoming man before they barrel in. It's absolutely critical to Sarah's safety that we take this slowly."

"Of course," he agreed, and he was gone into the darkness.

Joan's heart glowed with hope. Jake was here already, and the others were on the way. They might have a chance.

She crouched over the dead body, her gaze scanning the darkness, seeking for the second man. The torrential rain blurred her vision, and she wiped it away, straining all her senses.

Where was he?

A hint of movement caught her eye, and she stared at the corner of the mill. There. The faintest of shimmers, a lighter grey against a darker, as if a shark had slid up against a granite rock for a moment. She crept slowly toward him.

She was only two feet away when he heard something and spun toward her. His eyes widened in surprise; he dove at her, his dagger out. She dodged right, slipping the attack, spinning to keep him before her. He flipped his hilt in his grasp, changing the blade to point backward, then lunged again, this time in and up, aiming to carve open her stomach. She leant back, barely missing the strike, then lunged forward, aiming for his heart.

He pressed off with his forward foot to lunge backward and avoid the blow, but his body slammed into the sturdy bulk of Bossard. Bossard had traded in his tavern apron for a leather jerkin, and his wavy red hair was flattened by the pouring rain. Joan pinned the bandit to Bossard as neatly as if he were a new sign being nailed to a nearby oak. The wolf's head gasped in shock, then he slid down the length of Bossard's body to collapse at his feet.

Bossard reached down to twist Joan's dagger free, handing it back to her. His voice was low and serious. "My Aiden is in there," he informed her, "along with Sarah. We have to get them both out safely."

She patted him on the arm. "And we will," she vowed. "Gather up the incoming men. Get every bale of hay you can out of the stables. Pile them up beneath the mill's attic window. I want every option covered for those two."

"Will do," he agreed without hesitation, and he was gone.

Joan breathed in a sigh of relief. The reinforcements were arriving. They were whittling down the forces. There was still a chance for Sarah and Aiden.

She swept her head left and right for a long minute, but nothing else stirred on the ebony clearing before the mill. The only movement was the heavy, wet drops slamming into the earth, sending up small fountains of brown.

At last she crept forward cautiously, all attention on the closed door before her. As long as it did not open, she could then move to the window to the right and ease herself over its sill just as she had last time. And once she was inside –

The edge of a dagger pressed against her throat.

She froze.

A rough voice growled in her ear. "Not gonna be quite that easy, missy," he informed her. "Might be that Cecily has a few choice words for you. Perhaps a few interesting ways to teach you the error of your ways."

He drew the blade tight. A trickle of warm blood slithered down her neck.

His other hand moved to her neckline, and his voice took on a rougher cast. "Then again, maybe I could teach you a lesson or two myself, before I turned you over to her care."

Joan balanced herself on her left leg. If she could just get the angle right, one sure mule kick against the man's kneecap should send him to the ground. Of course, if she missed, there wouldn't be a second chance. She drew in a breath …

The man coughed, the blade's pressure eased on her neck, and then he spiraled down to the ground. The shimmering point of a dagger shone from the center of his chest.

Joan looked up to meet Norman's eyes. His grey hair gleamed in a flash of lightning, and his gaze was even. "I know you had everything under control," he commented smoothly, "but I needed some practice with my blade. I hope you don't mind."

She grinned at that, reaching out to clasp his arm. "Not at all."

Ymbert bounced up on his right, his eyes bright. "Might I assume that door is locked?"

She nodded. "And the window shutters too, I might imagine. If you could get both free without alerting the inhabitants, I would be most obliged."

He performed a sweeping bow. "Your wish is my command." He reached into a leather pouch at his waist, withdrew a pair of metal tools, and went to work on the door.

Sybil stepped up on Norman's other side. "This time, I will show you what my talents are all about," she promised. "I will go in through the door and distract them. You enter via the window and take them as the opportunity presents itself."

Ymbert raised a hand in victory. "One down," he called out, moving on to stand before the window's closed shutters. "Round two."

Joan turned to face Sybil, taking in the set look in the woman's eyes. "I should be able to handle them without risking you," she assured the woman.

Sybil shook her head. "Even if you could, there's no need for the extra risk," she pointed out. "You did all you could to save me when I needed help. Let me do my part to put this group to an end."

Ymbert moved to stand before them. "Your portals await, M'Ladies."

Joan went over to stand by the window, then nodded to Sybil. Sybil gave a wide smile, an amused wink, and then she stepped to the door.

Chapter 23

Joan carefully eased the window shutter open just enough to peer into the room beyond. Compared with the torrential cacophony of the outer world, the inside of the mill was a blissful oasis of calm. A crackling fire glowed in the fireplace. A wicker basket of crimson apples sat at the center of the wooden table. Her stomach rumbled, reminding her that she had not eaten much of anything since her departure from the tavern. It seemed like eons ago.

There was movement, and she held still, not wanting to catch an eye. After a minute she had located the occupants of the floor - a trio of burly, leather-garbed men. The blond with the long plait down his back hunched over in a chair by the table, sharpening his sword, his eye glancing occasionally at the front door. The second man, nearly bald, had gathered a stack of bread and cheese and was carefully packing leather sacks. The third, his hair a mat of greasy brown, was laying asleep against the far wall, sprawled beneath the larger window that Hugh had come in through the last time. He had his sword immediately beside him. By the looks of him, Joan had no doubt that he would come instantly awake at the first sound.

A firm knock sounded at the front door, and three pairs of eyes latched onto it. Three hands drew up swords and approached the door in a low crouch. The blond looked back at his two fellows, ensuring they were ready, before laying a hand on the latch.

He called out loudly to be heard over the storm. "Who goes out there?"

Sybil's voice came through with a tough edge. "It's Eve. Let me in. I have a present for Cecily."

The blond took another look behind him, getting the nod from both of his companions, before easing the door slightly and looking out into the rain.

He grinned in approval and stepped back, drawing the door wide. Sybil stepped through, her thin burgundy gown plastered against her body by the heavy rain. After her came Linota, her aqua dress even more revealing than Sybil's, her curling tendrils of short hair giving her a mermaid-like appearance.

Sybil looked around with sharp attention. "So, where is she? I think she'll be pleased with my latest gift to her. What do you think of her? Quite a beauty, eh?"

The blond soldier bumped the door shut with his hip, then slid his sword into its scabbard while he circled Linota. "Oh, she'll do quite nicely," he agreed. "Cecily is upstairs and gave strict orders not to be disturbed. The Bull Twins are up there on the second floor, to lend a hand if needed." A grin split his face. "So you'll just have to stay down here with us and keep us company for a while."

Sybil drew her brows together as she pondered this new information. "Well, I suppose we can wait a bit," she agreed at last. "How about this. You pour me a mug of ale, and I'll have this girl give you a demonstration of the dance she was doing down at the Spinning Lark."

The bald man had her ale poured and presented within a heartbeat. She took a long pull on it, then wiped her mouth off with her sleeve. "That hits the spot," she murmured with a smile. "Been a rough ride today."

The blond pushed the table to the far left wall while the greasy-haired soldier set up a trio of chairs facing the open area before the fireplace. The three men gathered up their mugs of ale and settled down with anticipation glowing on their faces.

Joan smiled at the men's easy distraction. She carefully pulled open the shutter, then eased over the sill into the darkness of the main workroom. The three men's backs were to her; every ounce of their attention was on the slender woman before them. Linota drew a fabric scarf from her waist, circling it around the frame of her face to hold back the hair. She looked to the blond and winked. "Keeps my mouth free this way."

He nodded mutely, his eyes tracing their way down her form.

She raised both arms over her head. "I call this dance, 'Do Not Scream'."

The bald man raised an eyebrow. "That's a funny name for a dance."

A hand clamped over Joan's mouth, and it took every ounce of self-control for her to swallow the cry which swelled from within her, as she recognized Hugh next to her and melted in to him.

Linota gave the bald man a wink. "Oh, believe me, when this dance reaches its climax you will understand perfectly what the name is all about."

He leant forward in anticipation, the mug of ale in his hands all but forgotten.

Hugh pointed a finger at her, then at the greasy man who was even now slicking his hair back in an attempt to neaten it. She shook her head firmly. There was no doubt Hugh was planning on taking on two men by himself, leaving her with only one. She pointed at the blond with the braid. If she was going to have only one man to deal with, better it be the leader.

Hugh frowned, but he took in the determination in her eyes, and his shoulders fell. He nodded, his eyes holding a clear message for her.

Be careful.

She nodded, drawing the dagger from her hip. His was already in his hand. They crept side by side from the deep shadows of the main workroom to the smaller dining area, where Linota whirled in a spiral, her hands waving in an undulating rhythm. Sybil stood against the fireplace, tapping time on the mantle, her eyes on Linota.

Her voice was a low murmur. "Now, watch this, boys. Watch this thing she does with her hips."

The three men on the chairs leant forward, their eyes glued to the dancer before them.

The blond was on the far left of the three. Joan took one last step to the side, giving Hugh room with which to work on the other two.

She pounced.

She drew the razor-sharp edge of the blade along his neck, severing the artery, and he flung his arms out wide, lunging at her. He grabbed a hold of her right forearm, bearing down on top of her as his life's blood pumped from his body. His weight slammed her into the floor, and for a moment the breath was knocked out of her. He inexorably twisted her arm, rotating the blade, pressing it ... pressing it ...

The desperate gleam in his eyes flared, faded, and then he collapsed on her, his bulk pinning her in place.

Joan could hear the grunts and heavy thuds of a fight, and she pressed furiously at the body. There was the sound of running feet, and Linota and Sybil were there, hefting the blond off of her. She sprang to her feet, turning to seek out Hugh.

The greasy-haired man lay sprawled next to his chair, blood flowing from beneath him in slow rivulets. The larger, bald bandit was circling Hugh, his eyes tiny with fury, his dagger in his hand. The man lunged forward with an arcing blow, but Hugh danced back, barely missing it.

Joan took a step forward, but Hugh shook his head without removing his gaze from the man before him. "Stay back," he warned her. "I'll take care of him."

There was a soft scratching at the door, and a smile crossed Joan's lips. She backed up to the door, her eyes never leaving the two men. She reached her hand back and pulled the door wide.

In from the ebony wetness stalked a pair of large, bristling wolves, their amber eyes gleaming in the firelight, their gaze focused on the bandit before them. A low growl emitted deep from their throats, and even Joan's neck hairs stood on end.

Linota and Sybil pressed themselves flat against the far wall, their eyes round in shock. It took the bald man an extra moment to turn his attention from Hugh, but when he did his mouth fell open in fear. His voice was a hoarse mutter. "Here, let's put aside our quarrel. Those monsters will tear us open!"

Joan smiled sweetly. "Their mother was slain by a swordsman," she informed the man. "They are driven to mad fury any time they see a blade."

He tossed his dagger toward the fire, holding his hands high. "See? No blade," he called out to the approaching animals. "No blade!"

Hugh spun him in place, pressing him up against the wall. Joan grabbed rope from the corner and came over to them, tying the man's hands behind him.

His voice was a frantic squeak. "The wolves will eat us all! Kill them!"

Joan winked at Hugh, then went over to her dogs. "Ah, my darling pups. Tracked us here, did you?" She knelt down and nuzzled Romulus. "And you are drenched."

The dog lapped her face, then gave himself a long, thorough shake which doused the few spots which had begun to dry with a fresh soaking.

She scrunched Remus behind the ears, and then gave them both a gentle shove toward the fire. They didn't need a second hint. They padded their way over, turned around a few times, and curled up in its warmth.

Hugh pushed the man down into the center chair, giving him a firm gaze. "Sit."

The man glanced at the two dogs, and they both raised their heads slightly, fixing the bandit with a steady gleam.

He nodded fervently. The dogs lowered their muzzles in between their paws again.

There was a cascade of thunder, and the walls vibrated. Hugh looked up at the central staircase, then back to Joan. "The Bull brothers are up there," he murmured.

She nodded. "I heard. But we have to get through them."

There were footsteps in the open doorway, and Joan turned. Lord Weston and Greslet stood there, side by side, their swords in hand. Lord Weston's gaze swept the room, then moved up the stairs toward the second floor. "Let us take care of that," he stated evenly. "You two need to get to Sarah."

Joan's instinct was to turn them down. She would not let anyone else shoulder the burden that was hers to bear. But Hugh stepped forward, gently laying his hand on her arm. "We are all in this together," he pointed out. He turned to the men. "Your help would be greatly appreciated."

Joan sighed, nodding in acceptance. "Yes, it would."

The two men settled their hilts in their hands, then Lord Weston led the way as they ascended the stairs. There was no need for careful placement of feet, not tonight with the steady thrumming of rain on every surface of the building, coupled with the unending crash of thunder. It would be a miracle if those upstairs had heard even the faintest sound of what went on below.

As the men reached the top of the stairs they gave one last nod to each other, then split. Lord Weston moved left, Greslet headed right. The clang of their first blows was a whisper beneath the thunderous force of the storm outside.

Hugh continued climbing the stairs to the attic, and Joan was right behind him. She hoped beyond all hope that they would find Sarah unhurt, that the woman had the nine lives of a cat to survive two such assaults on her home. She found her lips murmuring a prayer as they came up through the opening in the floor into the large room.

A few flickering lamps were set up in various corners. Joan's gaze swept the shadows, looking for movement. Her eyes swept to the window – and froze.

Chapter 24

The rain was thundering directly overhead, the walls were shaking with the pounding, and Joan could barely hear Cecily's tirade to Michael. The two stood near the large window, Cecily waving a hand in exasperation, Michael watching her as if she were an uninteresting exhibit at a dusty museum. He had his sword in one hand and idly traced circles in the dust while she raged.

Cecily's voice raised above the tumult of the storm for a moment. "And if you think I'm just going to sit around while you go back to that woman, you've got another think coming. Oh, I was fine while you played with your stable of whores. You've made your lifestyle clear enough over the years. But this goes *too far*!"

Joan glanced over to Hugh – and blinked in surprise. Hugh was standing as if transfixed, staring at Michael and Cecily. His sword arm wavered as if he had forgotten he held one. His gaze was distant, unfocused. He was completely disconnected with the current moment – lost somewhere in a distant past.

Michael turned. A wide smile split his face as he saw Hugh and Joan. "At last, there you are," he welcomed. "Certainly took you long enough to arrive." He gave a condescending nod to Cecily. "You see, my dear, there was no need to fret. Everything is working out just as I had planned."

Hugh's gaze sharpened, and he took a step forward. "I'm not sure your men downstairs would agree with that," he countered.

Michael laughed in amusement. "Took care of them for me? Exemplary. They were the last ones with a claim on a share of our prize here." He fondly patted the leather pouch at his side. "Now that you've handled that little problem, we have only a few minor issues to wrap up before I can head out."

Joan shook her head. "Your days of scheming are over, Michael."

He raised an eyebrow, then took a step to the left.

Joan sucked in her breath. Huddled immediately before the open window were Sarah and Aiden. Aiden had his arms wrapped around Sarah, and his eyes were glued on Michael.

Joan's heart skipped a beat. "Sarah, are you all right?"

Sarah nodded, her eyes wide. "We're both fine."

Michael casually raised his sword and pointed it at Sarah's chest. Aiden immediately moved so he had the tip of the sword against his chest, shielding Sarah with his body. The lad's voice shook, but rang clear. "If you want to hurt her, you'll have to go through me to do it."

Michael laughed. "That doesn't sound too bad to me. I could gut you both. Your screams could be the music we all dance to."

Joan stared at him in growing horror. "You? You're the reason Tobias became so violent these past few months? You're why he was planning the same end for Sarah when he held her hostage in this very attic?"

Michael gave a low bow. "Tobias was quite the student, as was Sheriff Elias and his other men. Really, though, I think of myself more as an artist than a mere teacher. Those men were rough clay. I molded them into something far superior."

Joan saw the gleam in his eye. She realized with shock that he would do it. He would spear the both of them through and then start the fight. Michael figured that the trauma of the two youngsters' agonizing deaths would distract her and Hugh enough to tilt the odds in his favor.

He probably figured correctly.

Joan moved her gaze to hold Sarah's eyes. She pitched her voice to be as steadying as she could. Everything depended on it.

"Sarah, do you trust me?"

Sarah instantly nodded.

Joan slid her gaze to Aiden. "And, Aiden, do you trust in Sarah fully? Do you love her?"

"Absolutely." Aiden folded his grasp into hers.

She looked between the two, wrapping her fingers slowly down the length of her hilt, settling it firmly into the groove of her palm.

There was no other choice.

"Jump!"

There was not a moment of hesitation. The two spun in place, stepped in unison up to the sill, and vanished into the thunderous darkness of the storm.

Michael stared after them with a look of abject shock and outrage. His mouth hung open for a long moment. Finally he slowly turned to stare at Joan in growing acceptance and amusement.

"After all these years, my dear, to think you have the capacity to amaze me. Never, in a lifetime of guessing, would I have imagined that you would willfully send those two to their death just to save your own skin. I always took you for someone who would battle any odds, would risk your life ten times over to rescue an innocent."

His smile widened. "I do say, I think I am finally starting to rub off on you. It has certainly taken long enough."

Joan's throat was tight. She hoped beyond all measure that Bossard had prepared a large enough hay pile to save his son and future daughter-in-law from critical damage. She stared at Michael. "The innocents are safe from your grasp, now, Michael. It is time to bring you and Cecily to justice."

He laughed, looking over her dismissively. "What, you and Hugh? Bring us in? Just when the final pieces are sliding into place?" He brought his sword up at his side. "You always did like watching a joust, my dear. Well, here's a show you won't want to miss. It's time I bring an end to this little affair of yours." He glanced at Cecily. "Do make sure she stays out of the way."

Cecily's eyes gleamed with determination. "Absolutely."

Michael looked to Hugh, and his gaze hardened. "What do you say, old partner? Joan was always mine – and I have always been the better man. But, not to worry, I'll take good care of her once you're gone."

Hugh's gaze flared with emotion, but he pressed his lips together, every ounce of attention on Michael's feet, on his stance.

Then Michael lunged, his sword arced, and they were a maelstrom.

Joan drove forward to help Hugh, but a sword slammed down against hers, and Cecily drove her back a few steps with heavy blows, separating her from the two men. Cecily's voice was a furious hiss. "Oh, no you don't," she challenged. "You won't interfere, not this time, not when I am so close to having everything I want." She spun in a circle with her sword out wide, driving Joan back another step. A pile of boxes tumbled between the two pairs of combatants. "Michael will take care of that boyfriend of yours, as he has taken care of every other impediment in our life. With a dagger to the gut."

Joan spared a glance for the two men. They were a blur in the shadows, a whirling progression of flashing blade and spinning limb. She could barely tell where one began and the other ended.

A sword was arcing toward her shoulder, and she leapt back. The tip sliced down her dress, rending it for a few inches.

Cecily gave a low laugh. "Oh, so sorry about that," she offered. "Just trying to keep you away from the fight. Accidents happen sometimes, you know." She dove forward, driving her blade straight at Joan's heart. Joan dodged left, feeling a whistle of air as the edge barely missed her arm.

A blow drove toward Joan's head, and she deflected to the right, ducked as the sword reversed and came back in again, then leapt back as the tip nearly ripped her stomach open. On the other side of the boxes she could hear the grunts of pain and clang of metal. It took all her willpower not to look over and see how Hugh was doing. She needed every ounce of her attention on the woman before her.

Cecily's blade whirled high over her head, Joan brought her sword up to block and –

Hugh's voice rang across the room. "Halt!"

Both women, startled, turned to look.

Michael was weaving by the window, swordless, blood streaming from a cut in his forehead. His left arm seemed broken and there were wounds on his legs as well. Hugh held his sword pointed at him. His left bicep was gashed and he seemed to be favoring his right leg.

Hugh's voice carried a clear command. "Cecily. Drop your sword immediately."

Cecily's eyes widened in disbelief, then darkened with all-encompassing fury.

"Never!"

She raced straight at Hugh, hurdling the boxes, her sword held high over her head.

Hugh waited until she was just at him, then leapt nimbly to the left. He whirled and gave her a solid push on the back as she stumbled past him.

She went sailing out the window, screaming, and then the noise abruptly ended. The steady thrum of the rain echoed along the roof.

Michael stared at the dark opening for a moment. When he turned to Hugh a coolness had sifted into his gaze. He nodded as Joan climbed over the boxes and came to stand alongside Hugh.

Michael's voice took on a note of rationality. "Two against one hardly seems fair," he pointed out. "Yes, Hugh might have won the first round, but this game is to the death. Let us see who is best in the ultimate contest."

Hugh shook his head. "No more games, Michael. Your foul machinations are at an end. You will be brought to justice."

Michael scoffed, looking between the two. "Justice for what? It is your word against mine. We are far from the Holy Land here. And, besides, you've killed off just about every witness that there was."

There was a quiet voice from behind Joan. "Not every witness."

Joan turned in surprise. Master Martin stood there, his eyes weary but steady. He strode up to stand between them, his gaze heavy on Michael.

Michael blinked as if he were seeing a ghost. "How can you be here?"

Master Martin held his gaze. "We are all a long way from where we started." His eyes shadowed. "You were once one of my greatest prides, Michael. Now ..." He gave a soft shrug.

Michael's brow darkened. "You have no right to judge me," he snapped. "You will never take me alive."

Hugh held his gaze. "You will be made to answer for all you have done."

Michael's eyes swept the three people before him. His face hardened. "Never. You remember this day, and remember how I escaped you all."

He turned then, launching himself out the window without a sound.

Joan raced to the window, Hugh and Master Martin close at her side. She stared down into the ebony rainfall.

A ring of lanterns flared into visibility as the covers were removed from them. Lord Weston and Greslet hauled Michael up out of the hay, the fallen man swearing up a streak which Joan could hear even from this height. Ymbert skipped forward with some rope, deftly tying the man's hands behind his back.

Joan could see Cecily standing to one side, her wrists bound, under tight guard from Norman. On the other side, Sarah, Aiden, and Bossard were all embracing, while Linota and Sybil handed around mugs of ale.

Joan folded against Hugh. His arms came up around her in a tender embrace. He pressed a long kiss against her forehead, and her world eased to a stop.

Master Martin's voice drifted into her reverie, a hint of amusement in it. "Well, if you two are going to be busy, I can always eat all those grape leaves and other delicacies myself. I will just be down –"

Joan's stomach growled loudly, Hugh swept her up in his arms, and she could swear she breathed in the delicious aromas as their feet echoed down the stairs.

Chapter 25

Joan sighed in angst as she looked across the smoldering embers which had once been her home. Remus and Romulus bounded with interest through the wreckage, sniffing at a corner here, digging in curiosity at a sagging patch there.

It was gone. Everything she had once loved was gone. Her few mementos, her stable gear, everything.

The tapestry was burnt beyond recognition.

Hugh's arm was steady around her waist, and he looked across the ruins with quiet acceptance. "We can rebuild."

Joan's voice ached with sorrow. "The tapestry is gone," she pointed out. "And your seagull. Those can never be replaced."

He turned her to face him, running a hand tenderly along her cheek. "Those were all we had, once, of a precious memory." His eyes shone. "Now we have each other. Those other objects, they are no longer necessary. We have the reality."

She smiled at that. Remus trotted up to her side carrying a stick; she flung it out past where the stables had once been. Aquila and Accipiter were hobbled by the clover, grazing quietly.

Hugh's face stayed steady. "With the reward money coming in from so many fronts, you could live anywhere you wished. Even return to the Holy Land."

She looked into his eyes. "Would I go alone?"

His breath left him, and he was quiet for a moment. When he spoke again, his voice was hoarse. "I would go with you to the ends of the earth, if you would have me. The Holy Land, Carthage, Rome, Cairo – it doesn't matter to me. Where you are, I will be."

She looked around the quiet clearing, a soft smile coming to her lips. "I'm not sure how Remus and Romulus would take to the heat of Carthage," she pondered. "They have fairly thick fur."

Romulus came up to rub against Hugh's leg, and he dropped a hand to run it along the dog's head. "That they do."

She glanced to the west. "And Sarah and Aiden will be married soon. I wouldn't want to miss those festivities."

Hugh's arm circled her waist. "Certainly not."

She tapped a finger to her lips. "And then at the autumn equinox Lord Weston promised to hold the largest race the county's seen in decades. I would disappoint a great many people if I did not ride Aquila in that and win them some money."

Hugh pressed his lips to her forehead. "It is almost your duty," he agreed.

She brought her gaze back to the ashes. "So I suppose it makes sense to rebuild here. After all, there's the well for water, clover for the horses, and friends all around."

He smiled down at her. "It does seem fairly ideal."

Her brow creased. "Although, we probably want to rebuild the new home with a few more bedrooms in it. So we all fit."

He raised an eyebrow. "We all?"

Her hand dropped to rest on her abdomen. The corners of her mouth tweaked up.

His eyes widened, he drew her up, and then they were spinning around, laughing. Joan could almost hear the joyful cry of a seagull, soaring in flight, realizing the dreams which had once seemed so far out of reach.

Chapter 26

One week later

Joan rode at Hugh's side, joy streaming out with every movement. The letter from Jessame and Berenger had arrived at the perfect time, carrying news of the couple's newborn son. It was the ideal opportunity for Joan and Hugh to go for a visit. It would give them one last, glorious ride through the English countryside before they settled down to rebuilding their home and preparing for their own new family.

They were now about half-way through their journey, riding into an impressively maintained keep. Joan doubted those walls had ever been breached.

Hugh chuckled as they reined in and dismounted. "The Bowyers are known for their skill at arms," he commented. "They have quite the reputation. Like us, they do their best to watch over the members of their community. And they're known for training both men and women well in use of sword."

Joan smiled. "Sounds like a perfect place to take our rest."

A pair of teen boys came out to gather up the horses, their eyes going round at the beauty of the steeds. Hugh gave them a wink. "Take good care of them and I might let you go for a ride."

By the look on the lads' faces, the horses were going to be treated like royalty.

A young girl, perhaps thirteen, was at the far side of the courtyard, practicing with a sword against a straw dummy. A woman, undoubtedly the girl's mother based on their similar looks, was watching from a distance, her eyes somber.

Joan walked over to her, Hugh staying at her side. "Greetings," Joan introduced. "We are Hugh and Joan Castillion, traveling through your area. We would ask permission to stay the night."

"I am Lady Bowyer," greeted the woman. "Where are you headed?"

"We are traveling through to visit our friend Terric, down in Somerset."

The woman turned with interest. "Was he a Crusader?"

Joan smiled. "How could you guess?"

She chuckled. "Your voice. You're hiding it well, but you still have the accent. Yes, I know Terric. He's a good man. It'll be a pleasure to have you here as long as you wish."

Her gaze went back to the young girl. "This is my daughter, Catherine. She's recovering from quite a blow. Someone tried to get at me by kidnapping her. Thank the Lord that she was able to get away, due to her training. She's thrown herself into her swordwork with a renewed focus."

Joan nodded. "I can understand why. I imagine you and your husband must have been quite worried."

Lady Bowyer's gaze shadowed. "My husband was slain two years ago during a treaty negotiation."

Joan glanced at Hugh. "I'm so sorry to hear that. Our condolences for your loss."

Lady Bowyer nodded, her eyes still on her daughter. "Catherine was always one to focus hard, but she has gone beyond even her own usual attentiveness, since she has come home to me. She's already destroyed three practice swords. I think she's ready for a true blade of her own." Her lips pressed together. "The girl will need it, if she continues down this path she's on. I think she may be hoping to become a protector of the weak."

Joan smiled. "That would be an admirable way to spend one's life."

"Admirable, but dangerous. I had hoped for something safer for my only child."

Joan twined her fingers into Hugh's. "Sometimes the path to happiness involves risk. But it is often worth it."

Lady Bowyer rolled her shoulders. "Worth it, but nerve-wracking for those who love her." She looked around. "In any case, the challenge will be to find a blade up to the task of keeping her safe."

There was a buzzing at Joan's hip, and she looked down.

She saw the blade that Jessame had gifted her with, when she first arrived at Dover.

She remembered clearly how she had felt that first day. How strange and unfamiliar everything had seemed. But Jessame had reassured her that, given time, she would find just where she fit in.

Joan leaned against Hugh, soaking in her warmth.

Now she knew.

And what was it that Jessame had said to her?

Do not become too fond of Andetnes. When you have at last found contentment, there will be another whose fate balances on the point of a pin. You will know when it is right. And the sword will have a new mistress.

Joan had no doubt at all what she should do.

She warmly patted Lady Bowyer on the arm. "Come, why not show us your fine home. I think we may have the perfect solution for your talented daughter. One which will keep her safe – and find her a path in life which brings her everything she dreams of.

* * *

The Sword of Glastonbury series continues with Book 10, *Badge of Honor* –

http://www.amazon.com/Badge-Honor-Medieval-Romance-
Glastonbury-ebook/dp/B007WMKZUY/

If you enjoyed *In A Glance*, please leave feedback on Amazon,
Goodreads, and any other systems you use. Together we can help
make a difference!

https://www.amazon.com/review/create-
review?ie=UTF8&asin=B00GCE9W0W#

Be sure to sign up for my free newsletter! You'll get alerts of free
books, discounts, and new releases. I run my own newsletter server –
nobody else will ever see your email address. I promise!

http://www.lisashea.com/lisabase/subscribe.html

As a special treat, as a warm thank-you for reading this book and supporting the cause of battered women, here's a sneak peek at the first chapter of *Badge of Honor*.

Badge of Honor Chapter 1

England - 1213

Honor is the reward of virtue.
-- Cicero

Catherine drew in a breath of the frigid night air. A thousand shards of ice lanced her throat; she bit off a moan, holding still against the pain. Winter had not yet released its glacial grip on the town. Arctic gusts caused her breath to puff out in frosty clouds of shimmering white. She snuggled the thick hood of her cloak closely in around her face, pressing tightly against the alley wall, seeking even the slightest shelter from the cutting wind. The warmth of the inn's fire was tantalizingly close, just around the corner and through a door, but she pushed the image from her mind, steeling her resolve. She would not abandon her watch post, not now, not with so much at stake. It was only a matter of time before the threat appeared, before she balanced on that knife's edge between courage and foolhardiness.

There – she caught the glimpse of movement in the distant shadows. A small group of rough mercenaries loped down the cobblestone alley facing her, one of the men blowing into his cupped hands to keep his fingers limber.

The group's leader came to a light-footed halt at the edge of the deserted square, and the men drew to his side. She watched them with careful appraisal, judging. They were now near where the alleyway opened up into a large cobblestone intersection, ringed on all four sides by multistory stone buildings. The courtyard was brightly lit by the waning gibbous moon. A brilliant exuberance of stars coated the clear January sky like a dense school of sparkling minnows in an ebony pond.

Catherine's eyes focused in on the man in front, and she shivered. Conrad. Of all the men to have been sent ... she shook her head. She knew him well, knew his cold heart, his ruthless sharpness, his clinical efficiency in dealing out death. A band of iron pulled tightly around her chest, and she let out a long breath, willing herself to relax. She had faced many challenges in her life, and as desperate as the odds seemed, she would see this through.

In a few days she would have to put this life behind her. If this was to be one of her last actions taken as Shadow, her alter-ego, she would make sure it represented her very best.

It seemed her opponent was taking no chances tonight. Conrad waited without moving, absently brushing the long mane of white-streaked hair out of his eyes with a gloved left hand. His sword hand held at the ready near the hilt. He stayed well in the shadows thrown by the edge of the building, his dark clothes helping him to blend in.

Catherine's eyes creased in confusion as she waited, motionless, looking over the group. Tall and haggard, Conrad had maintained his domination of the bandits for many years despite numerous attempts by rivals to unseat him. Now nearly forty, he usually disdained such trivial tasks as this. Why was he out with his crew on this desolate night, crossing her path?

Bitterness shadowed her heart; she pushed it away with fierce resolution. The man was a scorpion. She would have rather faced almost any other team than his. But he *was* here, and she had to ensure he did not succeed.

She could follow his gaze as Conrad's eyes roamed smoothly over the landscape, focusing carefully on potential danger spots. To his left a wooden sign hung from a pair of iron chains over a decrepit doorway. A black rooster was sloppily painted on the sign's cracked surface. The creaking of the rusty metal, swaying unsteadily in the breeze, was the only noise in this desolate corner of town. There were no signs of candles or movement in any of the windows. The other walls presented only dark windows and alleyways.

His voice was low, oily, but even so it carried to her across the crisp air of the courtyard. "Marc - that seems to be the only inn on the square," Conrad commented to his second-in-command, a wiry blond. Catherine glanced over at the shorter man, her eyes noting Marc's thinning hair and scrawny build. The flicker of a smile crossed her face. *No threat there,* she thought wryly, nodding. It was undoubtedly why Conrad had chosen Marc for his right-hand man.

Conrad was speaking again, and she pulled back her hood to make out the words over the brisk wind. "Let me make this clear, so we do not have a repeat of the Mercador debacle. We will search the inn room by room. When we find them, we will hogtie them, gag them, then haul them – kicking and screaming if need be - to the meeting point." The mercenary glanced up at the building, pausing for a moment. "If they are not there, then we start on other buildings in this area, clockwise, working our way outwards. Our orders were final. We have to find them tonight." His eyes swiveled to skewer Marc's. "No distractions this time," he added sharply.

Catherine had heard enough. In her experience half of any conflict was mental - the chess-game of setting expectations and bluffing power. It was time for her to begin. She pulled her scarf across her lower face, drew her hood down over her eyes, and pressed away from the shelter of the wall.

She slid out of the alleyway across from them, gliding through the open courtyard in silence.

Conrad froze as he sensed the motion. She watched as he scanned up her form with a practiced eye, judging the danger. She knew he was trying to ascertain her threat from her appearance. She had given him little to go by. She wore low, soft black leather boots, dark leggings, and a loose black tunic without adornment. A heavy black cloak was joined at her neck with a matte iron clasp. Her hood was up and pulled low, shielding her face from view, and her scarf completed the mask.

Her cloak swirled in a gust of wind as she smoothly crossed the center of the square, revealing the long scabbard at her left hip. She let them see the glimpse, then furled the cloak around her again, protecting her body from closer scrutiny.

As she approached, the group instinctively lowered their hands to their swords. Marc moved up alongside Conrad, his thin body tense. The rest of the wolves' heads looked to Conrad with curiosity, watching for a sign of how to react.

Conrad's hand, like that of his fellows, rested casually on the hilt of his blade. She drew to a stop, leaving about five feet between her and the men. It was close enough that they could talk quietly, yet far enough that they would have to take a step before a sword blow could reach her. The distance, along with the moon at her back, would help ensure her disguise remained intact.

Conrad flashed a wide, ingratiating smile, nodding in recognition. "Shadow, what a surprise," he welcomed. "What might you be doing in this particular corner of the world?" To hear his voice, the two might have been old friends catching up on news at a country wedding.

Catherine bowed her head in greeting, acknowledging the name of her alter-ego. She kept in the darkness while looking up at Conrad, who was a good five inches taller. "It has been a while," she gave in low reply, maintaining the same style of even tone. "You have admired my bluntness in the past; let us be so here. I am here on a job, as I imagine are you."

Her eyes moved past Conrad to scan the five men who stood behind him. "It is important that our assignments do not ... collide in any manner."

Conrad's grin grew toothy. "Well, now, let us see what we can do. Why not start by telling me what *you* are after."

Catherine's eyes returned back to meet Conrad's, considering for a moment. She let the pause linger, waiting until Conrad's brows narrowed, until she could see the tension pull in at his shoulders. Only then did her low voice rumble from the depths of the hood.

"Fair enough," she agreed, smiling inwardly as the tension released slightly, as she eased their strings like marionettes. In their eyes she had just made a concession. Their trust in her would ratchet up a minute amount. It was a game of inches, of subtle encroachments.

"I am here to protect a certain asset and to ensure that no ... local constabulary interference results. It is therefore critical to me that whatever it is you are up to is done quickly and quietly." She could not help herself, and added lightly, "Unlike, for example, the incident in Kidderminster."

Marc pushed forward, his shrill voice piping up with anger. "Hey, that was *not* our fault!" he shot out, his voice rising. "How were we supposed to know -"

Without looking, Conrad silenced him with a sharp wave of a hand. His eyes remained fixed on Catherine. "We will do what we have to do to get our job done," he replied smoothly, his smile icing slightly. "Now, if you do not mind, we have a task to perform." He nodded to his men and the group of six moved past Catherine toward the darkened inn.

"The priest is not there," offered Catherine with a soft chuckle.

Marc spun at this, his eyes blazing with fury. His hand dove toward his sword's hilt. "How did you know -"

Catherine reacted instinctively, knowing her control of the situation was all she had in her favor. Before he could complete his thought or action, Catherine's blade was glinting in the moonlight, the tip pressed tightly against the thin man's neck.

The group froze, all eyes caught by the tableau. Her sword was clearly of fine quality, but held no engravings, no markings of any kind. Catherine's black leather glove held the hilt in a gentle but firm grip, keeping the point steadily in position.

"You had better acquire a leash for your pet, Conrad," she suggested, her smile hidden by the scarf across her face but quite evident in her tone. "He might find himself injured."

"Marc, back off," ordered Conrad brusquely. Marc hesitated a moment, then pulled away from the sword, stepping back a pace, his face surly. Conrad kept his eyes locked on his opponent's, contemplating. "Now, why would you believe we were after a priest?"

Catherine resheathed the sword in a smooth movement and furled her cloak back tightly against the winter chill. "I know many things about your organization," came her inflectionless reply. "As for the priest, I have been watching this area of town for the past week. I made it my business to know who has been going in and out of these buildings."

Conrad eyed her speculatively. Without turning, he spoke to one of the smaller mercenaries who had been skulking in the back of the group. "Mouse. Go in and check out the inn - but do it *quietly*. If our quarry has truly flown, there is no sense in risking town watch involvement." Conrad's eyes flicked to Catherine for a moment, then he continued. "We will wait here with our ... friend."

Mouse nodded and ran with light-footed grace across the cobblestone square. Glancing around one last time, he eased open the inn's front door and slipped noiselessly inside.

Marc glared at Catherine with venom, absently fingering his sword hilt. "If this Shadow knows so much," he growled with quiet but clear anger to Conrad, "I say we give him a few cuts and convince him to tell us everything. Why trust his word?"

Catherine ran a steady eye down the line of five bandits. In addition to Conrad and Marc, the other three men were clearly seasoned warriors, in good shape despite their rough appearance and shaggy hair. She had no doubt they were well worth the coin paid to them. Each man wore leather armor and carried a scuffed longsword at his side.

To a man they appeared ready to draw on command and to take whatever action was required for the job. Catherine knew that any fight with this group would be a formidable task to win. Conrad alone had more assassinations to his credit than any man she knew of, living or dead.

Conrad glanced at his companions, then back at Catherine. "Interrogate Shadow. It is certainly a thought," he agreed, smiling with cold amusement.

Catherine flicked back a shoulder with a smooth motion and the swirling cloak exposed the sword blade's hilt. In the bright moonlight the men could see the moss-green-dyed leather wrap on the hilt, held in place with bronze wire. In the ensuing silence, one of the bandits murmured to the other, "He is a Bowyer."

Catherine nodded in agreement. It was time to increase the stakes. "I see you have heard of my clan and our sword fighting reputation. Let me assure you that if you try to prevent me in fulfilling my current assignment, I will spill the entrails of at least one of you. I may even slice open two or three of you, ensuring an agonizing death, before I am done." She created eye contact with each mercenary in turn, confirming with each man that he was her chosen first victim. When she spoke again, she pitched her tone to be a melding of ice and steel.

"Which of you will volunteer to be the first to die screaming?"

The silence stretched on for a few moments while the men eyed the potential threat speculatively, sizing up the challenge. Catherine did not move. A tense calm settled across the group. Each person there had been in many fights; there was no compunction about one more. It would only take a word from Conrad to start a fierce, coordinated flurry of swords.

Catherine knew she had little hope of taking on all five well trained mercenaries, but there was no backing down now. With practiced ease she first tensed then relaxed each muscle group, watching for any sign of movement. The command would come from Conrad; these men were too disciplined to move until the signal was given. She would need to subdue Conrad first – if such a thing were even possible.

The mercenaries had changed their stance subtly, settling into combat readiness. The four subordinate men were focused on Catherine, but clearly watched Conrad for a sign.

A movement came from the courtyard; all eyes instinctively turned toward it. Mouse came scurrying out of the inn and ran quickly across the cobblestones to Conrad's side. The smaller man seemed oblivious to the tension in the air and gave his news to his boss in a rapid, soft whisper.

"Shadow told the truth. There is no sign of the priest or his followers," he reported in his barely audible voice. "I checked every room. Now what?"

The mercenaries relaxed slightly at hearing this information. Conrad took his hand off his sword and glanced over at Catherine. "So, any other interesting information to share with us?" he asked, his smile glinting in the moonlight.

Catherine returned Conrad's gaze without saying a word. There was a long silence which Conrad made no move to break. When Catherine finally spoke, she pitched her voice to be low and reluctant, as if she were providing an unplanned concession.

"It is in my best interest to tell you, I suppose, as it will get you out of this area," she offered in a growl. "The priest and his entourage left the inn earlier today in a great hurry. They headed north; in that direction lies the old stone bridge."

Conrad eyed Catherine for a long while, considering. He crossed his arms, fingertips drumming on the heavy muscles of his forearm.

"Here is what I will do," he offered at last. "We will make our way to the bridge and see if we pick up the trail. Yes, I am sure it is in your best interest to have us leave, and I will take that at face value." His eyes sharpened. "However, if we find you have misled us for any reason, we will be back. When we find you - and we will - we will make sure you greatly regret having caused us to waste our time."

Catherine nodded amicably and stepped back. "Good hunting."

With an answering nod, Conrad turned on his heel and strode northwards. The mercenaries moved in closely after him.

Catherine remained motionless and carefully watched their movements until they had dissolved into the obsidian night. Then without a sound she turned and retreated down the alleyway in the opposite direction, regaining her watch position, furling herself back into the shadows.

* * *

In a window high over the square and opposite the Black Cock inn, Jack sat back in the ancient leather chair, its decaying hide crackling beneath him. He ran a hand through his thick hair, contemplating what he had seen.

The second floor room had been too high up to hear the conversation clearly, but an alliance between Conrad's well trained mercenaries and Shadow's sword prowess was definitely not a good thing.

Jack looked over at the elderly priest who lay slumbering peacefully in the corner of the room, surrounded by his three young acolytes. His brow furrowed as he considered his options.

He would be very happy when he had delivered the group safely to Worcester Cathedral.

http://www.amazon.com/Badge-Honor-Medieval-Romance-Glastonbury-ebook/dp/B007WMKZUY/

Medieval Dialogue

I've been fascinated by medieval languages since I was quite young. I grew up studying Spanish, English, and Latin, and loved the sound of reading Beowulf and the Canterbury Tales in their original languages. I adore the richness of medieval languages. How did medieval English people speak?

There are three aspects to this. The first is the difference between written records and spoken language. The second is the rich, multi-cultural aspect of medieval life. And the third is how to convey this to a modern-language audience.

Let's take the first. Sometimes modern people equate the way medieval folk would talk, hanging around a rustic tavern, with the way Chaucer wrote his famous *Canterbury Tales*. Something along the lines of this (note this is a modern translation, not the original Middle English version):

> *"Of weeping and wailing, care and other sorrow*
> *I know enough, at eventide and morrow,"*
> *The merchant said, "and so do many more*
> *Of married folk, I think, who this deplore,*
> *For well I know that it is so with me.*
> *I have a wife, the worst one that can be;*
> *For though the foul Fiend to her wedded were,*
> *She'd overmatch him, this I dare to swear."*

Sure, it seems elegant and rich. But did worn-down farmers sitting around a fireplace with mugs of ale really talk like this?

Do we think the London street-dwellers in the 1600s skulked down the dark alleys emoting like Shakespeare –

> *Two households, both alike in dignity*
> *In fair Verona, where we lay our scene*
> *From ancient grudge break to new mutiny*
> *Where civil blood makes civil hands unclean.*

And, in the 1920s in Vermont, did farmers really wander down their snowy lanes murmuring to their farming friends, a la Robert Frost:

Whose woods these are I think I know.
His house is in the village though;
He will not see me stopping here
To watch his woods fill up with snow.

As someone who lives in New England, I can pretty resolutely say "no" to that last one. And, given my research, I'm equally content saying "no" to the previous two. There is a big difference between poetry written with deliberate effort and the way "normal people" talked, flirted, cajoled, and laughed day in and day out. People simply did not talk in iambic pentameter. I'm a poet and even I don't talk in iambic pentameter :).

Modern people sometimes think of the medieval period in terms of the plays we see. We imagine actors on a stage, speaking in formal, stilted language, carefully moving from scene to scene. But medieval life wasn't like that. It was a rich cacophony of people struggling hard to survive amongst plagues and crusades, with strong pagan influences and the church trying to instill order. People fought off robbers and drove away wolves. They laughed and loved in multi-generational homes. It was a time of great flux.

England - A Melting Pot
England wasn't an isolated, walled-off island. It was continually experiencing influxes of new words and sounds. The Romans came and went. The Vikings came and went. The French invaded. Nearly all of the English men headed off to the Crusades, leaving behind women to gain strength and position. The men returned with even more languages. Pilgrims went to Jerusalem. Merchants arrived from all over. This was a true melting pot.

So, in part because of this, Middle English was a rich, fascinating language. People in this time period had a wealth of contractions, nicknames, abbreviations, and combinations of words they used. Often people could speak multiple languages - their old English, the incoming Norman language, Latin from church, and random other words from tinkers, merchants, and pilgrims they encountered. Medieval people had all sorts of words for drinking, for fighting, for prostitutes, you name it. They had slang and shortcuts just like any other language does. After all, these are the people who turned "forecastle" (on a ship) to "foc's'le" and who pronounce the word "Worcester" as "Woostah."

But, here's the trick. With the medieval language being so rich, varied, intricate, and full of fascinating words, how can we bring that to life for a modern audience?

Centuries of Change

Let's start with a basic issue - most modern readers simply cannot understand authentic medieval dialogue. They don't have the grounding in Middle English, French, and Latin that would be required. Even the fairly straightforward, basic Chaucer works look like this:

And Saluces this noble contree highte.

Modern readers generally wouldn't know that "highte" meant "was called" as in "And Saluces this noble country was called."

This happens over and over again. Words change meaning. In the Middle Ages, if you *abandoned* your wife it means you subjugated her. You got her under your thumb. It didn't mean you left her - quite the opposite. Awful meant *awe-ful* - as in stunning and wonderful. It had a positive connotation. Fantastic wasn't great - it was a fantasy; something that didn't exist. Nervous didn't mean worried or agitated - it meant strong and full of energy. Nice meant silly, and so on.

If a book was written with proper medieval words and meanings, first, even if the words are reasonably close to what we use now, modern readers would have to struggle with the spelling -

> *By that the Maunciple hadde his tale al ended,*
> *The sonne fro the south lyne was descended*
> *So lowe, that he nas nat to my sighte*
> *Degrees nyne and twenty as in highte.*

But, again, that is just the tip of the issue with medieval language. The word "bracelet" didn't exist until the 1400s. Necklace wasn't a word until 1590. The word "hug" wasn't around until the mid-1500s. We also didn't have the words tragedy, crisis, area, explain, fact, illicit, rogue, or even disagree! Shakespeare invented the words "baseless" and "dwindle" in the 1600s. Staircase is from 1620. A story written solely with words that existed in the year 1200 - and that still retain their modern meaning so modern readers could understand them - would be fairly basic.

(Speaking of which, the word "basic" didn't exist until the mid 1800s.)

Conversely, some words we might think of as thoroughly modern, like "puke", were also used in Shakespeare's time. "Booze" traces back to the 1500s. And these are just the proofs we have. While "shiner" for a black eye can be traced definitively to the 1700s, it could easily have been used for centuries before then and we just don't happen to have a letter or newspaper article which mentions it.

It's fair to say that people in medieval days did get black eyes and had a wealth of interesting terms for that situation. After all, it could be a rough life back then. Was one of the terms used "shiner"? Maybe, maybe not. Out of the ten fun phrases they used, probably nine of them would make zero sense to a modern reading audience. So authors strive to find phrases that provide meaning to a modern audience without being too *l33t* and techno-speak. It doesn't make sense to completely avoid the word "bracelet" simply because it technically didn't exist in the 1200s. Surely people in the 1200s had several words for "bracelet" and we are simply using the word modern readers understand. Similarly, people in medieval times hugged! They just called that action something else.

Medieval people loved playing with words. They called their kids "dillydowns" and "mitings" (little mites). They called sweethearts "my sweeting" and "my honey. They loved snapping out insults, from "dunce" to "idiot" to "pig filth" and "maggot pie." And, again, these are just the ones that happened to get recorded.

Medieval people loved contractions. There's a phrase "ne woot," meaning *knows not*. They'd simply say "noot". They did this with all sorts of words.

So writing in modern English should have this same sort of loose, fun sense to the writing. It's important to remember that even the kings, in this era, were rough fighters. They were out with soldiers, crossing multiple countries, and experiencing a range of languages. They weren't necessarily concerned about speaking in iambic pentameter. They were more concerned about breaking down their enemy's walls to plunder what lay within and then drinking themselves under the table to celebrate.

So, certainly, treasure the poetry and prose of the time. As a poet, I appreciate that immensely. But also keep in mind that people did not talk in poetry. They did not speak in fantasy-speak of *Lord of the Rings* or *Game of Thrones*. They talked and laughed, flirted and cursed, gossiped and cajoled in a rich, multi-lingual, contraction-filled, sobriquet-laden dialogue which mirrors how we talk in modern times.

About Medieval Life

When many of us think of medieval times, we bring to mind a drab reality-documentary image. We imagine people scrounging around in the mud, eating dirt. The people were under five feet tall and barely survived to age thirty. These poor, unfortunate souls had rotted teeth and never bathed.

Then you have the opposite, Hollywood Technicolor extreme. In the romantic version of medieval times, men were always strong and chivalrous. Women were dainty and sat around staring out the window all day, waiting for their knight to come riding in. Everybody wore purple robes or green tights.

The truth, of course, lies somewhere in the middle.

Living in Medieval Times

The years in the early medieval ages held a warm, pleasant climate. Crops grew exceedingly well, and there was plenty of food. As a result, their average height was on par with modern times. It's amazing how much nutrition influences our health!

The abundance of food also had an effect on the longevity of people. Chaucer (born 1340) lived to be 60. Petrarch (born 1304) died a day shy of 70. Eleanor of Aquitaine (born 1122) was 82 when she died. People could and did lead long lives. The average age of someone who survived childhood was 65.

What about their living conditions? The Romans adored baths and set up many in Britain. When they left, the natives could not keep them going, and it is true they then bathed less. However, by the Middle Ages, with the crusades and interaction with the Muslims, there was a renewed interest both in hygiene and medicine. Returning soldiers and those who took pilgrimages brought back with them an interest in regular bathing and cleanliness. This spread across the culture.

While people during other periods of English history ate poorly, often due to war conditions or climatic changes, the middle ages were a time of relative bounty. Villagers would grow fresh fruit and vegetables behind their homes, and had an array of herbs for seasoning. The local baker would bake bread for the village - most homes did not hold an oven, only an open fire. Villagers had easy access to fish, chicken, geese, and eggs. Pork was enjoyed at special meals like Easter.

Upper classes of course had a much wider range of foods - all game animals (rabbits, deer, and so on) belonged to them. The wealthy ate peacocks, veal, lamb, and even bear. Meals for all classes could be flavorful and well enjoyed.

Medieval Relationships

Some movies present a skewed version of life in the Middle Ages. They make it seem that women were meek, mild, and obediently did whatever their father or husband commanded.

This was *far* from the truth!

Medieval times were times of immense change. Men were off at the Crusades, leaving the women to run things. Christianity was trying to get a foothold, but many areas of Britain were still primarily pagan, with all the Goddess worship and female empowerment which had been tradition for centuries. The vast majority of brewers were female. Most innkeepers were female. Women's knowledge about herbs, health, and food was respected. Healthy women were treasured as the key to a child-rich partnership.

Medieval life was heavily focused on fertility. Farm animals had to be fertile in order to create meat to feed the family. Women had to be fertile to create helpers for the farm and household. Celebration after celebration in medieval times focused on fertility. These people weren't shy about the topic. They watched their horses, cows, and dogs continually engage in these activities. Their festivals focused on the topic with bawdy delight. Their songs lusted about it.

The church tried, again and again, to squelch this behavior so that all aspects of relationships could be regulated by the church. However, half of all medieval couples were together outside of a church marriage and, for those sanctified by the church, a large proportion were "sealing the deal" for a couple already pregnant.

This was the way the medieval people looked at it: they needed to know their partner could create children. This was a key consideration for a relationship.

The Medieval period was far from an era of Victorian prudity. Quite the opposite. People of this era celebrated fertility, felt it was wholly natural, and even felt it was unhealthy for a man or woman to go for too long without sex. The celibacy would block critical flows of the body.

It was considered natural that a male noble might take on mistresses and that unmarried couples might seek out partners. It was the same as someone needing food if they were hungry. It was a bodily function which had to be tended to for the health of the person.

So where does marriage fit in with this mindset?

Medieval Marriage

In medieval times, marriage was primarily about inheritance. It was almost separate from sexuality. Sexuality was an important part of bodily health, like eating well and getting enough exercise. Marriage, on the other hand, was about ensuring one's lands and chattel were cared for from generation to generation. Sex, within a marriage, was focused on creating family-line children to then tend to that wealth.

For this reason, wealthy families would put immense energy into arranging optimal marriages for their children. This was about the transfer of land far more than a love match. Parents wanted to ensure their land went to a family worthy of ownership - one with the resources to defend it from attack. It was not only their own family members they were concerned with. Each block of land had on it both free men and serfs. These people all depended on the nobles – with their skill, connections, and soldiers – to keep them safe from bandits and harm.

That being said, both the woman and man would be consulted about the match. Their input was a critical aspect of the decision. Choices were often made with intricate selection processes. Keep in mind that the woman and her suitors would have been raised from birth to think of this process as natural. They would participate in that choice-making with an eye as to how it would secure the stability of their future family.

Yes, villagers sometimes married for love. Even a few nobles would run off and follow their hearts. Even so, they would have first seriously considered the potentially catastrophic risks which could result from their actions.

Here is a modern example. Imagine you took over the family business which employed a hundred loyal workers. Those workers depend on your careful guidance of the company to ensure the income for their families. You might dream about running off to Bermuda and drinking martinis. But would you just sell your company to any random investor who came along? Would you risk all of those peoples' lives, people who had served you loyally for decades, to satisfy a whim of pleasure? It is more likely that you would research your options, map out a plan, and made a choice with suited both you and your responsibilities.

Medieval Women
In pagan days women held many rights and responsibilities. During the crusades, especially, with many men off at war, women ran the taverns, made the ale, and ran the government. In later years, as men returned home and Christianity rose in power, women were relegated to a more subservient role.

Still, women in medieval times were not meek and mild. That stereotype came in with the Victorian era, many centuries later. Back in medieval days, women had to be hearty and hard working. There were fields to tend, homes to maintain, and children to raise!

Women strove to be as healthy as they could because they faced a serious threat - a fifth of all women died during or just after childbirth. The church said that childbirth was the "pain of Eve" and instructed women to bear it without medicine or follow-up care. Of course, midwives did their best to skirt these rules, but childbirth still took an immense toll.

Childhood was rough in the Middle Ages – only forty percent of children survived the gauntlet of illnesses to adulthood. A woman who reached her marriageable years was a sturdy woman indeed.

You can see why fertility was so important to medieval people!

To summarize, in medieval days a woman could live a long, happy life, even into her eighties – as long as she was of the sturdy stock that made it through the challenges of childhood. She would be expected to be fertile and to have multiple children, which again weeded out the weaker ones. This was very much a time of 'survival of the fittest.' Medieval life quickly separated out the weak and frail. Those women who ran that gauntlet and survived were respected for that strength and for their wisdom in many areas of life.

So medieval women were strong - very strong. They had to be. They were respected. Still, would they fight?

Women and Weapons

Queen Boudicia, from Norwalk, was born around AD60. She personally – and successfully - led her troops against the Roman Empire. She had been flogged - and her daughters raped - spurring her to revenge. She was extremely intelligent and quite strategic. Her daughters rode in her chariot at her side.

Eleanor of Aquitaine, born in 1122, was brilliant and married first to a King of France and then to a King of England. She went on the Second Crusades as the leader of her troops - reportedly riding bare-breasted as an Amazon. At times she marched with her troops far ahead of her husband. When she divorced the King of France, she immediately married Henry II, who she passionately adored. He was eleven years her junior. When things went sour, Eleanor separated from him and actively led revolts against him.

Many historical accounts talk of women taking up arms to defend their villages and towns. Women would not passively let their children be slain or their homes burned. They were able and strong bodied from their daily work. They were well skilled with farm implements and knives, and used them with great talent against invaders.

Many of these defenses were successful, and the victories were celebrated as brave and proper, rather than dismissed as an unusual act for a woman. A mother was expected to defend her brood and to keep her home safe, just as a wolf mother protects her cubs.

Numerous women took their martial skills to a higher level. In 1301 a group of Italian women joined up to fight the crusade against the Turks. In 1348 at a tournament there were at least thirty women who participated, dressed as men.

This is not as unusual as you might think. In medieval times, all adults carried a knife at their belt for daily use in eating, chores, and defense. All knew how to use it. Being strong and safe was a necessary part of daily life.

Here is an interesting comparison. In modern times most women know how to drive, but few choose to invest themselves in the time and training to become race car drivers. In medieval times, most women knew how to defend themselves with a weapon. They had to. Few, though, actively sought the training to be swordswomen. Still, these women did exist, and did thrive as valued members of their communities.

So women in medieval times were far from shrinking violets. They were not mud-encrusted wretches huddling in straw huts. They were not pale damsels locked away in towers. They were strong, sturdy, and well versed in the use of knives. Many ran taverns, and most handled the brewing of ale. Those who made it through childhood and childbirth could expect to enjoy long, rich lives.

I hope you enjoy my tales of authentic, inspiring heroines!

Glossary

Ale - A style of beer which is made from barley and does not use hops. Ale was the common drink in medieval days. In the 1300s, 92% of brewers were female, and the women were known as "alewives". It was common for a tavern to be run by a widow and her children.

Blade - The metal slicing part of the sword.

Chemise - In medieval days, most people had only a few outfits. They would not want to wash their heavy main dress every time they wore it, just as in modern times we don't wash our jackets after each wearing. In order to keep the sweaty skin away from the dress, women wore a light, white under-dress which could then be washed more regularly. This was often slept in as well.

Drinking - In general, medieval sanitation was not great. People who drank milk had to drink it "raw" - pasteurization was not well known before the 1700s. Water was often unsafe to drink. For these reasons, all ages of medieval folk drank liquid with alcohol in it. The alcohol served as a natural sanitizer. This was even true as recently as colonial American times.

God's Teeth / God's Blood – Common oaths in the middle ages.

Grip - The part of the sword one holds, usually wrapped in leather or another substance to keep it firmly in the wielder's hand.

Guard - The crossed top of the sword's hilt which keeps the enemy's sword from sliding down and chopping off the wielder's fingers.

Hilt - The entire handle part of the sword; everything that is not blade.

Mead - A fermented beverage made from honey. Mead has been enjoyed for thousands of years and is mentioned in Beowulf.

Pommel - The bottom end of the sword, where the hilt ends.

Tip - The very end of the sword

Wolf's Head – a term for a bandit. The Latin legal term *caput gerat lupinum* meant they could be hunted and killed as legally as any dangerous wolf or wild animal that threatened the area.

Parts of a Sword

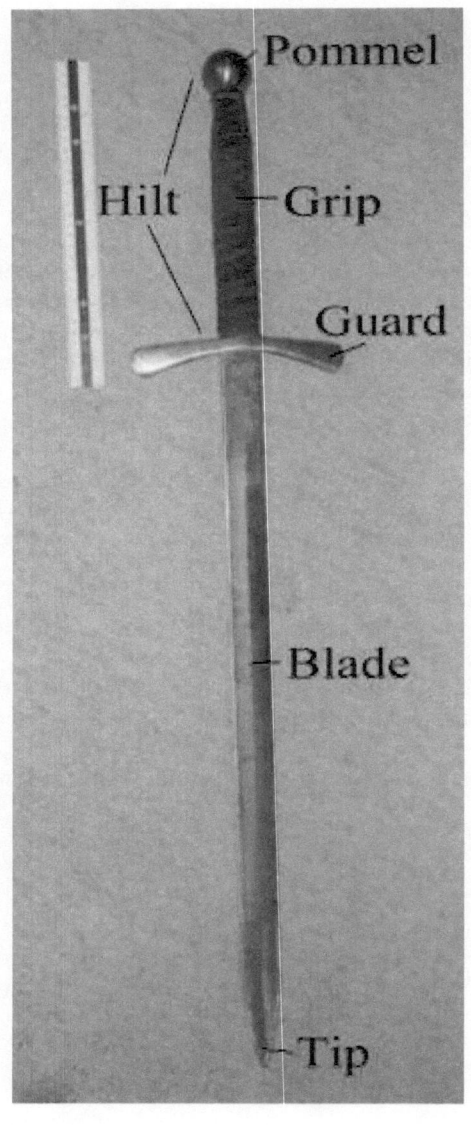

Medieval Clothing

Medieval people - despite modern stereotypes - did have noses and did like to stay clean. Public baths were popular, and people liked to swim as well. However, they did not have the luxury of bathing daily. Also, in medieval times people were often cold. Castles were damp and drafty. Fireplaces were not kept blazingly hot all night long. There is a reason that people wore many heavy layers including cloaks. That way they could add or remove layers as necessary to keep warm.

The basic under-layer was a chemise. This thin nightgown would be worn at night as well as during the day. Because it was against the body it kept the actual clothes clean from sweat. That way you could wash the chemise regularly and not have to wash your actual dress every day. Think of it like when you wear a turtleneck and a wool sweater. At the end of the day you would wash the turtleneck, but you would not wash the wool sweater after every wearing. If you wear a t-shirt under a jacket, you would toss the t-shirt into the washing machine but just hang the jacket on a hook again. The same is true for medieval outfits. The inner layer would be washed, while the other layer would be reused multiple days before it had to be washed.

The chemise was generally not meant to be seen, especially in colder months. It was underwear. There would always be an over-dress with a floor-length hem on top of that. Perhaps a glimpse of the chemise would show at the neckline or at the end-of-sleeve area. In hotter months the chemise might be more visible as the outer dress had short sleeves or no sleeves.

Men would typically wear a tunic over leggings. Men working in summer heat would sometimes wear simple linen "shorts" without anything else. Their chest and lower legs would be bare. This is a stark difference from how covered up women would be.

Both sexes would wear boots or shoes. There was no "left" or "right" - both halves would be made in the same oval shape.

Cloaks would be worn when going out into poor weather, to help keep you warm. These cloaks could be quite heavy if they were full circle cloaks, and incredibly warm.

Monks would wear similar clothing to non-religious men, but the monk's hair would be cut short and have a "tonsure" - or bald spot - shaved out of its center. The tonsure was a sign of their humility.

This illuminated image is from a 12th century manuscript at the library at Cambridge University.

Women's Clothing

A number of readers had specific questions about women's medieval clothing so I created this page with those specific details. To illustrate it, I have included a drawing done by Andreas Muller, a famous German artist known for his work restoring ancient paintings. This drawing was published back in 1861, so it's now out of copyright. As you might expect the drawing shows German people, not English, but the fashions are from the 1200s and are quite similar in style.

So, the basics. Women wore at least two layers of long dress. The bottom layer, or "chemise," was often plain white but could be fancier with nobles. This was what was against the skin, got sweaty, and would be washed. The chemise was often slept in, again especially if the person was poor.

The outer layer, what we would call the "dress," was the prettier layer. This would have the nicer stitching and designs. It could have embroidery or different fabrics stitched together to create designs. The outer dress could have long sleeves, short sleeves, or no sleeves, depending on how hot the weather was. In general, though, a woman's arms and legs were covered by the inner chemise and perhaps also by the outer dress as well. Women in medieval times did not tend to show skin from those parts of the body.

You might see images on the web with medieval women wearing long "trumpet" sleeves which made housework impractical. These were sometimes worn by French nobles who were showing off that they did not have to do menial labor. They were not a normal fashion in England or most other areas.

By the same token, women who had to work hard would wear shorter dresses - ending above the ankle rather than dragging on the floor. That was so their dresses did not catch or drag while they went about their work. Noblewomen who had a quiet day planned or a formal event would wear longer, floor-dragging dresses. These subtle differences helped to show off their status.

If it got even colder women would wear cloaks. These range from light, like the woman in the middle is wearing here, to heavy and full-circle, which could be amazingly warm. I have one of those.

Here is an illuminated image done between 1285 and 1292 which shows the famous poet Marie de France. Marie primarily wrote between 1160 to 1190 and was well known by nobility in France and England. Again, you can see how her outer long dress goes to the floor and the inner dress is visible at the arms. This copyright-free image comes via the National Library of France.

Women had an immense array of colorful dyes to choose from, some more expensive, some less expensive. So clothing could be quite bright and cheery. Just as in modern times, practicality had an aspect here. If someone was going to work in the pig pen all day long they'd probably wear something brown and old. If they were going to church they'd wear their best outfit they had.

In modern times we can sometimes think of dresses as "fancy" items we wear to "dress up" that are hard to move in. In medieval times, a dress was normal and natural! These were the outfits they wore every single day. Women made their dresses so they could do all their normal activities in them. To them a dress was like our modern t-shirt and sweatpants. So they're no question about "could they do chores in a dress" or "could they ride a horse in a dress." Of course they could - that's what the clothing was made for. Medieval women didn't generally hide out in tower rooms. Noblewomen would do archery and horseback riding for fun. Working women would scythe hay, ride to the market, and do a myriad of other chores in their dresses. It was what one wore. So those outfits absolutely were made to easily let them do those tasks. Dresses were loose to allow all of that. Women didn't ride side-saddle in medieval days - they simply put their legs on either side for stability. And their clothing was made for that. To ride, a woman could either tuck the skirt beneath her, like when one sits on a chair, or let it flow behind her. Either way works!

In terms of underclothes, most medieval women did not wear a bra. Their simple, straight dresses were meant to keep the body hidden rather than emphasized. A large breasted woman might wear a "binder" to keep the breasts from jiggling around while they tried to work. Current thought is that women didn't wear "underwear" (underpants) either. With their long multi-layer dresses it would be a challenge for underwear-wearing women to go to the bathroom. Instead, they would just move to a section of the field, fluff out their dresses, and go. Then they could get back to work. The same in the outhouses.

Even during the time of their periods, many researchers feel that the philosophy of the time was that binding or constricting a woman's flow would damage her fertility. So she simply bled into her underdress and that was washed. This free-flow practice continued long after medieval times. It was mentioned in doctors' journals in the 1800s. Even as recent as the 1900s there were cotton mills in the United States that had straw-strewn floors to absorb female workers' blood, so again this was not a short-term trend. And given that tampons can cause toxic shock syndrome, maybe those medieval women knew what they were doing :).

Let me know if you have any other questions about medieval women's clothing! I have a library of books here to help with research.

Dedication

To my mom, dad, siblings, and family members who encouraged me to indulge myself in medieval fantasies. I spent many long car rides creating epic tales of sword-wielding heroines and the strong men who stood by their sides. Jenn, Uncle Blake, and Dad were awesome proofers.

To Peter and Elizabeth May, who patiently toured me around England, Scotland, and France on three separate occasions. Elizabeth offered valuable tips on creating authentic scenes. Visiting the Berkhamsted motte and bailey was priceless.

To Jody, Leslie, Liz, Sarah, and Jenny, my friends who enjoy my eclectic ways and provide great suggestions. Becky was my first ever web-fan and her enthusiasm kept me going!

To the editors at BellaOnline, who inspire me daily to reach for my dreams and to aim for the stars. Lisa, Cheryll, Jeanne, Lizzie, Moe, Terrie, Ian, and Jilly provided insightful feedback to help my polishing efforts.

To the Massachusetts Mensa Writing Group for their feedback and enthusiastic support. Lynn, Tom, Ruth, Carmen, Al, and Dean all offered detailed, helpful advice!

To the Geek Girls, with their unflagging support for my expanding list of projects and enterprises. Debi's design talents are amazing. I simply adore the covers she created for me.

To the Academy of Knightly Arts for several years of in-depth training and combat experience with medieval swords and knives. I loved sparring with Nikki and Jo-Ann!

To B&R Stables who renewed my love of horseback riding and quiet forest trails.

To my son, James, whose insights into psychology help ground my characters in authentic behavior.

To Bob See, my partner in love for over 19 years and counting. He enthusiastically supports all of my new projects.

About the Author

Lisa Shea is a fervent fan of honor, loyalty, and chivalry. She brings to life worlds where men and women stand shoulder to shoulder, steady in their desire to make the world a better place for all. While her medieval heroines often wield a sword, they equally value the skilled use of their intelligence, wisdom, courage, and compassion.

Lisa has studied the Middle Ages since she was quite young. She has trained in medieval swordfighting for several years. She studied medieval dance and music with the SCA. She has been to England numerous times and loves exploring old castles and churches.

Please visit Lisa at LisaShea.com to learn more about her background and interests. Feedback is always appreciated!

You can also contact Lisa at her many social networking accounts:

Facebook - http://www.facebook.com/LisaSheaAuthor
Twitter - https://twitter.com/lisashea
Google+ https://plus.google.com/+LisaSheaAuthor/
GoodReads – https://www.goodreads.com/lisashea
Wattpad - https://www.wattpad.com/user/lisasheaauthor
Instagram - https://www.instagram.com/lisasheama/
Pinterest - https://www.pinterest.com/lisashealowcarb/

Free Ebooks

Do you enjoy free ebooks? I have 33 free ebooks that you can download and enjoy on your PC, tablet, smartphone, or other device!

If you have trouble locating any of these for free, just let me know and I'll lend a hand.

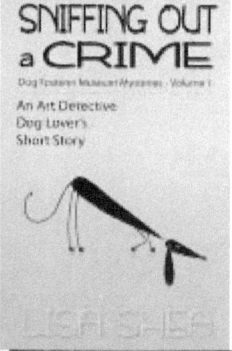

I may have added more free books since releasing this list here. For the most up to date version, be sure to visit:

http://www.lisashea.com/freebooks/

Thank you for supporting the cause!

Be the change you wish to see in the world.

Namaste Aloha Servus

Many languages have a single word that can be used both as a greeting and a farewell. I imagine it's because, in thoughtful relationships, the person is never really gone. They stay within your thoughts until the next time you are able to be together again. While there was technically a beginning, once that connection is made it is always there. There is a continuation of memory and care.

Over the years, countless people have helped me with my writing. My dedication earlier does not even come close to touching them all. Every time a new reader picks up a book and becomes part of the story process, their comments enrich our entire community. Often it's a random thought or idea from one reader which then causes improving changes in the storylines for future ones.

I then am able to pass along those ideas and suggestions to all the authors I help. That allows them to blossom and grow in their own projects.

If you have feedback on this or any of my stories, please share it! I'd love to hear from you.

Thank you so much to all my readers. Thank you to my fellow authors who encourage me. Thank you to the wonderful creative spirits who provide inspiration for me.

Perhaps most of all, I want to send my warmest of wishes to the battered and emotionally burdened women who struggle each day to face the world. All of the proceeds from this series support shelters. This mission is extremely important to me. It is tragic we still live in a world where those shelters are necessary. Until our society rises to a level where they're no longer needed, I will strive to do my part to support them.

We all share this big blue marble we call home. It's the only place we have to live. And we're only on it for the blink of an eye before we're gone again.

We should treasure each day.

We should care for those around us who have walked a rough road.

And we should be grateful for all we have.

Thank you for being a part of my journey.

Namaste.